Dr. Bones & Missy Grey

The Man-Eating Wendigo

Book III

Alex Ross Carol

Blue M

Blue M Publishing, LLC - CHICAGO

Library of Congress Cataloging-in-publication data
Names: Carol, Alex Ross.
Title: *Dr. Bones & Missy Grey: Book Three – The Man-eating Wendigo*

Description: First edition | Blue M Publishing, Chicago, IL [2023] | Series: Book three of monographic series | Contents: Fiction, Murder, Horror | Summary: A doctor and young woman go in search of an elusive man-eating monster in the Midwest. | Audience Note: Recommended for readers fifteen and older | Language Note: Infrequent, mildly offensive language. Some scenes of murder and bloodshed.

Identifiers: ISBN 978-1-945385-34-6
Subjects: LCSH: sh85047117 Historic fiction, American | BISAC: FIC061000 FICTION / Magical Realism | FICTION / Fantasy Contemporary | GSAFD: 00000cz a2200037n 45 0 155 Fantasy fiction | 455 Fantastic fiction | Genre/Form terms: gf2014026333 Fantasy fiction/Heroic fantasy fiction.
Classification: LCC PS370-380 | DDC 813/--dc23

Alex Ross Carol

Printed in the United States of America
www.blueMpublishing.com
Book Cover Design by Allendorf-Vigenere

Blue M Publishing
Chicago, IL 60525

Dr. Bones & Missy Grey
The Man-eating Wendigo

Book Summary

The date is 1883; the scene is the lake country of Minnesota.

Dr. Cook, Missy Grey, and Samuel, venture out again—this time to find the fierce, man-eating wendigo monster. In a rush to locate the creature before a private group of bounty hunters, Bones, Missy and Samuel are asked to follow the trail of a monster that has been spotted in the outland reaches of Minnesota.

This is where their journey begins ...

*****

Note to Readers:

This book is a work of fiction. Certain historical characters are included as well as other facts to further the narrative.

Contents

Dr. Bones & Missy Grey
The Man-Eating Wendigo

Definition: Wendigo

The wendigo is allegedly a supernatural cannibalistic monster believed by several Algonquin tribes – including the Ojibwe, Saulteaux, Cree, Naskapi, and Innu – to reside in the forests of the Atlantic Coast and Great Lakes regions of North America. Appearing in a form described as having some human characteristics or as an evil spirit that holds the power to transform a human into such a beast, a wendigo is said to be created through human cannibalism or by an individual overcome with avarice and greed.

There were few means known to be able to stop a wendigo. Native Americans believed it was best to avoid it at all costs and certainly not to seek it. If it were pursued, they believed that the hunter would likely become the hunted.

*****

Part I

CH 1 – Renewed Friendship

Date: Spring 1883

Dr. Reginald Cook, aka Dr. Bones, received an urgent telegram from William Tillson, an old friend from Washington, D.C. It had been two years since they had worked together on the Boggy Creek Monster case in Arkansas and a year since they had discussed his trip to New York City to help the police find a serial killer or a sewer monster that was terrorizing the metropolis. Both times, Bones had teamed with Missy Grey and her nephew, Samuel Stinson, to track the elusive creatures that were thought to be causing death and destruction with the locals.

Now, Tillson had been promoted to a directorship under the Secretary of the Interior, Henry M. Teller, and wielded some influence in the nation's capital. His friendship with Bones went back years, and the doctor was someone he greatly respected and trusted implicitly.

"William, it's good to see you," said Bones, as he greeted Tillson in his expansive office situated on the third floor of the Patent Office Building. "I'm glad I had a medical conference in town so I could stop in. I got your message. I hope all is well."

"Please," said Tillson, cutting to the chase and motioning for him to sit. "Yes, yes, it is, of course, good to see you as well Dr. Cook. But there are many things brewing here in Washington. As you can appreciate, things change often and yet they all stay the same. In this case, the players have changed but their motives have not."

"I understand. D.C. is quite an odd place. We don't understand you people who live here in our nation's capital. You're almost considered foreigners to the rest of the country."

"No place like this anywhere else in the world."

In some ways, it was the same old Tillson, too. He had always been serious and frank in his conversations—getting quickly to the point. When he had first arrived in Washington, he had an earnestness about him—a naivete that believed in the goodness of the system regardless of how flawed its leadership was. He often told Bones that it was necessary for the nation's elected leaders to remain steadfast to moral principles and not let them be compromised by the power bestowed on and entrusted to them in their political positions. Yet, at the same time, his years in the nation's capital had done nothing but erode those beliefs. The last time they had talked, Tillson had told the doctor he felt that he, and others in the bureaucracy, were just marionettes dancing at the ends of strings. He claimed there were others—the grand puppeteers, standing behind a dark and impenetrable curtain—who were the real power brokers.

"So, are the scales falling from your eyes?" Bones asked. "We all would like to think our politicians and bureaucrats are only looking out for our best interests. Yet, that isn't true, is it?"

"If only it were," Tillson answered. "I haven't grown completely apathetic, mind you. I still believe there is a chance we may succeed in this governing experiment of ours, but it shrinks daily I'm afraid."

"So, tell me what's on your mind."

"It's the Indians. As you know, we've been pushing them farther west, relocating them constantly from one state to the next. The unrest is growing—understandably so. But regardless of what I say, voicing my sentiments against the policy, no one cares to listen."

"Yes, your department has done a lot of resettlements."

"Yes, and deep down, I don't agree with it."

"Then why do you stay?"

"That's why I wanted to talk to you. I'm not. I've tendered my resignation, effective at the end of the year."

"Oh, well, that's quite a change. But I can understand why. The resettlements really are inhuman based on what I've read in the Boston papers," said Bones.

"Well, you must be getting different papers up north. The ones here in Washington all support it. They hide the truth about what's really happening to those poor people."

"So, where are you going?" asked Bones.

"I'm going elsewhere to try to make a difference."

"Are you leaving DC, then?"

"No, my wife wouldn't like that. She's made a lot of friends here. I couldn't uproot her and move back to New York. No, I've connected with a consortium of wealthy families who wish to support various causes I think are worth fighting for. There aren't many willing to risk their reputations though. The money and the power are still with the establishment—the millionaire tycoons who run most of America these days. All we can do is continue to fight them and fight for what is right."

"They pay a lot for senate votes these days, you know," said Bones.

"Yes, I know. But it's not just the programs against the Indians that they're paying for. There are other issues too."

"Like what?"

Tillson got up and poured two short glasses of brandy from a lead crystal decanter he kept on a low table near the window. He handed one to the doctor before sitting back at his desk.

"Last month, a certain wealthy group of businessmen approached our Secretary asking him to facilitate the capture of unusual beasts in the wild. They asked him to use the power of the Interior Department and, if necessary, the military to track them down and hand them over for use in commercial enterprises. The cover for the enterprise is to 'protect our citizenry' from these terrible and vicious beasts. However, the sole purpose is to tap into Uncle Sam's wallet to underwrite their exploits."

"How can they get by with that?" Bones asked.

"Like everything else. There's money in it for everyone involved, including people in this building. These businessmen are rich. They've been importing elephants, tigers, lions, leopards, rhinos, giraffes, orangutans, peacocks and many other wild animals from Africa, India and Indonesia, but they don't wish to stop there. Now, they've turned their attention to the United States. They plan to capture wild animals here and exploit them to make money. I find that reprehensible."

"I'm not sure I understand," Bones said. "What kinds of wild animals are there here that they could exploit? In the West there are still buffalo, bears and cougars, but those don't seem very exotic to me."

"No, not those kinds of animals, Dr. Cook. We're talking about the kind that *you* study and research."

"Legendary creatures?"

"Yes. For example, have you heard of the Wendigo?" asked Tillson.

"Of course. It's another monster legend—a beast that lives in the wilds of the Great Lakes, Northeast, and Canadian forests."

"That is true, but as you know, this legendary creature is one of the most brutal and blood-thirsty ever mentioned in folklore. It is alleged to roam those forests freely without the threat of man. But with more people settling in the West, there are increasing stories of whites being attacked by them."

"I see why you wanted to talk about this," said Bones.

"I thought you would be the best man for the job."

"What job?"

"You see, this group of powerful businessmen not only wants to find and capture this particular creature, it wants to bring it back to show it in New York City."

"New York City? To exhibit it in a cage?"

"I believe so, and that's why I need your help. Besides the fact that it's inhumane to put animals in a cage, just think of what might happen if that thing got loose in that city. You, of all people, would know what kind of damage a creature like that could cause in a place of over five million people. It might kill hundreds—maybe thousands—before being captured again. We just can't take that chance."

"William, I'm sure there is a good explanation for the attacks being reported in the west, and I can assure you they have nothing to do with a Wendigo."

Tillson smiled. "I guess you haven't changed much either then, have you Dr. Cook. You're still the same skeptic."

"Yes. I study the tales, but that doesn't mean I believe in them."

"Well, then, perhaps you could use this as an opportunity to do more research and collect more information on the legend. Wouldn't that be valuable?"

"Yes, of course. But I still don't know what you want me to do—aside from research. I'm not the U.S. Army. It's not like I can go find the creature for you."

"But that is precisely what I need you to do, doctor. I need you to find the creature *before* they do."

"Before a bunch of paid mercenaries does?"

"Yes."

Bones cleared his throat. "Even if this Wendigo creature does exist, that's asking a bit much, William."

"Yes. I know. But if anyone can do it, it's you," Tillson answered. "Tracking these things requires as much brain as it does brawn."

Bones nodded. "And who would be funding my expedition this time?"

"Like I said, I have my own group of wealthy families who donate to charities and good causes," said Tillson. "I've approached them, and they are eager to help. Most, as you can imagine, live in Manhattan and don't want to see such a creature caged and delivered into the heart of their city."

"I must tell you that I've had my fill of tracking monsters in New York City. I would not want to see that scenario play out again; that's for sure."

"So, you'll do it?"

Bones smiled. "I am easily persuaded, especially if it involves a new adventure."

"Wonderful, but you must go soon. The group pursuing this creature has already engaged people here in their scheme. They've sent a posse out there to find it. What's worse, they want Secretary Teller to request military aid from Lincoln—Robert Todd Lincoln, who controls the War Department—to give him a brigade to help with it."

"But you said there's a group already out there. Where?"

"I don't know. But when I find out, I will tell you straight away." Tillson leaned forward in his chair. "Dr. Cook, this must be kept secret. No one here can know that I'm working on something that is against what they're working on. Do you understand?"

"Of course."

"When do you think you'd be able to leave?" Tillson asked.

"I don't know yet, William, but once you advise me where I'm going, I can let you know within a day or two."

"And when you find it …"

"… *if* I find it." Bones corrected him.

"I want you to make sure the others are thrown off the scent. You know what I'm saying."

"To misdirect them?"

"Yes. They must not find or capture the animal."

"*If* the creature exists and *if* I find it ..." Bones said, correcting him, "... then what I'll likely do is invite it to sit down with me and have a beer. We'll find a tavern near the woods, and we'll chat for a while to figure out what's best for its long-term future within the boundaries of the United States. I'll make some suggestions, and it will thoughtfully contemplate them before making its own decision."

"You haven't lost your humor either, have you, doctor?"

"Nope," said Bones, "and I hope I never do."

*****

CH 2 – Report from Wadena

Reports hit the only paper in Wadena, Minnesota—a local rag called *The Northern Pacific Farmer*—that something strange had happened there. It was a small town only one hundred seventy miles from the nearest major city, Duluth, but with a population of only fifty-three, Wadena was tiny compared to the thirty-five hundred in its larger neighbor, which was exploding with settlers. Duluth's growth, and that of the surrounding area, had resulted primarily from the construction of the Great Northern Railroad and the discovery of iron ore in the Mesabi range nearby. By 1900, Duluth would have over fifty-two thousand people, over ten times the number it currently held.

As always, the front page of *The Northern Pacific Farmer* had the day's weather and mundane local news.

Weather

Gettin' cooler these days.
The air is thick as possum soup.
It was 45 degrees yesterday, so
we figure it will be close to that today.

In Other News:

Wadena carpenters have been busy on the Lutheran Church in town. As you recall, a fire last month destroyed the nave and part of the alter. The carpenters are also rebuilding a new alter and cross.

Eda Stenson was putting clothes on the line when she was flustered by three young boys roughhousing through her yard. If you have information about this, please contact Mrs. Stenson. She wishes for an apology …

And so, the news continued.

But one eye-catching headline was something not previously seen by the people of Wadena, and it sent a panic through that small community.

Man Witnesses Monster in Woods

From our local reporter:

Not far from Wadena, in Aiken County, a local man says he saw a monster out in the dense forest two nights ago. Jenkins Palmer, a long-time farmer and resident of Wadena, says he was out late on Thursday night returning home after visiting his nephew who lives in Barre Mills. He claims there were two red eyes glowing deep in the underbrush. It was around dusk when he witnessed the creature.

Jenkins claims the beast was hairy, about eight feet tall, and besides the red eyes, it had a long snout like a wolf and teeth like a bear. When asked whether it was a bear, Jenkins said, "No, it was too skinny for a d*** bear. It weren't nothin' like I'd ever seen before."

There have been stories told of such a creature in the woods in Aiken County—one many call a Wendigo. But no one has ever been able to capture the beast to prove it really exists. So, the legend continues.

***

The story would have died then had it not been for a member of the Palmer family who had cut it out and given it to a wayward traveler passing through Wadena on his way to Duluth. There he gave the clipping to someone who was traveling to Chicago and then on to Washington, D.C.

It had taken nearly a month, but the news of the sighting eventually reached the desk of the editor of the *Washington Post*, a relatively new paper to the nation's capital, established only a few years earlier in 1877. The editor and owner, Stilson Hutchins, seized the opportunity to sensationalize the story to increase circulation. It didn't make front page news, but it was included a page or two back. However, it still caught the eye of an astute business man who was in Washington to attend a few meetings. His name was Mr. Phineas.

Mr. Phineas was an older man in his seventies who had recently married a young woman forty years his junior after the death of his first wife. He had a squared-off face with deep-set eyes. In fact, his eye sockets had taken on a darkness which could only be described as sunken and mournful since his wife's passing. His wiry grey hair sprouted from every angle but revealed a considerable forehead which covered an equally considerable brain. He had a prominent nose combined with a smaller, less prominent, mouth—making his features irregular and oddly proportioned.

Wearing a gentleman's suit and ascot, Mr. Phineas was rich beyond measure, having accumulated his vast wealth in a variety of ventures. One alone which lasted only six months netted him over half a million dollars—some twenty million in monies of the current day.

Mr. Phineas could smell a business opportunity like a bloodhound could pickup the trace of a fox running for its life through a dense Yorkshire forest. And as his eyes scanned the article about the mysterious creature in Minnesota, his thoughts turned to dollar signs. Yet, it was a far-off place in 1883 (Minnesota had only become a state twenty-five years earlier in 1858), and although he was rich, he believed he would need more resources. With wealth comes connections, and Mr. Phineas had plenty of them. One happened to be the Deputy Director of the Interior, Cecil Bronson.

Bronson was a hardened Washington insider—a career politician who had been at the department since its inception and, before that, had spent his early years in the War Department. Only five foot three inches tall, Bronson was about as round as he was tall. Rotund and stubby, the deputy director played both sides of almost everything he viewed as an opportunity to make money.

"Cecil, it is good to see you. How are things here in Washington?" Mr. Phineas asked, making himself comfortable in Bronson's office in the Patent Building.

"Phineas, my dear old friend. How are you? I hear your enterprises are doing well. Your events certainly make the papers these days."

"Sometimes that's good and sometimes that's bad. But I suppose even bad publicity is good for business. As long as your name is out there and people hear it, it can't be too bad, right?"

"You've turned it into an art form, I must say," said Bronson. "So, what brings you to DC?"

Phineas handed Bronson the *Washington Post* article and let him read it.

"Interesting," said the director. "But there are crazies out there who think they see all kinds of things."

"Yes, but what if it's true? What if these legends are real?"

"What if they are?"

"Don't you see the hazards to the white settlers out there? A beast like this could cause untold harm to them. This would look very bad for the Administration, wouldn't it? It is the duty of the government to protect its people. I feel the Department of the Interior is where this belongs. It should get involved, together with the War Department. Fighting beasts like this should be every bit as important as fighting the Indian savages out West, I should think."

Bronson shook his head. "The chances are remote. This isn't something the federal government would get involved in Phineas. I'm sorry, but I'm not going to be able to help."

"Well, I think you're wrong about that Cecil."

"I tell you what. Let me discuss it here and see. In the meantime, you should form your own group to go out and find it. If it's as fierce and reclusive as you suggest, I'm sure people will pay a lot of money to see it."

"Yes, I've already thought of that," said Phineas. "It would just be nice to get some help from DC ... to protect the people, of course."

Bronson told Tillson about the matter to get his thoughts, and when Tillson categorically rejected offering any assistance, he dropped the matter.

Tillson, already disgusted by the department's policies on American Indians, decided he had seen and heard enough during his time there and tendered his resignation. Seeing a cause itself in this matter, he went to several wealthy families in the DC area and found interest in a new mission. To Tillson, this wasn't just an attempt to exploit one creature but rather a larger effort to exploit animals in general—whether for domesticated or not.

Phineas received a brief note from Bronson apologizing but stating that:

> *"... the matter of the Wendigo and all other such creatures of legend are outside the purview of the United States government. Therefore, it is the policy of the Department of the Interior not to become involved.*
>
> *Best wishes,*
> *Deputy Director*
> *Cecil Bronson"*

Shortly after, Mr. Phineas sent a telegram to one of his business partners.

URGENT MESSAGE STOP

Mr. McGinnis STOP I have received information on a beast discovered in Minnesota STOP I believe it would make a fine addition to our portfolio STOP It is time to form a posse and track the creature down STOP We will have two months to return it alive to New York City STOP This mission is vital to our mutual business interests STOP I will copy Cooper on this message and send details on a meeting to discuss STOP

*****

CH 3 – Conflict

In all the rush to ready himself for another trip west, Bones forgot about something very important—Samuel's graduation from Harvard medical school. Not only was he the nephew of someone very special to him—Missy Grey—but he had been one of Bones's best students at the school. Having spent a great deal of time with the young man during his mission to Texarkana and then again into the underground depths of New York City, Bones had developed a special relationship with him. They had become close, and to forget his graduation would have been unforgiveable—especially by the Grey family.

"So how are the plans going for Samuel's graduation party?" Marigold asked her mother. Marigold was Samuel's mother, and daughter of the matriarch of the Grey family and fortune, Esther Grey—more formally known as Madam Grey.

For Esther, it was a proud time. Although the family was extremely wealthy— akin to the titled aristocracy of England—they had never had a doctor in their legacy. And while those European aristocratic families would have considered such a profession to be plebian, the Greys embraced their hard work ethic in all manor and form.

"The celebration is all being arranged," answered Esther. "You need not worry about anything. We are having a catered affair here at the mansion. Invitations have been mailed, and we have already received three hundred acceptances."

"Wonderful!" said her middle daughter. "Samuel will be most pleased."

"I presume you sent one to Dr. Cook?" Missy asked, sitting with the others as they had their afternoon tea on the rear veranda. Missy was the youngest of Esther's three daughters.

Ever since the New York City incident, it had been a difficult time for the relationship between Bones and Missy. Intending to grow closer to him in New York City the year before, Missy had left the big city in tears. The entire affair had ended unhappily with a rather abrupt split between the two of them.

"Of course, we sent him one, child," said Madam Grey. "However, he has not yet responded. I trust he received the invitation. Have you talked to him lately?"

"No, Mother."

"I see. Well, I believe you should reach out to him and try to get things patched up. This is a wonderful opportunity to do that. You need to confirm with him that he is coming, although I'm sure he is. Samuel was his pupil after all."

"I don't know, Mother."

"You don't know what, dear?"

"I don't think I should contact him."

"Well, I do. You will go to him and talk to him. You must work this out, Missy. And, of course, the purpose of your reaching out to him will be to verify that he will be attending Samuel's graduation. I believe you can do that, can't you?"

For someone who prided her independence, the remarks rubbed Missy the wrong way, but she felt it was neither the time nor the place for a confrontation. So instead, she sighed and relented. She had hoped that Bones would have been the one to reach out to her—not the other way around. She struggled with having to do all the hard lifting in the relationship and wondered if there was anything left to salvage. Yet, for the sake of the family and Samuel, she would give it one more try.

***

There was a sharp knock at the front door, something unusual for the tiny flat where Bones lived. Normally, such a late-weekday intrusion meant either a student was panicking over an approaching final exam or one who was having second thoughts about the medical profession altogether. But when he opened the door, he found a more pleasant surprise.

"Missy! I wasn't expecting you," he muttered, straightening his hair with the palm of his hand. His expression was one of unexpected delight. "Please, please, come in."

"I am so sorry to intrude," said Missy. "I normally would have asked a good time to stop by, but my mother felt there was some urgency in the matter."

"What is it?" Bones asked, his mood growing more concerned and somber.

"It's about the graduation."

"The graduation?"

Missy was slightly taken aback by his reaction.

"Yes, Samuel's graduation from medical school. You did remember that, didn't you?"

20

Bones stared at her, as if she had just told him her mother had passed.

"I ... I completely forgot," he muttered. Strangely, he now looked both confused and embarrassed.

"What? How could you forget, Bones? For God's sake. You taught him. You knew he was graduating in the fall because of his little jaunt with you up to New York City."

Bones put up his hand. "Now, come on Missy. We both know it was the trip to Texarkana that put him behind in his studies. That's why he is graduating a late."

"Whatever! Still, how could you forget?"

"I'm sorry! Okay? I'm sorry. I just have a lot on my mind right now."

"Bones, you always have a lot on your mind, but that doesn't excuse you from thinking and caring about others in your life." Her words revealed much more than her feelings about his forgetting the graduation. She was quiet for a moment before adding, "And Mother is quite worried because you didn't respond to her invitation. I think she's rather insulted, actually."

"I'm not sure I've checked the post for the last few weeks," said the doctor. "I didn't mean to disrespect her or the family."

"What's going on, Bones. Why are you so preoccupied?"

He shook his head.

"Bones, talk to me."

"It's Claire."

"Your sister?"

"Yes."

"What is it?" Missy asked.

"We found out a few weeks ago she has ... she has TB."

"Consumption?"

"Yes."

"I'm sorry. I had no idea." Missy paused, now the one feeling insensitive and ashamed. Then, she said, "Bones, you of all people know that it's not inevitable. Not everyone ..." She stopped short of completing the sentence.

"You're right. It's not, but her chances of recovery are low. We all know many who have died from it."

"You must have faith, Bones. The Lord will take care of her."

Like his belief in tribal legends and their monsters, the doctor's acceptance of religion and a higher power was also weak.

"Ah, of course. Well, I know you believe in all that stuff, so perhaps you can say some prayers for her," he answered. "Perhaps if *you* do it, it will have some effect."

Missy frowned. There were many things about this man she wanted to change, but many more that she loved and wouldn't change for the world. She knew her mission was not to convert him to faith or anything else. If there was a mission left at all, it would be to help him see a new path—with religion and other things to which she felt he was blinded.

"I know you don't, Bones, but you should. He is the only one upon Whom you can always depend, except for me, of course." Missy reached for his arm and squeezed it affectionately. "There are many of us who care about you Bones. Please let us help."

Bones smiled and took her hand in his.

"You are so special, Missy. I can't tell you how much you mean to me."

"You can tell me." She laughed. "I certainly wouldn't mind."

Bones kissed her on the cheek.

"There's something else, too—not nearly as important, though," he said.

"Oh?"

"I have been approached by our friend William Tillson at the Interior Department in Washington. He wants me to go on another expedition."

"Really?"

"Yes, but this is not government sanctioned. He also wants me to leave within the next few days."

"But Claire? The graduation?"

"I know. I'm going to tell him that I can't do it right now," Bones answered, shaking his head. "I can't leave Claire, and I can't miss Samuel's graduation."

"Where is Claire now?" Missy asked.

"She's staying with my brother, Orville. But his brownstone is small, and he doesn't really know how to care for her. I've told her over and over to stay with me, but she says I'm too busy with the college. She's probably right."

"She will stay with Mother and me in the manor house." Missy was clear and decisive, her tone resolute.

"Oh, no," said Bones. "We can't risk your mother getting infected."

"We can put Claire in the east wing of the house until she recovers. Mother can provide 'round-the-clock care for her. I know she will insist once I tell her."

"I don't want to impose my family on yours," said the doctor. "It's not fair to do that. Anyway, I don't know if Claire would be up for that."

"The only way to find out is to ask," Missy answered. "In the meantime, Mother and I will make the arrangements."

*****

CH 4 — Recalibrating

Bones met again with Tillson and told him he would not be able to leave until the beginning of the summer. Although Tillson wasn't happy with the news, he accepted it.

"Do you wish to find someone else to take on this project?" Bones asked him. "I won't hold it against you if you do."

Tillson shook his head. "I'm afraid we may need to do that, Dr. Cook, but whoever we find, he won't be the caliber we've come to find in you."

"Your very kind."

"In the event we can't find an alternate, when do you think you'd be able to leave?"

"Within a month or two," Bones answered. "The graduation will be over, and we will see how my sister is doing at that point. If she is recovering, then I will accept your offer if it is still open."

"Not to be insensitive, but what if she is not recovering?"

"I don't know," Bones answered. "I think within two months, we will have our answer either way."

"Yes, yes, of course. Well then, we will wait and see. You will keep us apprised as you work through your situation. Evaluate whether you wish to take on this project. I will look to engage another as a backup just in case. But I assure you, Dr. Bones, that I'm hopeful your sister will recover and that you will be ready for a new adventure soon after."

"If there is such a creature, William, it is likely there is more than just one out there. Have you given that any thought?"

"Yes, but no one has captured even *one* before, and foreigners have occupied this country for more than three hundred years. It would be astonishing if *any* of you are able to find one, let alone an entire village of the beasts."

*****

CH 5 — Mr. Phineas

Mr. Phineas did not like to be kept waiting even when it was with his own partners. This was not a regular meeting, but rather a special one he had called to discuss urgent business matters, including the urgent message he had sent to McGinnis.

"It's about time you two showed up!" Phineas remarked. "Was there a queue of carriages in the road keeping you from being on time?"

James McGinnis and James E. Cooper took off their suitcoats and hats and draped them over the waiting arms of the young staff attendant before entering Phineas's office.

"I apologize Phineas, but Cooper here insisted on taking a new route to your office."

"It is quicker," said Cooper, extracting a heavy armchair from the sizeable, oval-shaped conference table.

"Not this time," answered Phineas. "Now, may we get started?" The old man was noticeably irritated and in a foul mood—not something either McGinnis or Cooper relished. "We have some decisions to make."

"Is this about your message?" McGinnis asked, opening his already bulging satchel to retrieve some papers.

"It's about the future of our business. I believe we need to expand it to include other things—things that will attract more patrons."

"Like what?" asked Cooper. "Wild beasts in the West?"

"More unique things, or, more precisely, things that would shock the ordinary person."

"We already have that," Cooper answered. "That's why we merged our businesses, so we could take advantage of what our companies have to offer the general public."

"I don't believe we've taken it far enough," said Phineas. "I think there is a huge piece of untouched business that we … and in fact, no one … has yet brought to the people. People like shows. People like to be amazed and dumbfounded. People want to see things they've never seen before. It's more than being entertained. Hell, they can do that just playing the fiddle, and

25

drinking and dancing around like fools. No, I'm talking about things that are memorable—*shockingly* memorable."

"But the common man is stupid. It doesn't take much to entertain him," said McGinnis.

"Yes, that's generally true, but sooner or later they tire of the same things. You can't show them the same stuff year after year. They will want more. We already have competitors, you know. You've worked in this industry long enough to know that, McGinnis. You and I both understand that we have to keep things fresh to keep an audience. It's always got to be something new."

"But we travel from town to town, Phineas," said McGinnis. "They don't see our shows every year. We don't have to change them that often. Plus, it's costly to start something from scratch. You know how expensive it is!"

"No, I don't, and I don't care. The financial part of the business is for you to handle. I'm the one who has to find a way to get people in to see what we have to offer. And from where I stand, I think our next big thing will be in New York City."

"Why the big city?" asked Cooper. "We've never done events in big cities before. People there have plenty of other venues to find entertainment."

"Because, my dear friend, there is a World Exposition scheduled for Chicago within the next few years, and I want to be part of it. We need to make a splash in a big city before that so we're ready for the global stage. I want our exhibition to *wow* the people of the world, not just America. Just think how grand that would be! We will be world-famous, not just in America."

"So, what is this next big thing?" asked McGinnis. "Is it this creature in Minnesota?"

"Legendary beasts," said Phineas. "All kinds of them—not just the one in Minnesota. You have to think bigger than that, McGinnis."

"What? Like unicorns and dragons?" laughed Cooper. "Where are you going to find those?"

"You may laugh, but there *are* such creatures, as I cited in my note. They are within this country too—not roaming some foreign shore."

"So, you're not talking about werewolves or vampires, then," added McGinnis, no longer smiling. "You're serious about this wendigee or wendigrow, thing?"

26

"I'm dead serious," said Phineas. Phineas pulled out the article from his desk drawer and shot them across the table to his colleagues. "Here, this is what my message was about. Take a look. This is the type of creature I think would make a splash—a sensation—for us."

McGinnis and Cooper glanced at the article.

"Well, I'll be damned," said McGinnis. "I never knew there were creatures like that out there."

"But how do we know this is true?" asked Cooper. "How do we know this man isn't making this stuff up?"

"We don't. But I've already begun making inquiries. We'll need to setup a group of trackers to go and find it. McGinnis, that will be your job. Put a team together and have them talk to the man who said he saw the beast. If it checks out, they'll need to find it and bring it back to New York City for us to put on exhibit."

"And what do you want from me?" asked Cooper.

"You're the business guy here, James. You come up with a way to fund it. I need that creature in New York City no later than the end of the year. I want to go into 1884 with something new—something no one has ever seen before and something people will pay a lot of money to see again and again."

*****

CH 6 – Time with Claire

Although there was no hesitation by Madam Grey in inviting Claire to her manor, Bones was concerned that Claire would reject the offer out of benevolence—not wishing to put anyone outside the family at risk. So, Claire sent word back through Bones and Missy responding that she was "politely and respectfully" declining the offer.

"I will not stand for it!" said Esther, hearing of Claire's reluctance. "The poor child has no mother or father, and if I must impose myself as a maternal figure in the matter, I will. Now, Dr. Cook, you must tell your sister that I will be most offended if she refuses my offer to stay with us. She will be of no hardship to us, and I will respect her privacy and give her most of the east wing of the house. My private doctor will look after her, and I have more than enough servants to attend to her needs. Now go. Tell her my wishes and that I don't want to be disappointed in her next response."

Bones went back to his brother's place and discussed it once more with his sister. Finally, Claire relented, sending a handwritten note back to Esther telling her how much she appreciated her generosity.

When she arrived at the stately manor the following week, she was pale and weak. She had tried to swirl her long, chestnut brown hair up on her head in the fashion of the day to make a "proper" presentation to her hostess , but Orville had been needed to help her. As a result, the final twirl hadn't stayed intact and by the time she reached the front doorstep, it dangled loosely on the side of her head.

Claire had always looked more like her mother and her side of the family than that of her father. With deep-set, dark eyes, high cheeks, and a broad, inviting smile, Claire was a beauty, and while Bones and Orville had thick, sturdy frames like their father, Claire's was more delicate and fragile. What all the siblings shared were their parents' tough spirit and unquenchable resilience. Both had been achievers in life and had encouraged their children to persevere, even during the hardest of times.

Bones's sister had been engaged to be married but had broken off the nuptials when she had become ill. Her betrothed, Harris Peabody, said he would stand by her regardless of what disease she had, but she pushed him away. She had told him she no longer loved him, even in truth, she was afraid he would contract the consumption from her. She couldn't bear that thought.

28

To a fault, she was a caring, giving young woman. Having gotten her divinity degree from Boston University, she had secured a position with a downtown church, Trinity Methodist. There she had been responsible for the outreach programs to the poor and the soup kitchens that kept that community alive. Religion had become a strong part of her life, and she lamented her brothers' rejection of it. Still, she tolerated their agnosticism as much as they accepted her dedication to the faith.

"Claire," said Esther, greeting the ailing, young lady at the door of her estate, "Clarence will take you to your quarters upstairs. Dr. Cook, will you help your sister in case she needs support going up the staircase?"

As they made their way up the grand staircase, Madam Grey called up to them, "Oh, and although we usually have supper at seven o'clock, you shouldn't feel pressure to come down and join us. I know you don't feel well. This is a time for you to recover and convalesce. We are all here for you, dear. Please make yourself at home. You may stay as long as you like."

"Thank you, Madam Grey," Claire answered. "I so much appreciate your hospitality. My brother has told me so much about you and your family that I feel I already know you."

"Well, you will get to know us much better during the coming days, and we're not always a model of the perfect family, I can assure you."

Bones helped his sister upstairs while Clarence carried her bags. At the bottom of the staircase, Missy turned to her mother. "She looks dreadful! I know Bones said she had contracted the illness some time ago, but I never expected her to be in such a poor state as this."

"Yes, it is sad," Esther answered. "I've had several friends succumb to the disease. It is a horrible thing too. It is slow and relentless—every day stealing more and more energy from the body. Hopefully, that won't be the case with this poor dear. I pray she has the strength to fight it."

The days passed, and Claire grew weaker. For the first few days, she had come down for supper and eaten with them. It hadn't been much, but she had pushed around some peas and roasted squash on her plate none-the-less. At one sitting she had managed to eat half a bowl of cioppino soup—a thick seafood dish which was becoming increasingly popular in the area. However, by day five, she no longer ventured downstairs, mostly staying in her room and either sleeping of staring out the window. Bones had suggested she read—a favorite pastime of hers—but she shook her head, claiming she had neither the energy nor the interest.

"What does your mother's doctor say?" Orville asked Missy one day while stopping by to check on his sister.

"He says the disease is spreading—consuming her lungs," Missy answered.

"And what about my brother?"

"You haven't talked to your brother about it?"

"Not lately. He's been in his own little world. I've raised the question, but he avoids it. He doesn't want to talk about it."

"He's in denial," said Missy.

"Yes. I'm afraid we all are," Orville said. "We can't bear the thought of ... well, you know."

"Yes. I can understand. And Orville, you are welcome to stop by anytime. You know that, right?"

"You and your family are so kind taking care of her this way. I don't know how we can ever repay you."

"There is no need," Missy answered. "We consider all of you part of our family."

*****

CH 7 – A Minister Is Summoned

After Tillson learned more details about the Minnesota sighting, he sent an urgent message to Bones to find out if and when he would be able to leave. Only weeks earlier, Bones had told him of his delay; however, things had become much more urgent during the interim.

> Dear Dr. Cook,
>
> I trust you and your family are doing better and that your sister is beginning to recover from the frightful disease with which we are all faced these days.
>
> Although I continue to look for a suitable replacement for you, I still hold out hope you will be able to take up my offer. I have more information on the location of that animal we discussed while you were here. Apparently, it was seen near Wadena, Minnesota, near Duluth. The sighting was over a month ago, so it is difficult to know whether there have been others.
>
> I can only surmise that the businessmen involved in tracking the beast and bringing it to a major East Coast city are well engaged by this point. It looks like my former employer, the Department of the Interior, has decline the request to get involved.
>
> Please advise me immediately of your status as I need to move expeditiously.
>
> Very truly,
>
> William Tillson

Bones received the letter, and promptly responded.

> Dear Mr. Tillson,
>
> I received your post and understand your predicament. Unfortunately, at this time my sister is still suffering immeasurably from tuberculosis; therefore, I will be unable to take up the mission we discussed.
>
> I apologize for any inconvenience this may cause; however, I know my time is best placed here with my family.
>
> Sincerely yours,
>
> Reginald Cook

Although it was difficult for Bones to turn down this unique opportunity, he knew it was the right thing and quietly accepted the call to his family that he'd been given.

Samuel's graduation from medical school had gone without a hitch. He had graduated with high honors and earned his medical degree. Comically, he had quipped that he would only require that everyone in his family call him *doctor* until the glow had faded from his face, which he added, "might be never."

"And how long do you think it will take for the glow to dissipate?" Missy had asked Bones, jokingly.

"Oh, about five minutes after he receives his first patient, I should think."

Yet, despite the happiness and celebration, there was darkness in Bones's life. His sister, Claire, was not improving, and as the days and weeks passed, things only worsened. Orville stopped by the Grey estate now and again to check on her, but it was Bones who took to Claire's bedside, remaining there in a vigil to monitor her vitals and care for her needs.

Finally, her situation began to deteriorate quickly, and her condition became grave.

"I think we should send for a priest," said Esther, coming down the stairs and speaking to her youngest daughter. She had just come out of Claire's room and engaged Missy as she reached the main landing.

"She's that bad then?" Missy asked.

"Yes, I think so, dear. I don't believe it will be long."

"Shouldn't we call for Orville?"

"Yes, contact him right away. He left only an hour ago to get some rest, but I think he should be here."

"What about her doctor—*your* doctor?"

"I think that time has come and gone," said Esther soberly. "Dr. Moorhead won't be able to save her now. Only He can do that."

Missy went to the room and found Bones kneeling next to the bed. His sister's face was grey and sallow; her eyes were closed; and she was breathing ever so lightly through her open mouth. Missy put her hand on his as they surprisingly remained folded in prayer. As she looked at him, she saw a tear trickle down his cheek before dropping off his chin and onto the wool rug beneath the bed.

"I'm so sorry," Missy said to him. "I wish there were something more I could do."

Bones gave her a feeble smile and shook his head without saying a word. He didn't have to.

Orville arrived within the hour, and the minister, Reverend Thaddeus Benton came through the front door only a few minutes later, donning his white alb and red chasuble before placing a violet stole around his neck. He went upstairs and approached Claire with an open Bible resting in his palm, making the sign of the cross once he reached her bedside.

"In the name of the Father, and of the Son, and of the Holy Spirit," the reverend began.

Esther and Clarence came up to be with them as Claire's Last Rites were performed. They remained quiet as the reverend started through the readings.

"Through this holy anointing may the Lord in His love and mercy help you with the grace of the Holy Spirit. May the Lord who frees you from sin save you and raise you up."

But before he could utter another word, Claire opened her eyes. It was the first time in days she had done so. Bones and everyone else in the room sat up, surprised. They had no idea what to think or what to do at the moment, and all parked their enthusiasm, watching carefully how the preacher would react to the change. However, as the priest continued with the Last Rites unabated, as if he hadn't realized the change.

"Uh, Reverend Benton," said Orville. "I think she's …"

Benton looked up from his reading. He too seemed surprised by what he was seeing. There had been a marked pinking in the color of Claire's face; suddenly, it became flushed with rosy hues.

"Claire?" asked Bones. "Claire, how are you feeling?"

"I … I think I'm better," she said haltingly. She tried to raise her head but listlessly let it fall back onto her pillow. She was too weak to talk further, but she raised her hand to stop the priest from reading any further.

"Yes?" asked Reverend Benton, waiting for Claire to say something to him.

"Reverend, I think she's feeling better," Oliver muttered. "Maybe we should pause the rites for now. What do you think?"

The minister looked at Orville with astonishment. "I've seen some things in my time, but this is extraordinary," he answered.

Bones took his sister's hand. "Claire, do you feel like eating or drinking something? You haven't had anything for days."

His sister gently pushed herself higher on the pillow as Missy and Bones helped her, fluffing her cushion and re-situating her on the feather mattress.

"Clarence," said Esther, turning to her butler, "why don't you get her some cool water."

Clarence left, as the others continued to gape in amazement at the astonishing recovery of someone who, only moments earlier, was thought to be at Death's doorstep.

"I do feel like some water," Claire said. "My mouth is a bit parched."

Reverend Benton instead turned to another piece of scripture and applied holy oil to Claire's forehead. Finishing the passage, he said, "And may the Lord shine upon thee and give thee peace," he said, making the sign of the cross once more. "In the name of the Father, the Son and the Holy Spirit. Amen."

Esther's physician, Dr. Moorhead, was summoned promptly, and he hurried up the stairs to the room where Claire now rested comfortably. Opening his black bag, he took out his stethoscope and listened to her heart and lungs, asking her to take deep breaths each time he moved it. Then he looked into her eyes to judge whether they were dilated or had any unusual milkiness or redness.

"Well?" asked Bones, knowing he too could have examined his sister; however, practicing medicine on one's own family member was frowned upon.

Taking off the stethoscope, Dr. Moorhead answered. "I must say," he began, his wispy eyebrows bobbing up and down as he talked, "I've not seen anything quite like it. If I didn't know better, I'd say she never had TB. I can't hear anything in her lungs. Here, take a listen." Moorhead handed Bones his stethoscope and stepped aside. "I can't explain it," he continued. "I don't hear anything congestion at all."

Bones asked Claire to take some deep breaths and then asked again after he placed the monitor at various points on her back.

"I don't hear anything either," said Bones. "There is no indication of disease or fluid in her lungs. They are clear. How can that be?"

"I don't have an answer either," said Esther's doctor.

"So, what do we do now?" Missy asked.

"She should rest," responded Moorhead. "Give her plenty of liquids and let her eat what she feels she can keep down. We just need to monitor her for the next several days. I don't want to get ahead of ourselves on this."

"So, she's not cured then?" Esther asked.

"I don't know," said Moorhead. "Again, I've never seen this before. I will go back to my office and see if there is anything in the journals on this type of thing. I'll let you know."

The doctor leaned in and peered closely at Claire one more time. "You look much better," he said. "Your color is back, anyway."

Indeed, during the next several days, Claire seemed to be recovering well. By the third day, she was joining the others downstairs for supper, and by the end of the week, she told her brother, Bones, she was ready to go home.

"It's been so nice of you to provide a place for me to stay as well as your doctor's services," said Claire, as she stood at the doorway with both brothers, readying to leave. Orville held one bag; Bones held another, and Clarence and another house attendant began taking her trunk out to the waiting coach.

"It was the least we could do," said Esther. "We certainly weren't going to let you lie there at your brother's place without some motherly attention."

"Well, thank you again. You have been most gracious and charitable."

Bones left with his siblings and a renewed sense of optimism. He felt good about things—the first time in a long time—and later that day he penned a quick note to William Tillson. It had only been two weeks since their last exchange of letters, and Bones hoped the offer to go to Minnesota was still available.

Tillson's reply was prompt.

> Dr. Cook,
>
> It is quite serendipitous that I received your letter when I did. You see, the fellow I finally found to replace you telegrammed me yesterday and informed me that he too would be unable to undertake the task. He said that he was contacted by someone in New York City who made it clear that under no circumstances should he interpose himself into this matter.
>
> I feel compelled to share this with you, as I do believe this mission comes with more risk than we had originally thought. Therefore, if you decide to accept this project, you must understand this. I have my suspicions from where these threats are emanating, but I fear stating that openly in a post.
>
> Please confirm that you still wish to pursue this with me. I will be most grateful if you accept and believe that millions of people in New York City would feel the same if they only knew.
>
> Very truly,
>
> William Tillson

CH 8 — Old Enough

With the help of his grandmother, who pulled some strings and helped fund him, Samuel Stinson was able to acquire a medical practice on Merrimac Street in Central Boston. Esther had arranged for her grandson to work with Dr. Moorhead upon graduating from Harvard. Then, when Dr. Moorhead retired, the plan was for Samuel to take over the practice. Moorhead had wished to retire earlier but believed it would take three to five years to break-in the young Stinson to ensure his patients were well cared for. Fishing had long been the doctor's passion, and since the death of his wife, he had thought of little else.

"Now, Samuel, you'll need to consider whether the patient has a wet cough or a dry cough. It can mean different things, you know," said Moorhead.

"Yes, doctor," Samuel answered, already well aware of the difference and its meaning. He had learned much in medical school and was anxious to put his skills to practice. Although his grandmother and mother were eager for him to take over Dr. Moorhead's practice, Samuel wasn't so sure. He was still young, and the adventures with Bones had sparked something else inside him.

"A surgeon?" said Bones, listening to the newly minted doctor. "You now want to be a surgeon? Why?"

"Yes," Samuel answered, "I think I'd like to be a surgeon. That's a very up-and-coming field of medicine, and I'd like to be a part of it. I think it would exciting."

"I suppose you're right," commented Bones. "Ever since Long and Simpson began using ether and chloroform on patients to anesthetize them, things have changed greatly in that world. No longer do we have to strap people to tables or chairs to saw or cut into them."

"I know I can discover the next greatest thing in medicine too, Dr. Cook. I want to try."

"Well, why don't you learn all you can from Dr. Moorhead for now," Bones said. "You are still young and new to medicine. There is much he can teach you. You should do that before you launch off into something else."

Samuel nodded, although he seemed unconvinced.

"But I must tell you, and I will tell your aunt and your grandmother, that I am leaving Boston for a while," said Bones. "I may not be back for several months."

"Where are you going?" Samuel asked.

"I have matters to attend to in Minnesota," said Bones.

"Minnesota? What could you possibly have to do way out there?"

"Business," Bones said without further explanation. He knew that if he told Samuel everything, he would want to come with him like the last time. Bones felt it more important that Samuel get himself established in his medical practice before he did anything else. The last thing Bones felt he should do was chase after more monsters in the western hinterlands.

"I understand," answered Samuel, giving Bones a skeptical look. "But you know that I can help you like I did the last time. You wouldn't be here, you know, if I hadn't …"

"Samuel, stop right there," admonished Bones. "I know what you're saying but this is different."

"How is it different?"

"For one thing, it's not in a big city. It's out in the wilds of the West. Hell, the Indians still roam out there."

"But I helped you in Texarkana too, if you don't recall," said Samuel, standing his ground.

"Yes, you did. And I thank you for both of those efforts. And both times you were lucky you weren't killed. Right?"

"I know what I'm getting into."

"No, you don't. We were lucky. Heck, in Texarkana you didn't even know how to shoot a gun."

"But I learned."

"Yeah, you did. But you don't even know what this project is," countered Bones.

"No, I don't, but …"

"It's not about some leafy, green gnomes wandering the sewers chewing on bark and ginkgo root."

"What's ginkgo root?"

"See! That's what I mean, Samuel. This is very serious business. This thing is man-eating—not mushroom-eating."

"Ah ha!" shouted Samuel. "I knew it. You're going after another monster, aren't you?"

"Samuel!"

"Dr. Cook—with all due respect—you need me," Samuel stated resolutely.

Bones huffed. He knew how headstrong Samuel could be, but he also knew how unforgiving Madam Grey could be. He was caught between Charybdis and Scylla, and it made him uncomfortable.

"If I let you come with me, your mother and grandmother will have my neck!" said Bones.

"Better *they* have your neck than the Reaper has your soul," said Samuel.

Bones shook his head. He knew he had taught this young man well. Now, he was thinking that it had been *too* well.

***

Bones didn't have to think very long as Samuel's persistence eventually wore him down. However, he dreaded telling Madam Grey and her middle daughter, Marigold. What would be worse was sharing the news with Missy—particularly since he hadn't offered her the same chance.

"You're not taking him!" shouted Marigold, wagging her finger at the doctor.

"Mother! I'm old enough to make these decisions on my own," said Samuel, standing in the crossfire.

"No, you're not!" Marigold shot back. "I'm your mother, and I will not have you put in harm's way like this. Especially a *third* time."

"Marigold, I assure you that your son will be in good hands," said Bones. "I will be taking a security guard with me as added protection. He will be with us throughout the trip. He's done many missions like this, so he knows what to expect."

Bones was stretching the truth a bit as his "security guard" had been in the military and attained the rank of major but had not seen any active engagements. He was the brother of Tillson, but Bones was confident that if Tillson were recommending him, he must be of sound character. He certainly came from good stock with the Tillson family heritage.

Marigold crossed her arms and huffed.

"I share my daughter's concern, Dr. Cook," said Esther, chiming in. "I didn't want Samuel to go to New York City either, if you recall. I didn't know about it until after the fact, but had I known, I would have stopped it. You almost got him killed there!"

"That's why we're telling you now, Madam Grey—Marigold," said Bones, addressing each of them. "I didn't want you to think …"

Samuel was standing in the group stewing. "I'm sorry mother—grandmother, but this is *my* life, and I control it—not you. Although I respect what you're saying and appreciate your concern for me, *I* will make this decision—that is, I have already *made* this decision."

Marigold stormed out of the room while Esther gave Bones a cold stare. "You are not on my most-favored list, Dr. Cook. I want to make myself perfectly clear about that," she said.

"I'm sorry, madam. I echo Samuel's thoughts that I too respect your opinion on the matter. Having been in Samuel's shoes before when I was younger, I understand his point of view as well. He is a man now, and sometimes one must make tough decisions that go against other people's wishes. He wants to live his life—not the one you and your daughter wish him to have. With no disrespect, I have allowed Samuel to exercise his right to make this decision on his own. I will not stand in his way."

"Well then, Dr. Cook, you may see yourself out," Esther answered frostily.

She turned on her heels and started to leave the room but suddenly glanced back at him. "And if anything happens to my grandson, doctor, you will have Hell to pay for it!"

After Esther left, Samuel looked at Bones and said, "I think that went pretty well, don't you?"

*****

CH 9 — Thaddeus Dalrymple

Although others "in the know" at the Department of the Interior were interested in what was going on with the hunt for the Wendigo, there was another who was approached specifically to assist in it.

Thaddeus Dalrymple was a mid-level bureaucrat who worked for Land Commissioner, Randolph Preston--then directly under the relatively new Secretary Henry Teller. He was responsible for granting and processing land requests under the Timber Culture Act of 1873. The Act was intended to give 160 acres of land to homesteaders who had already received an initial 160 acres under the Homestead Act of 1862—lands west of the Mississippi River and east of the Rocky Mountains.

However, Dalrymple was not satisfied with such a low-level position and had befriended James McGinnis while on a train to New York City. By then, McGinnis had an extensive empire of businesses, not the least of which involved the partnership with James Cooper and Mr. Phineas.

Standing nearly six feet two inches tall, Dalrymple was a large presence in any room. His ego and disposition were only surpassed by that of Mr. Phineas, who had few equals in those categories. Yet, Dalrymple soon became an important and useful tool of Mr. McGinnis, and in the spring of 1883, he agreed to assist the Phineas-McGinnis-Cooper partnership in locating and returning a Wendigo for its unique and specialized shows.

Oversized and overbearing, Dalrymple had a long frame with equally long arms and legs. His hands and fingers would have made a concert pianist jealous, and his feet were narrow and high-arched to support the size and mass above them. At the same time, his severe myopia forced him to wear silver-rimmed glasses at all times—the thick lenses making him appear more like an accountant than a surveyor by trade. Aside from his dark eyes and bushy brows, his face was rather plain with an average sized nose but a broad mouth framed by very thin lips. What was extraordinary was his overly thick, and some would say gnarly beard which hung below his Adam's apple.

"Thaddeus," said McGinnis as the middle-aged man came into his study, "it's good to see you. Where have you been hiding?"

Dalrymple laughed—more for the benefit of his patron than reflecting any internal enjoyment at the remark. "I've been under a rock," he answered, hoping to get the same response.

McGinnis didn't disappoint, uttering a guffaw that could be heard throughout the expansive manor. "Good one," he said. "Well, I hope to pull you out from under that rock, as we have some business for you to attend to."

Although McGinnis was about the same age as Dalrymple—both men were in their late thirties—McGinnis had money. He hadn't been born with it but instead worked hard as an entrepreneur to get to a position where his life—and that of his family—was easier. At a young age, he had lost both his mother and father to disease. His older sister had tried to raise him by herself, but her harsh, disciplinary approach had pushed him away, causing him to leave her house and its security at the age of only sixteen. He eventually found a job and through attention to detail and good business instincts became a partner with James Cooper, a man almost twice his age who was very experienced and successful in his own right. It was a few years later when they merged their business dealings with those of another seasoned entrepreneur—Mr. Phineas.

McGinnis could have been a ladies' man—as he was handsome and well mannered—but he was more introverted than his more flamboyant partner, Mr. Phineas. His face was sculpted and prominent like a Greek god's, and his meticulously groomed beard framed his face like a wet blanket on a mare. But even in his early thirties, McGinnis was showing signs of baldness, and by 1883 his hairline had retreated mightily, showing off a glistening pate with only two legacy sprouts over the ears as reminders of a more youthful past.

"What do you have for me?" Dalrymple asked. "You asked that I quit my job at the department, but I need some assurance that you have something that will pay me what I'm worth."

"I do. I have some business in the West that needs attention," began McGinnis. "It has some urgency, I'm afraid. We are looking for someone who can lead a private group of, well, bounty hunters of sorts. However, they aren't out tracking a human; they'll be seeking a wild animal."

"You need trappers, then?"

"Yes, you may call them that."

"Good. I just hope the pay is commensurate with my exertion," said Dalrymple, responding to the intriguing proposal thrown out by McGinnis.

"Oh, I think it will be worth your time. Anything is more than the fifteen hundred a year you make at the Interior, am I right?"

"I have been struggling with the earnings, yes. If I am to give up my career at Interior, I'll need a big increase," Dalrymple responded.

"Let's get down to brass tacks, then, shall we? Thaddeus we need you to go to Minnesota. Like I said, there is an animal there that we need you to find and return."

"Why do you need someone like me from DC to go all the way out there for that? Can't you find trappers in Minnesota?"

"What I need is someone like you to spearhead this. I need someone I can trust. I need someone who can gather a group of trappers from the area and track down this creature. It's been seen near Duluth, Minnesota recently. I need my own man out there who will report back and keep this thing on track. Are you interested?"

"What kind of animal is it? Bear? Coyote?"

"It's called a Wendigo by the Indians, and it has a long and mysterious past. You'll need extra men to capture it and put it in a sturdy cage for transport."

"Is it dangerous?"

"Some say it is, but I don't believe it's any more dangerous than your normal, everyday black bear, Thaddeus. You'll need to gather some experienced trappers, though. No one has ever been able to capture one." McGinnis paused and walked to the window of his study which overlooked a beautiful garden in the back of his manor. Looking out, he continued. "Thaddeus, I won't tell you it will be easy. They say the animal is cunning and elusive. You'll need to keep your wits about you and make sure you take armed men with you, just in case."

"I can handle it," said Dalrymple. "This shouldn't be too hard."

"Good. Then, you'll leave tomorrow. Your travel and expenses will be paid for, of course."

"What does it pay?" asked Dalrymple.

"We will give you a thousand dollars in advance and another thousand when you return the animal. You'll make more in a few months than you make in a year at Interior. Do you have a family, Thaddeus?"

"No, my wife died a few years ago, and we never had any children."

"Then this little jaunt won't be much of an inconvenience. When you return, we will pay you another thousand dollars if you bring back the Wendigo alive. That's three thousand, Thaddeus."

"And if it's dead?"

"You'll at least get the two thousand. The beast isn't worth as much to us if it's dead."

"All right. I will bring it back alive, sir."

It was good that Dalrymple didn't ask more questions about the creature. McGinnis wasn't above lying to him, but he preferred not to. In this case, it wasn't necessary, and he didn't have to mention the chances of Dalrymple or his men returning more dead than alive. Dalrymple might not have liked the answer.

*****

CH 10 – Strange Behavior

Orville took Claire back to his townhouse, telling her that she should stay there for a few days or weeks until she felt well enough to return home. But it was already during the second day that Orville experienced a run-in with his sister.

"Orville, why can't you keep your place clean! It's a pig stye," she said loudly—something most out of character for the diminutive young woman.

"I'm sorry if my housekeeping offends you," he said rather defensively. "It is *my* place after all." Then, realizing the harshness of his tone, he backed down, adding, "But for you, Claire, I will try to clean up after myself a little better. All right?"

Claire walked into the kitchen and picked up a dirty plate from the sink. It was one of many dirty dishes that hadn't been cleaned for at least a day or two.

"Disgusting!" she exclaimed before hurling the plate across the room where it smashed against the wall and fell into hundreds of fragments on the parquet floor.

"Why did you do that?" Orville shouted at her, engaged again. "That was one of Mother's fine China pieces. You knew that. Why did you break it?"

"Because it was Mother's," she answered.

As she mouthed the words, Orville could see her face twist and contort in a way he'd never seen before. Her mouth was taut and stringent, and her nostrils flared. This was a temper he'd not witnessed by his sister, and it troubled him.

"Claire, listen, I think you may be coming down with something again. Perhaps you should get some rest. Why don't you go into the guest room and lie down. If you don't feel better in the morning, I can take you back to the doctor. Is that all right?"

Claire's face softened, and her body relaxed. She gave her brother a slight smile and nodded.

"Perhaps you're right, Orville. I … I don't feel like myself right now. It's probably from being pent-up in that room in the Grey mansion for all those weeks. It's finally caught up with me. I think I will go lie down."

She gave her brother a quick peck on the cheek and left the room to lie down. Later, Orville went to check on her, but she was still sleeping. Electing to let her rest, he shut the door softly and went back to the kitchen to clean up.

Claire seemed better after her rest, and there were no more incidents—at least not that week. She felt well enough to go into town and do some shopping on her own.

Seeing her improvement, Orville suggested that she contact her former fiancé, Harris Peabody. He had learned of her remarkable recovery and had immediately left her a note letting her know that he had stopped by to visit. However, she had not answered him. Orville knew of this exchange only by accident when he discovered Peabody's note tucked into the door of her flat one day. He had gone to check on any posts or other correspondence left there while she convalesced at the Grey's place. Although he had given his sister the note, she hadn't written back to him.

"I do think Mr. Peabody would like to hear from you," Orville had pressed her.

"In time, my brother. In time."

It was very unlike her to be so fickle and unconcerned about others. Normally, she went out of her way to accommodate people, especially those close to her. Still, Orville was hopeful that the two would be reunited as he greatly admired the well-healed and charismatic young man.

But when Claire still hadn't responded to Mr. Peabody's note after some time, Orville took it upon himself to pay the young man a call.

"I am so glad to hear that she has recovered," said Peabody after welcoming Orville into his home in a posh district of Boston near Back Bay. "You don't know how worried I am about her."

"We all are," Orville answered. "But I think all is better now."

Peabody was a tall man—six feet three and one-half inches, in fact. He towered over the shorter Cook brother. Yet, he was not thin and lanky, like his parents, but instead had some girth. Weighing in at some two hundred sixty pounds, he had difficulty finding a good tailor for suits and trousers. But Harris was a kind man. He never raised his voice when a tailor got it wrong. His benevolent, blue eyes always looked kindly on them and asked gently that they "take another look."

"When Claire told me she no longer loved me, I thought my life was over," said Harris. "I believed her. Then, later, I found out the real reason—she was protecting me from her consumption. I loved her even more after that knowing that she was only thinking of me. She's like that you know—loving and caring."

"Yes, I know," said Orville. "I've been lucky enough to have her as my sister for nearly twenty-six years. She was like that as child too—always looking after other people before herself."

"So, has she fully recovered?" Peabody asked eagerly.

"Yes. The doctor says she has anyway."

"Yet she hasn't contacted me. I'm a bit bewildered by that, you know. I sent a note to her. Perhaps she didn't see it?"

"Perhaps," said Orville, lying. "She is still trying to get her life back on track after being so near death. Things like that can have an effect on you."

"In what way?"

"I've heard some people reassess their lives when they think they are going to die but somehow survive. Maybe that's what she's doing now. She's just working through it."

"Do you think she's changed her mind about me?" Harris asked nervously.

Orville shook his head. "Oh, I don't think so, Harris. She loves you. You two were meant for each other. Trust me. She'll come around. It just may take a little more time."

"I'll give her as much time as she needs," said Peabody. "But I'd like to see her. Do you think she would see me if I stopped by to visit?"

"I'd give her a little more time. As I said, she's recovered, but she isn't one hundred percent. I will remind her to get a hold of you. She will. Just don't push things too fast. Fair?"

"Yes. I understand," said Peabody dutifully. "I will await further direction from you, Orville. You've always been a good friend and a kind soul. Thanks."

*****

CH 11 — Palmer Jenkins

Palmer Jenkins was a family man and a farmer. He was born and raised in Aiken County even though his parents had come from England and settled there in 1824. He had married his wife, Abagail, in 1847 and had four children with her before she died from cholera in 1855 during the epidemic that had afflicted travelers passing through, heading to California to resettle. He alone had raised the children and tried to make the farm work to support all of them. Then, tragedy had struck again in 1858 when his youngest, Isaac, had died at the age of four. Lilly, his only daughter, had died the year after, at age eight. But with help from the few neighbors in the area, he had managed to raise his other two sons, Jacob and Eli. Both still lived in the area, were married, and had families of their own.

Even with all the tragedy, Jenkins had remained on his property, working the farm to make a living and hiring local hands to help with the more arduous chores. Often, he would venture out to hunt pheasant or wild boar to keep fresh provisions on the table.

However, it was he who had seen and reported the red-eyed monster in the woods as he was returning from Perham to visit with his sister, Amelia. He had been shocked by sighting. Never before had he witnessed anything like it or felt the cold evil that had invaded his body when he stared back at it. Although he had tried to move his legs to escape, to flee, to save himself, he found himself frozen in place—paralyzed with fear of a monster so large, hairy and abominable that its image haunted him for weeks after. It wasn't until the horrible red eyes lost interest and moved on deeper into the woods that he regained his senses and began to run.

He ran faster than he had ever run before back to his cabin, locking the doors and shuttering the windows. He had grabbed his Hollis & Sheath 10-gauge, double barrel shotgun and prepared for the worst. Shaking, he had watched the windows and listened at the door, but it never came. After downing two shots of whiskey, he had fallen asleep with his head resting on the gunstock as the sun peaked in through an uncovered window on the east side of the house. He had dreaded the return of nightfall when the woods would grow quiet and dark once more, setting free the beast to pursue its evil intents. Ever since that day, he hadn't slept—his face aged with dark circles beneath his eyes and a sudden, nervous twitch in his left eye.

Yet, his story was all the people of the tiny town of Wadena could talk about for the next three months. And when it reached the big newspaper in Washington, D.C., Jenkins became a local celebrity of sorts.

"Jenkins, seen any monsters lately?" asked Willy Martin, the sole saloon owner in town, taunting his neighbor. "Ya' know, I get a lot of that in here, but it usually only comes after they're stone drunk and staggering home!"

Jenkins would often get ridiculed in town by ill-mannered town folk who had nothing better to do than to torment well-meaning residents. However, he would just smile, shrug and say, "Monsters? Nope. Haven't seen any today."

Even after news reporters from Duluth had come and gone, Jenkins didn't lose his sense of modesty. He had seen and experience too much in his life to let this one incident define him—for good or for bad.

But one day, he got a knock on his door that changed all that.

"Yes?" he said, answering.

"Mr. Palmer?" said the man, misusing Jenkin's first name as his surname.

"That's me. How can I help you gents?"

The man at the door had a massive frame, and he looked even more intimidating with his long, thick, gnarly brown beard. At the same time, his extensive facial growth was tempered by his rather plain face and a pair of silver-rimmed glasses

"I'm Thaddeus Dalrymple, and I'm here on behalf of the U.S. government. We are investigating the sighting you had of a monster in the woods not long ago. You are the Jenkins Palmer who reported that event, are you not?"

"The name is Palmer Jenkins, sir," said Jenkins, correcting him.

"Fine, then we need to chat."

But before Jenkins could question the nature of their inquiry, the man and all of his companions were inside his cabin making themselves at home. The man called Dalrymple took a seat in Jenkins's main chair and put his dusty black boots up on the table in front of him. He pulled out a hand-rolled cigar and struck a match on the bottom of his boot to light it before puffing away without an ashtray in sight.

"So, tell me about this monster of yours. Where did you see it?" asked Dalrymple.

Although kind-hearted, Jenkins was not a man to put up with rudeness, so he walked over and pushed the man's boots off his table before he too sat down in a chair next to him.

"I saw it down the road yonder," Jenkins said pointing at one of the closed windows that offered a view out the front of the place.

"Where exactly? I need to know the *exact* place you saw it, old man." The stranger's voice quickly turned fiery and hostile.

Jenkins could tell the men were up to no good, but there was little he could do but play their game until they left. Besides now questioning whether they were really from the US government, he was sorely outnumbered.

"You said you were from the government," said Jenkins. "Can I see some proof?"

"I don't need to give you proof!" said Dalrymple. "But if you want proof, here!"

He shoved his Department of the Interior credentials at Jenkins just long enough for him to catch the masthead logo of the department and his name but not enough time to see that it had expired.

"Well, all right then. I'll tell you what I remember."

Jenkins began his story, and when he'd finished, he looked at the group's leader. But instead of nodding in understanding, Dalrymple's face remained cold and dispassionate as he continued puffing intently on his cigar.

"Is there anything else you want to know?" Jenkins asked.

"Yes. We'll need you to take us there—where you saw the creature," said Dalrymple.

"Well, I can do that. I'd say the day after tomorrow works for me."

"No, Mr. Jenkins. I mean *now!*" The man's face remained unmoved and determined.

Jenkins smiled. "I'm sorry, but I have a church meeting tonight. I can do it tomorrow if that's …."

Dalrymple suddenly pulled out his revolver and held it menacingly in his hand, pointing it directly at Jenkins's chest. "I guess you didn't hear me clearly old man. I said, 'we go *now'*."

Jenkins looked up at the other men. All were wearing gun belts and itching to put a few slugs of lead into him. So, he rose, but as he did, the men in the group drew their guns as well—all directed right at him.

"I was just going to get my hat," Jenkins said. "That's all."

They handcuffed the old man and put on the back of one of their agitated horses while its rider hopped on in front of him, slipping his Smith & Wesson rifle into its saddle harness and buckling it securing with a strap.

"Now then, Mr. Palmer," said Dalrymple, "where did you say you saw the creature?"

*****

CH 12 – Onboard the Bones Express

The Midwest was still considered "wild" country in the 1880s. Although Minnesota had become a state only twenty-five years earlier, the land to its west was still open territory. In fact, it was known as the Dakota Territory which included lands that would one day become North and South Dakota, and much of Montana and Wyoming. The twin states of North and South Dakota would not be created for another six years, in 1889.

Getting to Minnesota was far easier in 1883 than it had been only five years earlier. The Pacific Union and the Baltimore Ohio (B&O) railroads had crisscrossed the eastern states for many years before branching out to the Midwest. This expansion had greatly facilitated commerce as well as general travel from the East Coast to the West.

After traveling from Boston south to Washington, D.C., Bones and his party would take the B&O to Pittsburgh and then past Columbus and Toledo in Ohio before angling west to Chicago. From there, they would shift to the Burlington Quincy Line which would shoot north to Milwaukee where they would catch the Wisconsin Central Line before again heading northwest to Minneapolis-St. Paul. Beyond the Twin Cities, there was a small branch on the Burlington Quincy RR that ran directly to Duluth, Minnesota—very near the area of special interest. It was certainly not a direct route; however, it was much faster than taking a stagecoach from Boston which would have tripled the time if not more. All told, it would take a week to travel to their destination, largely by rail. After traveling to Texarkana two years earlier, they at least had some idea of what to expect —or at least that is what they thought.

At South Station in Boston, Marigold stood sadly, watching her eldest son— now a doctor—carry his nice leather duffel bag to the boarding platform. There stood Dr. Cook already anxiously looking at his silver pocket watch to assess how much time they had left before the train would move on toward Washington and intervening stops. Madam Grey had refused to see them off, instead telling Marigold to give her best to her nephew and intentionally omitting any reference to Bones.

"Now, you take care of yourself," said Marigold, clutching her son as if he were going off to war. "If you see some monster out in the woods, you know what to do."

"Yeah, we're supposed to capture it," said Samuel, smiling.

"No! You're to run, Samuel! Run!" said his mother, realizing her words would fall on deaf ears.

"Come on, Samuel," Bones called out, "we need to get on board. The train will be leaving soon."

Samuel kissed his mother on the cheek. "I'll be fine, Mother. I'll write."

He climbed onboard and took his seat next to Bones in first class.

"I could get used to this," said Bones making himself comfortable in his plush seat.

"Yeah, I guess I've grown up with it, so it's not that unusual for me," Samuel answered.

Bones nodded and then lay back, closing his eyes and waiting for the sudden jolt from the railcar indicating they had left the station. But it wasn't long before his eyes flew open again.

"Hello, Bones," came a familiar voice hovering over him.

The doctor quickly sat up in his seat. "Missy?"

"Of course. Who did you think it would be?" she answered throwing a bag into the compartment overhead and taking a seat across from him.

"What are you doing here?"

"Going with you. You didn't think I'd let you go with my nephew and leave me out of all the fun, did you?"

"But ..."

"And yes, I'm still very angry at you," she stated, her eyes drilling holes through him.

"About?"

"About? You have to ask? Let me see ... about New York City and ignoring me the entire time, about this little adventure of yours and not inviting me. Why wouldn't you tell me you were going on this trip, Bones? You told my mother and my sister, but not me. "

Bones sat quietly, struggling to find words—any words.

"Well, I'm not going to stand for it," she continued. "I'm not going to let you treat me that way."

"Missy, I didn't tell you because I didn't want you to be in ... in danger."

Missy stared at him in disbelief. "Really? You expect me to believe that?"

"Yes, why not? It's true."

"Then why are you letting Samuel here go with you. You're not worried about *him* being in danger?"

"I am worried. But I had no choice."

"What do you mean 'you had no choice'?"

"Samuel insisted on going. I couldn't talk him out of it. Isn't that right, Samuel?"

"Yep. I insisted all right," said Samuel, his eyes closed and merely parroting what Bones had said.

"What if I had insisted too?" Missy asked. "Would you have let me come?"

"I ... I don't know," Bones answered vaguely. It was weak, and he winced as he uttered the words. She had cornered him, and he could find no quick escape.

"You don't know. You don't *know*?" she pressed.

"It's hard to explain," Bones said finally. "I care for you ... a lot."

"Don't give me that *crap*!" Missy said, speaking frankly and out of character. "I'm going with you whether you like it or not, and you'll be glad you have me around too, if I may say so."

"Funny," Bones answered, "that's what Samuel told me too. If it's coming from both of you, I suppose I should listen." He paused and extended his hand. "Welcome aboard."

Missy's pouty face turned into a mischievous smile. She started to reach out with her hand to shake his but then slapped him with it instead.

"Ow!" Bones said, rubbing his cheek.

"You deserved that!"

"Yeah, I probably did. Still, I'm glad you're here. Did you bring your Winchester?"

"Of course. A girl can't let the boys have all the fun, now can she. I brought it and something else even more fun."

"So, what did you bring?" asked Samuel, opening his eyes and looking interested.

"Just for the occasion, I bought a four-barrel, Enfield .476 pistol." She pulled it out of her bag. It was a big gun--chrome with wood inlay and a crescent-shaped grip. The gun harnessed considerable fire power having four sizeable chambers. "Ain't she a beauty?" Missy asked, proudly showing it off.

"You can fire that thing?" Samuel asked.

"Sure as hell, I can!" she answered.

Bones shook his head. "Well, I'll be damned. Samuel, I think you and I could have left our pieces at home if she's packin' that!"

"Yeah, who needs the U.S. Army when you've got my aunt around to protect you," said Samuel, grinning.

*****

CH 13 – The Church

Claire remained with her brother even though she insisted that she was feeling completely normal again. At first, Orville was skeptical, but gradually he saw that she was recuperating well—or at least well enough—to return to her work at the Trinity Church. Having received her degree from Boston University's Theological Seminary, she had tried to find a position as an associate pastor at a church in town; however, no one would hire her as a woman in the position. So, she got a job helping with Trinity's outreach program.

Loved by her congregation, Claire had developed close relationships with the small group of parishioners, numbering only one hundred sixty-three. While they had a pastor who had served them for many years, it was Claire with whom most bonded. She was likeable and held confidences, and all knew that her word was as good as gold.

Orville also attended her church and enjoyed listening to the homilies of the senior pastor, Reverend Thaddeus Benton. In his late fifties, the fiery Benton could generate a great deal of heat from his pulpit on Sunday mornings, warning his congregation not to embrace the growing materialism that was taking hold in America—particularly as a result of the Second Industrial Revolution which was still transforming life all around them.

"God does not look kindly on those who turn away from Him and seek only the material riches of this world," said the reverend. "As it is said, it is easier for a camel to pass through the eye of a needle than for a rich man to pass through the golden gates of Heaven."

After the service, the pastor greeted the parishioners as they filed out of the church nave.

"Good seeing you, Mrs. Clyburn," he said, taking the hand of the middle-aged woman while placing his other on top of both. "How's your daughter feeling? I heard she had an awful cold last week and missed school. Is she better?"

"Why yes, pastor," answered Jennifer Clyburn, the daughter of Elijah Clyburn who was a major donor to the church. "She is better. She went to school on Thursday and has been acting herself again. Thank you for asking."

As Orville approached, the reverend smiled. "Orville, glad you could come. We always like having you here. You give us the pleasure of your nice singing voice, and I assure you that it helps the others when they know at least *someone* can carry the tune."

Orville laughed. "Why thank you pastor, I think that's the first time anyone has told me that."

"Well, it's true," Benton answered. Then he drew the young man closer and whispered to him. "But you know, Orville, I've been meaning to talk to you about your sister for several weeks now that she's back with us. Let me know when we can chat."

Orville was surprised. Benton had been the one to give Claire the Last Rites and had been instrumental in helping her convalesce afterward. He had assured her there would still be a place for her at the church when she got back on her feet, and so far, Orville was not aware there had been any problems.

"Uh, sure, reverend," said Orville. "What about later this afternoon? I can stop by and talk then."

Orville returned to Copley Square where the magnificent church had been rebuilt from the ashes of the 1872 Boston fire. Resembling a medieval castle with its rough-hewn stones, clay roof, Gothic arches, and soaring towers, the Romanesque architecture and grand, ornate interior made it one of the great churches of the country.

Orville knocked and then opened the creaky, walnut door of the reverend's study to find Reverend Benton standing by the window looking outside. The shades were up, and the window panes were open. There was a nice, cool breeze blowing in from the green courtyard that stood as a barrier between the church and its historical cemetery.

"What a glorious day, isn't it?" said the pastor, taking a deep breath.

Reverend Benton was a big man—nearly six feet two inches with a chest as broad as his smile. With a thick mane of greying hair, he showed few other signs of age. His face was long and narrow, covered by a heavy gray beard that made him look like St. Nicholas or Sinter Klaas, if not a close relative. Big boned with legs like tree-trunks and forearms nearly as large, he hobbled with a black, hickory cane due to an injury he had suffered as a young Union soldier during the Battle of Chancellorsville in Virginia. Unable to return to the fight, Benton had found a spiritual calling and followed that to the pulpit.

"Every day God makes is glorious, isn't it?" Orville answered.

Benton turned, grinning. "You have that right, son. Please have a seat."

Orville took a chair in front of the pastor's small, utility table and tried to make himself more at ease. With a raw cane-woven seat and no cushions, the chair was only settling for someone who sported extra padding on their posterior of which Orville had little.

"So, what concerns you, pastor?" Orville asked, still trying to get comfortable.

"Orville, ever since your sister had her bout with consumption, she's not been the same, has she?"

"It's been a long road to recovery, if that's what you mean."

"When she first came to this church she glowed with the Spirit inside her. Now, I know your family wasn't deeply religious, but ..."

"Our parents were religious, reverend. We always went to church on Sundays—we had to. Mother would not have let us do anything else but go, find an open pew, sing the hymns and listen to the Gospel. It was my brother, Reggie, who has drifted away from the Word. He doesn't believe at all. I think he got that way after he graduated from medical school. In fact, I think there are few things besides science that he does believe in."

"Yes, but your brother is a project for another time, don't you agree?"

"Yes, quite right. As for my sister, Clair—yes, she has been a beacon of light for the family. She has been a religious bedrock for me, anyway."

"But wouldn't you agree that this glow has all but vanished? She goes through the motions, but I don't think her heart is in it anymore. I can't understand it. Usually, a person's faith grows stronger after something like that. Have you noticed this too?" Benton asked.

"Right after her battle with the disease, I did see her acting differently. She was more feisty than I've ever seen her before. I just chalked it up to her fighting off whatever was left inside her from the consumption. I'm not a doctor, so I don't really know. Recently, I can tell you that I haven't seen anything strange. She's been pretty normal—back to her old self."

"Well good. Perhaps it's just my imagination, then. Let me know if you notice anything change. I'll still be praying for her and your family."

***

Across town Claire left the apothecary in a hurry. She wanted to return to her brother's brownstone before her brother got back from the church. *****

CH 14 – Journey to Minnesota

The journey to Duluth took more than the few days they had expected. After the train broke down between towns in Pennsylvania, Bones, Missy and Samuel slept on the railcar overnight until someone arrived to fix it. A burst compressor ring had caused the problem, and they were lucky the mechanic happened to carry in his wagon an assortment of rings and other parts that often failed on the engines.

In Chicago, they arrived on the Baltimore -Ohio Rail at Grand Central Station. But delays in getting their luggage off the train cost them their transfer to Chicago's Union Station about five blocks away, missing their next train by minutes. Yet another day was spent waiting for a train to leave for Milwaukee, Wisconsin, on the Burlington Rail.

Finally, they passed through Milwaukee and the twin cities, Minneapolis and St. Paul, and arrived in Duluth, a middle-sized town of about twenty thousand. Not wishing to continue on any smaller rails, the three got off and hired a coach to take them the rest of the way—to Wadena, about one hundred eighty miles west. Although more comfortable than riding on horseback, the coach was slower, and it took another five days to reach Wadena.

"Here's your stop," called the coach driver. "This is the great metropolis of Wadena. I hope you enjoy your stay."

Samuel wasn't sure whether the driver was being sincere or sarcastic, but once he got out of the coach, he could tell it was the latter. Wadena made Texarkana seem like New York City or Chicago. With a population of two hundred, it was a small, rural farm community just trying to make life work.

There was no official lodging in Wadena, but the three found temporary quarters with an elderly man who lived alone in town. His wife had passed several years earlier, and his children had moved to Duluth to find better opportunities for work. He was quite happy to receive company and offered his place free of charge. However, Bones insisted on paying something, and they agreed on a small fee of a dollar and a half per night.

"Say, Mr. Lindstrom," Bones said to the proprietor, "We're looking for a man named Palmer Jenkins. Do you happen to know where he lives?"

Lindstrom nodded, and, using his black cane he ambled toward the door. After opening it, he pointed down the dirt road with the same black stick.

"Across that way, you'll find an old road that leads south out of town. Palmer's is the first house on the left. But, come to think of it, I haven't seen ole' Palmer for several days now."

"He was the gentleman who saw that monster in the woods nearby, wasn't he?" Bones asked.

"Yes, he's a real celebrity around here—or at least he was for a while. Some people believed him. Others didn't and gave him a devil of a time over it. He isn't a showy person. He mainly keeps to himself. As a matter of fact, I owe him a visit."

"Do you mind if we tag along?" asked Missy.

"No, I'd be glad to have you. Let me get my wagon, and we'll trot on over."

When they arrived, they found Jenkins's horse in the weathered barn and his barely-working wagon just outside next to a series of empty pig troughs. None of the animals looked like they had been fed or watered for days, so Bones had Samuel help him with the hay and refilling the water troughs from the well in back.

Lindstrom went inside after knocking. "Palmer? Palmer, are you here?" But he got no reply. That was when Bones, Missy and Samuel joined him.

"Everything looks like it usually does," said Lindstrom looking around the place. "Maybe he's in town."

"Without a horse?" asked Bones. "Does he have others?"

"No, that's the only one. So, you're right, I don't quite know where he is. Maybe he's out hunting in the woods nearby. He sometimes does that too. Let's wait here and see if he comes back."

They waited and waited. After three hours, the group from Boston was becoming impatient.

"I don't think he's coming back any time soon," said Missy. "Why don't we go back to your house. We'll try again later."

While the others went back to Lindstrom's place, Bones rode into the small, town center. There was a General Store that doubled as a drug store, a small ammunitions shop that doubled as a barber shop, and a post office that also had a Western telegraph operator. And that was it.

Bones went into the General Store and saw two young ladies at the counter buying some iron kitchen pots. The store owner was a man in his forties with a long, black mustache and hair down over his ears. He wore an apron that had been white at one time in its life but now was stained with tea, coffee, and who knew what else.

Bones approached the three and politely interrupted. "Excuse me. I'm very sorry to interrupt. I'm from out of town, and I was wondering if any of you have seen Mr. Jenkins recently?"

One of the two women giggled and shook her head while the other only smiled. The man behind the counter did not find it amusing, and rather directly said, "I'm afraid I haven't seen Mr. Jenkins. As a matter of fact, I haven't seen him in quite some time."

"He's probably out hunting red-eyed monsters," said one of the women, laughing.

"Now, that's enough," said the man behind the counter. "Poor old Palmer deserves better than that. He and his family have lived here in Wadena for decades. We don't talk about people like that here. You two should be ashamed or yourselves."

"I didn't mean nothin' by it," said one of the young ladies. "Everyone knows Mr. Jenkins is a bit off though, ya' know."

"He's had a hard life—something neither of you knows anything about. Now take your pots and go home, or I'll tell you parents what you said."

The two women left abruptly as Bones approached the counter. "Do you believe he saw something?" the doctor asked. "A monster, that is."

"I don't know," said the shopkeeper. "It isn't for me to judge. He believes he did. He's seen enough during his life to make me think that if he said he did, he likely did. He knows the difference between a black bear and something else—something unusual. Hell, we've all we've seen things in the woods a time or two. At least Palmer is man enough to say he *thought* he saw something. He didn't do it for the publicity, that's for sure."

"Why do you say that?" asked Bones.

"He's a quiet man. He keeps to himself. He doesn't like the spotlight and prefers to be left alone in his cabin out there."

"We're staying with Mr. Lindstrom here in town, and …"

"Oh, Mr. Lindstrom is about the nicest man you'll ever meet. Be kind to him. He does a lot for others in town. He's a special person, ya' know."

"Yes, I can tell. He took us up to see Mr. Jenkins but, as I said, he wasn't home. Mr. Lindstrom is worried about him."

"I'm sure he's all right. He's able to take care of himself pretty good," said the owner.

"Well, if you see Mr. Jenkins, please let Mr. Lindstrom know too. That will go a long way to calm his anxiety."

Bones left the General Store. He tried the post office, but no one was there. Next door, he found no one at the ammo store either. Without further success, Bones headed back to Mr. Lindstrom's where he found the old man cooking away in the kitchen.

"Why aren't you helping him?" Bones asked the other two who were sitting comfortably on chairs by the fire that was burning actively in the fireplace.

"He said he doesn't want any," said Samuel, turning the pages of a book he was reading. "He said he's been doing it by himself for the last thirty years, and no one is going to show him anything he doesn't already know or doesn't need."

Bones smiled. "That's the way they do things out here. That's what they call rugged individualism."

*****

CH 15 – Meeting with the Senators

Yet, even though Tillson's meetings with two wealthy families in Washington yielded the funding for Bones trip to stop, or at least stymie, efforts to capture the wild Wendigo, he sought something more.

Seeing the development of children's and animal rights in New York state, Tillson believed he could accomplish the same at a national level. Getting passage of federal laws would satisfy his long desire to make a difference and effect the kind of change he felt was badly needed in the country. Early on during his tenure at the Interior Department, he realized that Washington was where change came to die rather than thrive. That was the very type of "change" that he wanted to change.

"I'm sorry, but I don't share your concerns," said Senator Thomas Ferry, sitting in the fine drawing room of his mansion which graced the magnificent boulevard known as Massachusetts Avenue. There Tillson had gathered several of the prominent leaders on Capitol Hill to discuss the matter of rights for those unable to stand up for themselves—both children and animals.

Thomas Ferry, who had been Acting Vice President from 1875 to 1877 after the death of Vice President Henry Wilson, had recently retired from politics and was hesitant to re-engage in the melee.

"Well, I'm grateful that you agreed to host this affair so we can, at least, exchange our ideas on the subject," said Tillson.

"If there are such beasts in the wild," Ferry continued, "and if it were in my home state of Michigan, I would certainly want the thing captured, and preferably, killed. But it's not. Therefore, I'm sorry, Mr. Tillson, but I'll abstain."

"How can you say such a thing!" exclaimed Melvina, the wife of Senator Philetus Sawyer from Wisconsin. "How could you kill a harmless creature that hasn't done anything to anyone. Every creature has the right to live peaceably in the wild. Does it not?"

"Peaceably, yes," answered Philetus Sawyer, her husband, "but Mr. Tillson is telling us that this creature is allegedly a blood-thirsty beast, not some harmless kitten meowing for milk in the forest. It eats humans. Is that not right, Mr. Tillson?"

"It has never been found to do such a thing, no," said Tillson.

"Has it killed anyone?" asked Anna Coswell whose husband was a Congressman from Wisconsin and was not at the gathering.

"No ma'am, but there will be an outcry from people asking for our heads if someone *is* killed," said Senator Sawyer. "They will demand to know why we didn't do something about this when we learned of it. I don't want to take that chance. I think we should let these men capture it and kill it, just like Tom said."

"Well, any way you look at it, this is a *state* issue, not a federal one," said Sam McMillan, the senator from Minnesota. He lifted his teacup and took a long sip before continuing. "If we've learned anything these past years, it's that Washington can't fix every problem."

"Why not?" answered Melvina. "I don't see that the states are prepared to take on significant issues. It's the federal government that has the money and the manpower."

"Since when is the Wendigo a *significant* issue?" asked Senator Ferry.

"If I may interject," said Tillson. "I only raised the Wendigo as an example. There are far more serious issues with other animals and how they are treated. I think that is the bigger issue here."

"What do you mean, William?" asked Melvina.

"There are many instances of domesticated animals being subjected to terrible treatment, if not torture, by their owners."

"Give us an example," asked Senator Sawyer.

"You've heard of cock fights and dog fights, I presume. These are events that are arranged by bookies for betting purposes. People of low income—those who can hardly afford it—are solicited to come to these fights to wager their hard-earned money. Then, these animals are affixed with razors or other sharp objects and provoked to attack each other. The fights are to the death. These are horrible scenes that should not be allowed!"

"Ew!" cried Anna. "That's disgusting! How could anyone permit such a thing?"

"Those fights have been going on since Adam was in the Garden with Eve," said Ferry. "And they will continue to go on. There's not much we can do about it."

"Why not?" asked Melvina. "I think this is a good example of something we *can* do to stop such cruelty!"

The group continued their discussion for the better part of an hour before Senator Sawyer glanced at his pocket watch. "I must say, it's getting late. I sorry, but I must be off."

The party disbanded, but it was a learning experience for Tillson. This wasn't an issue that would be universally supported. There were clear divisions, even at the top. The women tended to look more favorably at government intervention to protect animals from cruelty by their owners; the men, not so much. If he wanted to press this issue and make a difference, he knew what he needed to do next.

As a result, the next gathering Tillson arranged was not with the husbands but rather with their wives. In addition to Anna Coswell, Melvina Sawyer, and Harriet McMillan, Senator McMillan's wife, Tillson asked three others to join him: notably Elizabeth Blackwell, Susan Anthony, and Elizabeth Stanton.

Elizabeth Blackwell was the first physician in America, getting her degree in 1849. Susan Anthony, along with her friend Elizabeth Stanton, were in the midst of a long-fought battle for women's rights. Both Elizabeths and Susan were delighted to join the small group.

"I think freedom and rights are important everywhere," said Anthony. "As you know, I've gotten a lot of push-back over the years—those with power don't like to give it up so easily. They don't even like to share!"

"But it's a fight you will eventually win," said Tillson, encouragingly, "at least with respect to women's rights. I can see the softening of many in Congress already. Those who remain with hardened hearts will never come around, but those with some morsel of compassion will. Trust me."

"That's easy for you—being a man and all," said Anthony.

Although offensive, the remark didn't trigger Tillson. Instead, he merely smiled and moved on. "This issue with animals is another that should be addressed in the legislature at the federal level. New York is but one state. It would take many years to get the other thirty-seven states to adopt the same laws."

"Listen, I realize this issue is a small one," cried Anna Coswell, "but I believe there is widespread mistreatment of all sorts of animals. The circuses that are popping up everywhere—they are the worst! They keep those poor creatures locked in cages and feed them the bare minimum. That's what I've been told. It's inhumane!"

"I agree," said Harriet McMillan. "This is something Congress should address. It says in the Bible that man is the steward of the animal kingdom. It says that man shall not brutalize or torture animals in any way. But this, I think, is far worse. It's brutalizing them for years, and it must be stopped."

"Well, New York gave us a good start with the laws they passed back in 1866," said Tillson. "That's when they started the SPCA—the Society for the Prevention of Cruelty to Animals."

"Yes, but it doesn't even extend to horses," said Coswell. "And there's still cruelty to cattle during transport, and other animals on farms. There's a lot of mistreatment out there on all different fronts. We can't look at this issue too narrowly."

"What's strange is that animal rights came before those for our children," said Stanton. "They didn't pass animal legislation—as meager as it was—until just a few years ago, and laws protecting children only came later."

"I think it was 1874," said Tillson, "and you're right. It was after the legislation to protect animals."

"Shameful," said Anthony.

"So, what more can we do about this situation in Minnesota?" asked Stanton. "I worry about that poor creature too."

"We may need some more funding," said Tillson. "I have a widely acclaimed doctor heading up a team that's traveling to the Midwest to see about that poor animal that the group from New York is ruthlessly trying to track and capture. My team may need more help."

"You mean, Dr. Cook?" Elizabeth exclaimed. "He's an outstanding professor from what I understand."

"Yes, and he knows someone in Boston who may be able to help us underwrite this bigger cause for animal protection."

"Who's that?" asked Stanton.

"Esther Grey."

"The Grey's?" said Blackwell, joining in. "Esther is very philanthropic. I believe she's given generously to many medical projects too."

"Yes, Esther's daughter Missy has worked with the professor on other assignments, so I'm sure there will be no problem getting a gift from her. I have received support from the Posts—Meriwether Post and others."

"I'm in," said Blackwell.

"So am I," answered Anthony.

The rest joined in in solidarity.

"Thank you. Thank you all. Now, if I could just get your husbands to do something about women's suffrage on Capitol Hill …" said Stanton, looking over at the senators' wives.

"In time, dear. In time," McMillan answered.

*****

CH 16 – Over a Brandy

It wasn't often that McGinnis, Cooper and Phineas met to discuss business matters as Phineas gave his partners free rein to run the finances and operations of the company while he focused on promotion. However, periodically, they would schedule a review to assess where they were and where they wanted to go. Generally, it was Phineas who had the long-term vision of where he wanted to take the company even though he was the eldest of the three owners. And while Cooper was practical and methodical, McGinnis had the keen, quick business mind and the critical thinking skills they needed to assess the crazy ideas Phineas often had. Yet, even when they quarreled over the long-term, they also fussed over the short-term when there were big issues brewing on the horizon.

"Have you heard what's going on in Washington?" Phineas asked, swirling a short glass of Armagnac brandy.

"No, should I?" answered McGinnis, pouring his first drink of the afternoon.

"I believe so, my dear sir. There is a group that is hell-bent on pressing Congress to pass legislation outlawing the use of animals for entertainment purposes. They've already started petitioning members of the House to initiate a bill to prevent the harmful treatment of animals. They consider *everything* a mistreatment of animals, of course. It's all ridiculous. Animals aren't human beings. We shouldn't start treating them that way."

"They've already passed some animal protection laws in New York, and other states are starting to adopt them too, I believe," said Cooper. "I agree. I think this needs to be nipped in the bud before it goes too far."

"These people are insane. Pretty soon they'll make us invite our horses, chickens, cows, and hogs into the house and cook them dinner!" cried Phineas. "This world is becoming unhinged by the day. The insanity of it all!"

"So, what are we going to do about it?" asked McGinnis. "Do you think the proposed legislation has a real chance of becoming law?"

"I don't know, but we've come too far to let some group of petty, conniving women change what's been perfectly fine for over a thousand years," said the eldest partner. "Those b*tches want to change everything. They want women's rights. They want children's rights. They want pigs' rights. It's all preposterous. Soon, I fear we'll be letting women *vote* for God's sake! What a disaster that would be!"

"We might as well let our horses vote too," quipped McGinnis, already finishing his first drink while Phineas was still nursing his.

"Well, that's what Julius Caesar Germanicus did," said Cooper.

"Who?"

"His nickname was Caligula," said Cooper. "He contracted a disease early in his rein which warped him psychologically. He was only in power four years, but during that time he had a horse named Incitatus, which he loved dearly, and allegedly made a Roman consul. Caligula was quite mad. It didn't' take long for the Roman Praetorian Guard to do away with him—and his family."

"Perhaps these women are descendants of him," snickered Phineas.

McGinnis laughed too. "Perhaps so. If that's the case, I would suggest you ride your most handsome steed down to Washington and have a chat with this group of activists. Who knows, perhaps they will fall in love too."

"With me?" asked Phineas.

"No, with your horse!"

*****

CH 17 – Sudden Illness

Claire smiled as the congregation rose to sing the first hymn, *Whom Shall I Send?* It was nearing the season of Lent, and the church was in a festive spirit. The snug, white church stalls were filled with gay parishioners, and with the warmer weather and improved mood, all the ladies were wearing their finest spring fashions.

Reverend Benton delivered a sermon much toned-down from his usual fire and brimstone this particular Sunday, having delivered soul pounding homilies during the previous weeks. His intent was to keep the people in line with obedience to God but was careful not to go too far and alienate them. After the readings and sermon, the pastor prepared the wine and bread for communion. The ciborium, chalice and grape juice were extracted from the tabernacle, along with white linens, and the pastor blessed them.

"Take this and eat it. This is My Body which will be given up for you," said the reverend, holding a bread wafer between his fingers. He repeated the phrase, instructing his congregation to drink the grape juice which he lifted in a small glass as a symbol of Christ's Blood.

As the parishioners approached the altar, they took a morsel of bread and dipped it into the purple grape juice before eating it. It was increasingly more common for a Methodist church to use grape juice rather than the customary red wine for communion as the Temperance Movement was gaining more followers by the day. Once finished, the reverend cleaned the chalice and the paten before returning all to the tabernacle on the altar. Then, he said the final prayers.

"We humbly beseech You, almighty god, to grant that those whom You refresh with Your sacraments may serve You worthily by a life well pleasing to You. Through our Lord Jesus Christ, Your Son, who lives and reigns, world without end. Amen."

After the service, it was customary to hold a brief gathering of the congregation for fellowship and revelry. Many often stayed after the service on Sunday to share a simple lunch of local meats, cheeses, and either tea or coffee and to catch up on news and gossip of what was happening in their community.

"… and did you hear about Gladys's niece?" said Mildred Creighton, one of the senior members of the congregation and also one known for ensuring all news was spread as quickly as possible to anyone within ear shot. "Well, she was going to be married to a man from Duluth, but a month before the wedding, she called it off."

"Why?" asked one of the other three ladies crowded around a circle listening in on the gossip.

"She told him he just wasn't the right kind of man for her. At least that's what I heard," said Mildred.

"I heard she found another man in St. Paul," said Waverly Pettis. "He had more money and influence than that one in Duluth."

"That's not right," said Mabel Haskins. "I'm not saying you have to marry for love, but to drop someone because they aren't wealthy doesn't seem right."

"You have to marry a man who can support ya'," said Mildred. "Think of the children. Life is hard enough as it is. You don't want them to grow up with a deadbeat father who turns into a drunk and a wife beater, now do ya'?"

"Who said anything about a deadbeat or a wife beater?" asked Pauline Benton, the wife of the reverend and one of the more reasonable of the group. "You're just speculating. You don't know that! Perhaps the young man was hard working and church going. Just because he might have grown up in a poor family doesn't mean he would have been an abusive father and husband."

Claire was attentive to all the women as they chatted. Even though she had an opinion, she rarely gave it. Instead, she chose to be one who listened to others and was seen as empathetic to their plights rather than weigh in with her own advice or preaching.

However, the conversation was suddenly interrupted when one in the congregation approached Claire and Mrs. Benton.

"Mrs. Benton - Pastor Claire, I'm sorry to have to leave, but my husband isn't feeling well. I'm sure you understand." It was Mrs. Hornsby who had her husband and eight-year-old daughter next to her. His eyes were half closed, and his face looked chalky white. He leaned on his wife for support as they headed out the church doors. "Please tell the reverend he gave an excellent sermon, as he always does," she added, helping her husband outside and down the stairs to their wagon.

"I hope he feels better," Pauline called out, turning back to the group.

"He didn't look so good," said Mildred. "I hope he isn't too sick."

"He'll be fine, I'm sure," Claire said. "It might be the little bug that's been going around town lately. He should recover quickly."

Later, a few others left early as well, but none of the ladies, nor the reverend, thought much about it.

It was only later that Reverend Benton learned that Adrian Hornsby died that night. The family doctor hadn't been able to figure out what had killed him.

*****

CH 18 – Tracking the Beast

Dalrymple's posse plodded up the dusty, seldom-traveled road with Jenkins, bound in leather straps, on the back of one of the men's horses. By now, they were miles from the old man's homestead.

"We can go as long as it takes," said Dalrymple. "You just need to tell us where you saw it."

"Right in here," said Jenkins, lifting his two tied wrists in unison.

"Are you sure?"

"Yeah, I'm sure. It was right in here."

"Look around for tracks, boys," said their leader, chewing on a day-old cigar butt. "We'd better find something soon, there Palmer, or you'll have worse things to worry about."

Dismounting, the men roamed the thick woods looking for any signs of a wild beast. They were experienced trackers, but they weren't sure what kind of tracks they were looking for. Most knew the tracks of deer, bear, and even the occasional cougar that might be residents of the neighborhood. Anything their size would have left obvious tracks, but ones they would recognize. This beast was something they had never seen or come across before. Its tracks would be ones unlike anything they'd ever seen before.

While they looked, they tied Jenkins to a nearby tree. They were gone for over an hour, and the old man began to fear not only a Wendigo, but a big, black bear that would find him and decide he needed an afternoon snack.

"Find anythin'?" Dalrymple called out to his men who were scavenging the woods.

"No, boss. Nothin' yet," said Eddie, one of his men.

"Keep lookin' then." Dalrymple said as he steadied his rifle and walked back to where they had tied Jenkins. He placed the cold muzzle against the old man's head and cocked the trigger. "We haven't found nothin'!" he shouted. "I think you're lyin'!"

"No, I'm sure I saw it right in here," Jenkin's answered, nodding in the direction in front of him.

"You'd better not be lyin'. If you're lyin', I'm gunna unload this gun directly into your forehead. Do you understand?"

Jenkins's eyes grew big. "I ... I *think* it was here."

"You *think*? Or you know?"

"I could be wrong, I guess," said Jenkins. "It could have been farther down the road."

"Let's go, boys. We're gunna' move down the road a spell and see if there isn't somethin' more interesting. Mr. Palmer here says he's being forthright and cooperative with us. We'll take him at his word—*this time*. Untie him and saddle up."

They got back on their horses and continued down the trail.

"You tell me when we're there, Mr. Palmer," said Dalrymple. "But let me stress that I'm getting very impatient."

Their horses continued walking for a several more miles. By then it was late, and the crickets were chirping madly farther out in the brush. Also out in abundance were the mosquitos, some the size of a walnut, all buzzing their ears and those of their horses, causing great annoyance and irritation.

"Damned things!" shouted Dalrymple, swatting wildly at the flying vampires as he slipped from side to side on his saddle.

"Are we close?" asked Clyde, another of the men. "I'm gettin' eaten alive out here!"

Clyde was a master complainer. He had grown up in Wadena as a child but moved with his family to Duluth shortly after his kid brother was shot and killed in the town.

"Well, Mr. Palmer?" asked Dalrymple.

"Yeah, I think we're close," Jenkins mumbled.

"You know that *this* time, if we don't find any tracks, we're gonna strip you naked and tie you to a tree so those hungry mosquitos can feed on you all night long. Now, won't that be enjoyable?" His voice was threatening and sinister, as if relishing the thought of such a sadistic act.

Once more they got off their horses and began to look. This area was swampy and had a wide, shallow marsh surrounded by thick brush and white pines on three sides. They tied up their horses next to a patch of willowy cattails

73

growing along the shoreline before the men began scouring the earth and the nearby environs for any signs of a monstrous beast.

Nearly an hour passed as the fading rays of light grew dimmer, filtering more and more feebly through the forest canopy.

Jenkins sat on his horse which was tied to a nearby tree and couldn't run off. His face twitched in nervous anticipation watching the others as they combed the woods.

"Got anythin'?" asked their leader.

"Nope."

"What about you Clyde?"

"No, I ain't seen nothin' either. Only white tails and one black bear, but nothin' other than that."

Dalrymple pulled Jenkins from the horse and frog marched him down to the marsh.

"Strip!" he yelled, pointing his gun at the man.

"Please, no! I saw it! I really saw it!"

"Where?"

"Right in here, I swear!" pleaded Jenkins.

"You're lyin'," said Dalrymple. "I don't take kindly to a liar, and neither does my boss." He cocked the trigger.

"All right! All right!" exclaimed Jenkins, starting to take off his shirt and trousers. When he was down to his undershorts, Dalrymple's men dragged him into the cold waters of the marsh and tied him to a half-rotted stump.

"But I'll die out here!" shouted the old man.

"Maybe you'll get lucky, and that beast you say you saw will untie you instead of eating you. Let's go boys."

The men rode off, leaving Jenkins in the marsh; he shivered uncontrollably and watched in despair as the posse vanished into the darkness of night.

Dalrymple and his men headed back to town, but it was only a few miles from the marsh when they heard an awful sound—like a bull moose trying to free itself from a trap. But they all knew it was no bull moose. The horses bucked and brayed, trying to free themselves from their riders, but the men held them fast.

"Let's go," said Dalrymple, pointing in the direction of the sound. "I think we may have found it after all."

Furiously, they rode their mounts off the trail and into the woods following the sound. Hearing nothing more, they stopped and listened for another outburst, but after ten minutes all they heard were the chirping of crickets, the flapping of bat wings, and occasional hoots from a Great Horned Owl nearby.

"Do ya' think the old man was right?" asked Eddie, another of the men. "Should we go back and free him?"

Eddie was an unusual tracker—one who was scared of his own shadow most of the time. Although experienced, he had phobias that no one but his mother fully understood.

"Naw, no need. He's not worth the effort. I'm thinkin' it was a black bear after all."

"I don't know, boss," said Clyde skeptically.

"Well, I don't care what you think. I say it was a bear. Anyway, somebody will find him sooner or later—whatever's left, that is, after the bear and the leeches and mosquitos are done with him."

"What do we do now then, boss?" Jeeter asked.

Of all the men, Jeeter was the youngest and the one most likely to make a bad decision. He had hutzpah, but he had little experience to back it up.

"We'll camp out here for the night."

"What if that thing is out here?" asked Eddie. "What if wasn't no bear?"

"We'll be fine tonight, men. Tomorrow, we'll head back to Wadena and resupply."

"Aren't we supposed to bring that thing back alive?" asked Jack Peters. Peters had been in almost every war since the Mexican War of 1846. He'd been wounded twice during the Civil War but had never shrunk from a fight. He was the man's man, and few messed with him.

"Alive would be great," said Dalrymple, "but I'm not optimistic about that. I'm thinkin' we'll have to kill it to get it back. I think I can convince my bosses it's worth somethin' even if it's not crawlin' around in a cage for 'em."

"I don' know," said Eddie, nervously.

"What are ya' afraid of?" Peters asked.

"No! 'Course not!" said Eddie, defensively.

"Well, if it nibbles on your arm, you may have to fire your pistol at it, ya' know." Peters was smirking, enjoying his time making fun of his fellow posse member.

"Stop it!" shouted Dalrymple. "We have enough to deal with out here without you two sniping at each other. Now, let's set some traps and setup camp. We'll see what we find in the morning."

Meanwhile, a mile away, Jenkins was still alive, but fighting for his life. It was cold, dark, and the only thing he could hear were the frogs croaking for mates in the marsh. However, soon after, even that noise ended abruptly, and it became eerily quiet—the silence every bit more frightening than any howling he'd ever heard in the woods.

Then, Jenkins thought he heard something slushing its way through the cold waters of the marsh—something on two legs and heading toward him.

"Dalrymple?" he called out.

The last thing he heard was the shrieking of a wild beast—the same sound he had heard a few months earlier, but by the time he saw the two red eyes, it was too late.

******

CH 19 – Tillson the Activist

It wasn't long before Tillson became subsumed into the activism promoted by the ladies at the tea he had arranged. *Certainly, women's suffrage was an issue, and needed to be addressed,* he thought*, and so were the rights of children and animals. They were all important.* Anthony and Stanton were working day and night to bend ears on Capitol Hill, and they were having small, but steady, success. Yet, change was a patient man's challenge, and these were marathon races, not sprints. *Those who could sustain long-term pressure even against mighty adversity and continue to push for what was right and just would ultimately prevail*—at least that's what Tillson's father had always told him.

While Tillson was sympathetic to the other movements—women's and children's rights—he believed he had to focus on just one: animal rights. He thought that without such a focus he would most certainly, and inevitably, fail.

Yet, even though his attention was on animal treatment, he took notice of how progress was being made with the other movements—as well as the setbacks. Some states had adopted regulations for maximum hours that children could work per day, but those were rarely regulated and enforced. He realized that passing laws that weren't enforced was worse than passing no laws at all.

Children as young as six, were working in dangerous conditions in industrial sweatshops to supplement their family's earnings. With the average factory worker making only $1.37 per day, it was hardly enough for a family of four to live on. So for many to be able to eat, the families sent them off to work instead of off to school to learn.

But that was in the urban areas.

In rural regions, families would have multiple children because of high mortality rates and to help work the farms. Schools would go on hiatus during the planting season in the spring and the harvesting season in the fall. When not in the fields, those between the ages of six and sixteen at least got some education. It was the basics in the three *R*s, but it was better than nothing and often better than their parents received—many of whom were illiterate.

Like child labor laws, animal protection laws were not ubiquitous throughout the country, and those that were in effect varied greatly in scope among the states that had them on the books. Animals were still abused—sometimes savagely—and without regard to the degree of pain inflicted. Again, the laws were not always enforced. Both farm animals and those domesticated for households were often treated as inanimate objects or property to be used or misused as the owner saw fit. Many times, the local district attorney would not bring charges, fearing his own reputation in the community.

The issue of animal cruelty in America and attempts to control it extended back to the seventeenth century. In 1641, the Massachusetts General Court enacted its comprehensive legal code, the "Body of Liberties." Within it were sections that prohibited *"... any Tirranny or Crueltie towards any bruite Creature which are usuallie kept for man's use"* and *"... mandated periodic rest and refreshment for any Cattel driven or led."* The Puritans of the Northeast believed that cruel dominion was a consequence of Adam and Eve's fall from the Garden of Eden. They promoted a kinder stewardship of the world and its animals—something toward which they believed all men should strive.

Yet, egregious acts of cruelty were still common, even during the latter part of the nineteenth century. The transport of livestock to stockyards and processes within slaughterhouses were particularly abysmal as animals were crammed together so tightly that they could hardly breathe.

Then, there was the *intentional* mistreatment of animals. In major cities, there was the staging of dog and cock fights as well as the terrible living conditions of animals that were used to entertain audiences. Put in small cages barely large enough for them to move around, animals were subjected to a confinement worse than death, and when the cages were larger, the animals paced back and forth for hours every day, unable to cope with the lack of freedom they had once enjoyed. Use of these poor creatures in shows often resulted in their death or irreparable harm. However, the most heinous of all was the vivisection of animals for experimentation and research—an unconscionable act of performing surgery or experiments on animals while they were alive and without anesthesia.

"Let's bring this meeting to order, shall we?" said Tillson, banging his gavel lightly against the hard plate on his podium.

There were more than fifty people seated closely together on armless wooden chairs that were filed in neat rows within St. Anthony's fellowship hall. Hoping he would need the space, Tillson had asked a friend, Reverend Horas Talmun, if he could use the church for his meeting. He had posted flyers around in the surrounding neighborhoods hoping to arouse interest and support for the cause of animal protection, and he hadn't been disappointed.

Tillson was looking particularly dapper as he took command of the event. He had grown his sideburns long in the then-current style of the muttonchop and wore a gray morning coat and vest over a white, starch-collared shirt that held a long narrow, black-striped tie. Together with pinstriped trousers, he fit in well with the mainly upper-class audience he was addressing. Seated at his side was his wife, Amanda. The two had been through a lot together—first, in the cut-throat legal world of New York City and then in the similarly vicious bureaucratic morass of Washington, D.C.

Amanda was much shorter than he, standing only five feet, four inches in two-inch heels. She wore little makeup, but then she didn't need much. A beauty in her own right, she had dark, voluptuous auburn hair that cascaded down her shoulders; big, chestnut brown eyes; a small, charming sprite of a nose; and a broad, glowing smile framed by naturally plump, red lips. Faithful and earnest, Amanda was often in the shadows at parties where she allowed her husband to do the business of making connections while she chatted with a close-knit circle of friends she knew well.

"Now, this won't be a formal meeting, so I'll get right down to business," said Tillson.

"Mr. Tillson? Will this meeting go longer than an hour? My daughter is coming home for the holidays, and I want to make sure I'm home to meet her," said a middle-aged man who was dressed less formally than most others, suggesting he worked a patronage job for the government.

"No, Mr. Watkins, I don't plan to make this a long meeting. Of course, you may leave at any time, if I get long-winded." The audience laughed. "Now, I want to start by saying this is a very important topic, and it affects all of us. This country has been around for over one hundred years, and in that time, we have not properly addressed the mistreatment of animals in this country—the stewardship of which has been entrusted to us by the Most High. One would think that this would be high on our list of priorities, but alas, that hasn't been the case. Those in Congress have put things like dredging rivers, barring Chinese immigrants, 'encouraging' steam engine knowledge, selling some timberland in the west, and other such trivial matters as issues with higher import. Why is it more important to sell some timber, than to protect this Earth's precious resource of animals—whether wild or domesticated?"

Many in the crowd began nodding in agreement and uttering sounds of support.

"So, I thought about the best way to get your attention with this, but I should warn you that if you have a weak constitution or are offended by graphic descriptions of mistreatment, then you may wish to leave the hall now." A few did, indeed, get up and leave the hall, but the majority stayed to listen. "All right. Then, I will tell you some horrific stories about the treatment of animals in our own backyard—here in Washington, D.C."

Tillson spent the next thirty minutes describing three instances that had been reported to the local authorities within the previous six months. Two involved the treatment of domestic pets—one in Georgetown, an area near the marshy bog area that was drained in developing the nation's capital, and one in Alexandria, which had been a central hub for the slave trade, just over the border in Virginia.

One of the pets had been chained to a stake outside a home during a brutal winter's day in February and had frozen to death. It was reported by a neighbor who had pleaded with the owner next door to take the poor dog inside, but he had refused. Another pet had been sold to a syndicate that staged dog fights just outside of town. The group had organized the fights into a lucrative gaming business; however, the dogs were the ones who paid the price.

"Oh my!" exclaimed Mildred Owens. "That's truly awful! Those people should be thrown in prison!"

"They should be shot!" shouted Darien Coxwald, a retired military man who had served gallantly for the Union during the Civil War. "I never treated a prison of war like that—never! What kind of monsters do we have living among us?"

It wasn't Tillson's intent to incite a vigilante movement, and he was quick to quiet the group. Putting up his hands, he admonished, "We shouldn't take these matters into our own hands. We can't run out and string up people even if they commit these heinous acts. No, we need to talk to our legislators on Capitol Hill. We must pressure them to pass laws to protect animals from mistreatment just as we are starting to do for children and the infirmed. Only that will force them to go back to their home states and push for such laws or, better yet, to pass a federal law."

"We need to do something now!" someone cried out.

"No animal should be subjected to that kind of cruelty!" shouted another from the back of the room.

"Then, after the meeting, you should come to the front desk and sign our petition," said Tillson. "The more signatures, the greater impact we'll have on our elected officials."

At the end of the meeting, Amanda distributed an information sheet telling people to whom they should write to push for legislation while her husband manned the signature desk. He encouraged everyone to write to members of their families too, especially in other states, and persuade them to form activist groups to press their states' governors.

At the end of the night, those attending filed out through the front door where Amanda stood, thanking them for coming.

"Thank you," said Amanda, smiling meekly and awkwardly as they left the church. "I hope you will make a difference and follow up with your congressman. William really appreciates your support."

"He should run for office!" said a middle-aged man whom all knew to be a local attorney. "I think he has a real knack for it."

"I'll let him know," Amanda answered.

After everyone left, Tillson sighed. "Well, I think that went well," he said. As he began moving the chairs back toward the walls from where they'd come. "Amanda, what do you think?"

"Yes," she answered before pausing. Then she asked, "William? Have you ever thought about running for office? Someone tonight told me you should. They said you'd make a great congressman on the Hill."

"Yes," he answered her, "but I didn't think that would be something you would want."

Amanda put her hand on his arm. "William, I don't want to hold you back. I'm your wife. We are team."

"I love you," he answered warmly. "But still, I don't know if it's right for us. I've seen what politics can do to a person—to their family. It's brutal, and we've been through a lot of brutality already, both here and New York."

"Well, if you change your mind, we can talk about it."

Tillson smiled. His mind was turning. Yet, for now, he had a more immediate mission in life, and he intended to push for it—heart and soul.

*****

CH 20 – His Condition Worsens

Things were strained at the Methodist Church as more of the congregation were falling ill with each passing Sunday. Initially, it was thought there was another outbreak of cholera—a disease that had infected and afflicted many communities throughout the ages. Boston was a large metropolis, and it was conceivable that it, like London, New York City and other large population centers, had been struck. But the three deaths and others who became ill had only been from the church. No one else in the community had contracted whatever was killing them.

Not knowing where else to turn, Reverend Benton contacted the local police chief to see if he could get some help.

"Chief Sinclair," the reverend began, "we've been experiencing a wave of illnesses at our church recently."

"Well, we have seen an uptick in sickness in Boston," the chief answered. "Doctor McClary—up there at Boston City—told me he's seen a lot of influenza already this fall."

"You mean the public hospital in the South End?"

"Yes. I've known Doc McClary for over twenty years."

"The doctors who treated my parishioners said it wasn't influenza or anything else they'd seen. They weren't sure what caused it."

"Then why are you coming to me?" asked the chief.

"What if someone at the church is causing it?"

"Intentionally?"

"Yes."

"Do you have anybody in mind?"

"Maybe, but I'd rather not point any fingers. Could you look into it?"

The chief took up the matter but first asked the city sanitation inspector to examine the well behind the church to see if it were contaminated. When nothing was found, the chief began questioning the parishioners. Benton had asked that the investigation be done discreetly so as not to stoke any more anxiety than they had already experienced. However, as soon as the questioning began, the illnesses stopped.

Orville continued to go to the church despite the health problems reported. He had known each of the victims: Adrian Hornsby, Myra Tanner, and Miss Laura Acheson, who was only eighteen. In each case, they had participated in that Sunday's services and communion.

"I only wish my brother were here," Orville had said to the reverend. "As a doctor, he might have helped us with this."

"Orville, I must ask you a difficult question," Benton began, taking a seat at his desk.

"What is it?"

"I'm sure it's crossed your mind—as it has mine—that there is no mere coincidence between the illnesses at the church and your sister."

Orville felt sick to his stomach. Indeed, he had thought about it, but had pushed it to the back of his thoughts, telling himself that it was, merely, a coincidence.

"I ... well ... I ..."

"I know. It's hard to process. We don't want to think it's possible, perhaps it's not. But I think we must consider the possibility."

"Claire would never do to such a thing. She wouldn't hurt anyone."

"The old Claire wouldn't. What about the new Claire?"

"I think she's just having a difficult time getting back to her old self. But there's a big difference between that and believing that she would try to hurt someone," said Orville.

Benton sighed. "I hope you're right, Orville. I pray you're right."

The deaths had been devastating to the families and their friends both inside and outside the church. Worse was the lack of answers. Some at Trinity thought it was just a disease that had come to the parish from outside their community. Others believed it was God who was punishing them for something they had done or failed to do.

Reverend Benton could feel the heat too; he began to fear it was something he had done or not done that was causing God to retaliate against him. He had contemplated resigning but decided to stay on to help find answers. Then, when the illnesses stopped, he postponed his decision to leave, making it conditional on nothing further happening.

One day, Orville came home early from work. He had been laboring to develop a new engineering design for his employer, the Boston and Albany Railroad or the B&A, as it was known. The company had been through several mergers during the previous ten years, and the engineering department had swelled in ranks to keep up with the expansion of the company's reach. Yet, that afternoon Orville had noticed his hands trembling and going into spasms. Not only that, but his vision had become blurry, and he was having trouble making smooth, precise lines on his drafting paper. His "jitters" just wouldn't stop. So, he told his boss he wasn't feeling well, packed up his things, and went home.

"What brings you home early?" asked Claire as he came through the door.

"I'm just not feeling well," he answered. "I think I'll just go upstairs and take little nap. Wake me when it's time for supper."

But when it was time for dinner and he didn't come down, Claire went to check on him. She found him sound asleep, but instead of waking him, she decided to let him rest. By the next morning, he still hadn't come down for breakfast, so she looked in on him again.

"Orville, Orville," she said shaking him. He was lying on his back in the bed, his eyes closed, his breathing shallow. "Wake up, Orville!"

Orville's eyes fluttered, but he continued to lay there, still and unresponsive.

"I brought you your morning tea, Orville. Here, take a few sips. It will make you feel better," she said helping him sit-up. She puffed his pillow and straightened his bed sheets before lifting the white cup to his mouth.

Orville opened his mouth and took some of the tea before lying back down.

"How do you feel?" she asked.

Her brother shook his head. "I can't go to work today," he exclaimed. "Would you send a messenger to my office for me?"

Claire went downstairs and wrote a message, finding a courier to take it to the B&A Rail headquarters and deliver it promptly to Orville's supervisor. But the more days that passed, the worse Orville's condition became. Finally, Orville rolled over and mumbled, "I think we should summon my doctor. I'm not getting better."

"I'm waiting for Reggie to stop by," Claire answered. "I wrote him about you, and I thought he would have hurried here to visit you. It's terrible that he doesn't have time for his own brother."

"I think he's out of town."

"Perhaps that's it, then. I wondered why we hadn't heard from him." She glanced at the pale, gray face of her sibling; yet, there was only a ghastly wight looking back at her—not the full-of-life, robust family member with whom she'd grown up.

The next day, Claire heard a brisk knock at the door, and standing on the porch were two people—both familiar to her.

"Madam Gray, Dr. Moorhead … well this is a surprise," Claire stuttered.

"Claire, hello," said Esther, taking it upon herself to cross the threshold and enter the house. "I heard in town that Orville hasn't been to work in weeks. They said he was sick, so I was worried. I thought I would bring Dr. Moorhead over to see what's wrong with him."

"Ah, yes, Dr. Moorhead. It's good to see you again," said Claire, timidly.

"I'd like to see your brother. Is he in his room?" asked the doctor.

"Uh, yes, of course. This way."

Claire took them to Orville's bedroom where he was curled up in a ball on his bed. He didn't move when they came in. Shifting him onto his back, Moorhead examined the young man, and within a few minutes he put down his stethoscope and shook his head.

"What do you think?" Esther asked the doctor.

"I don't know," Moorhead exclaimed. "It seems like he's fighting a toxin of some sort, but I have no idea what it might be." The doctor turned his attention back to Claire. "Do you know of anything he's eaten lately that might have caused him to react this way? Has he been out of the city—out in the woods? Could he have been bitten by a spider or something?"

"I have no idea," Claire answered. "He was perfectly fine, and then he came home early from work one afternoon—now two weeks ago—and he hasn't been the same since."

"Where does he work?"

"He's an engineer at the Boston & Albany Railroad downtown."

"Does he work in the office or on the rail?"

"He's one of their senior engineers, so he works in the office, I think."

"Is he around any poisons or chemicals that might cause something like this?"

"Not that I know of," Claire answered.

"We should talk to the manager down there and see what he can tell us," said Esther. "Maybe Orville is working with something that's hurting him. It's a place to start."

The next day Esther and Dr. Moorhead went to visit the main B&A Railroad building. It was an imposing edifice some five floors high but with a massive, stone footprint that stretched for nearly a city block. On the second floor, they found Orville's manager, a man named Franz Bollenbach. Bollenbach was a first-generation German who had emigrated from Hamburg only ten years earlier. He was a bright man—tall and beefy—but his English was still rough.

"Thank you for seeing us," said Dr. Moorhead. "One of your employees, Orville Cook, is my patient, and as you know he has fallen ill. I'm trying to figure out what the cause of his illness is, but so far, I've been stymied. We were wondering if you could help."

"I very busy, as you see," said Bollenbach curtly, not rising from his desk which was piled with stacks of papers that seemed to lack any form or organization. "I not have much time for d'is."

"It won't take long," said Esther. "We just need to know if Orville was … is … working on something that might expose him to a poison of some kind."

"A poison? V'ee don't v'urk vit' poisons here," said Bollenbach abruptly.

"Sometimes people can work with substances they don't know are poisonous," said Moorhead. "That could be the case here."

"Or," interjected Esther, "maybe it's something to which he is simply allergic."

"I don't know v'aht you say. Allergies?"

"Yes, there has been a lot of scientific work on allergies within the last few years. Dr. Bostock discovered hay fever some seventy years ago, and doctors have been studying it ever since," said Moorhead.

"V'ee don't v'urk vit' anyt'ing like d'at here," said the manager dismissively. "Orville pushes a pencil. D'ats it."

"Has anyone else here become sick?" asked the doctor.

"No."

"No one in the last few weeks?"

"I said, no! Now, if you excuse me, I have v'urk to do."

Bollenbach left his office and didn't return.

On the way out of the building, Esther said to Moorhead, "He wasn't very friendly, was he?"

"Nor was he helpful," answered her doctor.

"Do you think he's hiding something?"

"I don't know. Perhaps that's just his way. Some people are like that you know. They care more for themselves and their careers. Let's just say he's not a people person."

*****

CH 21 - Dalrymple

The terrible fact was that no one would ever see or hear from Palmer Jenkins again.

The town talked about it for many weeks and even years later, but his body was never found. Some believed he was taken by the very same Wendigo that he'd seen on his way back from Barre Mills. They thought he must have ventured out to find it with those strangers who had come into town and, unfortunately, had found it. Others thought he had just gotten lost in the woods even though Jenkins had lived in the area almost his entire life. Still others believed the Indians had gotten him. The Chippawa were the predominant tribe in the area, but then it could have been the Croix many thought. Neither tribe was known for violence, but their "kind" was always suspected of being up to no good by many of the local white settlers.

As for Dalrymple, he and his men had returned to Wadena after failing to find the creature the first time out. They needed more supplies and decided to build a crate just in case they were able to capture the wild beast. A live creature would mean more money for all of them.

The men camped outside of Wadena so as not to raise suspicions of the town folk. Dalrymple didn't want to bring trouble as he feared people of the town might connect his presence with Mr. Jenkins's disappearance. They stole wood and supplies from the General Store to build a sturdy crate and then "borrowed" a wagon from a family not far from their campsite.

Just as they were ready to venture back into the woods to continue their search for the Wendigo, they were unexpectedly stopped yet again. Heavy rains began pummeling the Midwest's Upper Peninsula which included parts of Minnesota, Wisconsin and Michigan. Although it brought needed relief to the parched summer weather the farmers and ranchers had been experiencing, it further delayed the posse from its mission. As a result, the rains turned the dusty dirt roads into impassible, thick pits of mud much like the La Brea Tar Pits had been for the Wolly Mammoth.

Dalrymple stopped by the post office to send a telegram update to his patrons in New York City. But as he was dictating the message to a young Western Union clerk, another in the office overhead the exchange

"You say you're Thaddeus Dalrymple?" asked the middle-aged man.

"Why yes. Why do you ask?" Dalrymple replied.

"I have some telegrams for you."

The clerk left and then returned with a handful of papers, all telegrams from McGinnis.

"Here. These are for you. Sign here."

Dalrymple finished the telegram to New York and began opening the messages he'd just gotten in return. The first was from McGinnis.

> Mr. Dalrymple STOP I must know how soon you will be apprehending the creature STOP Please advise at once STOP

Dalrymple sighed. His boss was demanding, and with his success, he had only become more so. The next one read:

> Mr. Dalrymple STOP We have not received a progress report in some time STOP Please respond STOP

As he went through the remainder of the messages, they all said the same thing, although in increasingly harsh tones.

"Young, sir," said Dalrymple, calling out for the young man who had taken his earlier message to send, "I'd like to change that message to New York. Instead, please send the following."

> Mr. McGinnis STOP We have encountered the beast and know exactly where to find it STOP We are procuring supplies and a cage to pursue and capture it STOP It will not take long to apprehend and return it to New York STOP I will keep you apprised of our progress STOP In the meantime I will be unavailable to receive messages for the time we are in the woods STOP Please consider this when attempting to contact me STOP

It was an exaggeration to say that they had "encountered" the beast, but Dalrymple felt it important to soothe the anxiety of Mr. McGinnis and his other partners, Mr. Phineas and Mr. Cooper, as well as get them off his back.

"You say you've found a beast in the woods?" said the clerk at the Western Union office. "Is that right?"

Dalrymple laughed. "No, that's just the name we gave to one of my partner's cousins who lives out here. She's a real piece of work."

"Ha!" said the man. "That's a good one. At first, I thought you were talking about the creature Old Man Jenkins says he saw."

"I know nothin' about it," said Dalrymple. "Now, if you'll excuse me. I must be on my way."

***

"All loaded up?" Dalrymple called out only a day after the rains had ceased. The roads were still buried in several inches of mud, but Dalrymple wouldn't wait any longer. He looked over the men and materiel he had for the next attempt and sighed. "We got six men, seven horses, a wagon, a crate, and a bunch of guns. That should be enough to get this beast. Don't you think?"

Little did he know that it would not be enough—not by a long shot.

Dalrymple's first stop would be to visit the Indian village not far from Wadena. It was not on a reservation and was considered by the Indian Affairs Office under the Interior Department in Washington to be a nuisance. Most other tribes had been relocated to Iowa or the Dakotas, but there were what the federal authorities called "squatters" who still occupied lands their families had used as ancestral hunting grounds for centuries.

Dalrymple was not interested in the legal status of the tribe. He cared only about one thing: finding a Wendigo.

Riding cautiously into the humble Indian village of wood and grass huts, the white leader raised his hand to halt his entourage. They met no resistance coming into the town, as the leader, Chief Kewaydin, and his warriors knew better than to pick an unprovoked fight with a white man.

Dalrymple got off his horse when he spotted a young man of not more than thirteen who was watching them as he tended to the village livestock.

"Where is your chief?" Dalrymple asked tersely.

The young man spoke a little English, but instead of replying, he simply nodded and took them to a larger, more distinguished, timbered hut where their chief and his family lived. The Indian put out his hand to stop them before disappearing inside the hut. A few minutes later, he re-emerged with another man—this one older, with long silver hair and keen, perceptive eyes—ones that had seen many changes during his lifetime.

"I am Chief Kewaydin," said the old man. "What is your business here?"

"We need to talk to you," said Dalrymple, giving no courtesy or respect to the elder.

Rather than resisting, the chief showed them inside where three women sat on colorfully striped blankets on the floor. Two of them appeared to be his daughters—young and beautiful—and the third, an older woman about the chief's age, presumably his wife.

"Chief, we need to find a Wendigo that's reported to live in the woods near here. We've already made one attempt to find it, but we obviously didn't. We took a man named Palmer with us who said he saw the creature, but I don't believe he ever did 'cause he couldn't lead us back to it. I'm here because I figure if there is anyone in these parts who has seen it, it would be you or someone in your tribe. So, tell me where it is."

The chief stood beside a stack of rich beaver pellets which one of his sons had brought in earlier that morning. The lad was busy examining them as the Dalrymple talked.

"The Wendigo is very hard to find," said the chief. "You must understand this as you have tried once already and failed. Why do you pursue it so?"

"I have my reasons, chief. I just need to know where it is. I'm sure you or your savages here have seen it. Where is it?"

The chief smiled, ignoring the slight.

"There are many beasts in the forest. Some are evil; others are sacred. However, they are all creatures of Mother Earth. We don't share secrets of Mother Earth with white man. He can never be trusted."

Dalrymple pulled his revolver and pointed it at the chief's forehead. The young man who had led them to the chief's hut jumped up, pulling a blade from its sheath, but the chief waved him off. "There is no need for violence," the chief said calmly. "Put away your weapons."

Dalrymple hesitated, but when the young man next to the chief obeyed, returning the knife to its casing, the east coaster grunted and re-holstered his own.

"I still need to know," the posse leader said belligerently. "If you don't tell me, other white men will come, and they won't be as nice. I can tell you that."

"I'm sure you right. Many white men not nice, although not all." The chief stopped and thought for a moment before continuing. "The creature you seek can be in many places at the same time. However, it is most often seen in the hills surrounding Black River Falls, north of here."

"That's sixty miles away," said Clyde, standing behind his leader.

"Yes. It's a two-to-three-day journey through dense woods. But that's where you will find it."

"If you're lyin' to me chief, I'll come back and scalp you myself," said Dalrymple caustically. Then he turned to his posse. "Let's mount up. We have a ride ahead of us." As he was leaving, he glanced back at Kewaydin, giving him an evil eye. "Like I said chief, if you're lyin', you'll pay for it. Ya' hear me?"

The group rode north, cutting along an old Indian trail that meandered through the less-often traveled hinterlands of northern Minnesota. Not well populated, there were few towns of any kind farther north. Travelers were largely on their own and had to find all their food and water in the wild once their provisions ran low. A few days passed, and they finally arrived in the area known as Black River Falls where the river cascaded through a series of roaring rapids before disappearing over a twenty-five-foot waterfall.

"I think it's time we start huntin' some fresh game," said Leroy, one in the posse. "I've had all I can take of them beans and hash."

"I'll go round up something," said Clyde, grabbing his Springfield. "Maybe I can find a skunk or 'possum for ya'."

"Real funny, Clyde. It better be a white tail. I love venison over an open pit."

Clyde vanished into the thick brush. It wasn't yet dark, but the inky blackness of the moonless night was fast approaching.

While Clyde was gone, the rest of the men set camp and built a fire for the evening supper and to keep off the evening chill. With growling stomachs and growing impatience, they decided not to wait and opened up some more bags of hash and beans to cook—not waiting for their friend to return with anything better. After supper, they broke out the traditional bottle of rotgut whiskey they called Ole' Snakehead. It had its name for a reason and was almost as lethal as a wild Wendigo. It didn't matter what it tasted like; it all had the same effect, and within the hour everyone was in a better mood.

"So, Leroy, is this the farthest west you've ever been?" Jeeter Parsons asked as he took another gulp directly from the whiskey bottle.

"Naw. I've been all the way to Fargo—visited there with my pappa when I was a kid. I've also been to St. Paul, the state capital, and shook hands with the governor, ya' know. I bet that's somethin' you've never done."

"Well, you're right about that. The closest thing I ever came to a damned politician was sittin' next to our mayor at a fundraiser. All he could do was prattle on about hisself and ask for money. I think I gave him a Shield nickel, and he didn't even say 'thanks.'"

Dalrymple laughed but then put down his flask, looking around the campfire. "Say, where's Clyde? What's takin' him so long?" he asked.

"It hasn't been that long, has it?" asked Leroy.

"I don't have a watch, but it seems like it's been a while. Leroy, why don't you and Jeeter go check on him. He should have bagged something for us by now. It's a little late for tonight's supper, but maybe we can roast it up in the morning."

Leroy and Jeeter headed out into the woods. It was dark by then, and the forest was filled with the chirping of crickets, the buzzing of mosquitos, the nonstop blinking of fireflies, and the croaking of bull frogs in a pond not far away. Occasionally, there was a hoot from a barn owl on the prowl, but it wasn't anything unnerving to men so accustomed to living in the great outdoors.

But after another half hour, Dalrymple began to worry—not only about Clyde, but about the other two he had sent out after him.

"Eddie, maybe me and you need to …" began Dalrymple, but just as he uttered the words, there was a flurry of activity in the brush.

"Who is it?" asked Dalrymple, jumping up and pointing his double-barrel shotgun into the darkness.

"Boss!" came the cry. "Don' shoot!"

Sprinting out of the woods were two white-faced, panicked men who looked as though they'd seen a ghost.

"What is it? What's wrong?"

"It's Clyde … or what we think is him," stuttered Jeeter collapsing by the fire. "I … I …" then Jeeter passed out, leaving the rest to stare in disbelief at his buddy, Leroy, who was ghostly white and whose eyes were filled with abject terror.

"Well," asked Dalrymple, nervously, "what's happened?"

Leroy shook his head and muttered.

"What? What are you saying?" shouted their leader. "Talk to me!"

But Leroy couldn't. His mind and body had shut down. The shock of whatever he had seen and heard had been too much for him to take.

*****

CH 22 - Decisions

It was another day in Wadena before Bones learned the identity of the man hired by Mr. Phineas and his company to capture the Wendigo and return it to New York City.

"You say it's a Mr. Thaddeus Dalrymple?" the Bones asked. He was talking to Baldridge Mason, a short, stout man with a coarse, gray beard and tiny, beady eyes. He was one of the wealthiest landowners in the area, having come from a family of furriers starting with his grandfather, Nathan Myrick, a local legend as an expert trapper and fur trader.

"Yes, sir," answered Mason. "He was here with some other men about a week ago. They were all outsiders, you know—not from these parts. He was asking the same questions around town that you are now. When I asked the man his name, he told me 'Dalrymple, Thaddeus Dalrymple,' but he said he was from St. Paul, not Washington. I didn't believe him—not a word. He spoke like one of you's from the East Coast."

"He had an accent?"

"He had a funny accent, but not like you do," said Mason, laughing.

"Did he tell anyone that he was working for the government?"

"No," said Mason. "He just said he was working for some furrier out east and wanted to find new pellets they could sell."

"What else can you tell me about him?"

"He told me he needed to find the Croix tribal village near here. He wanted to ask the chief some questions about a creature we know as a Wendigo. Then, I heard later he was asking where to find Palmer Jenkins's place. No one wanted to tell him, but it sounds like he found out eventually. Poor Palmer. I sure hope he's all right."

"Do you know if this Dalrymple went searching for the chief?"

"Yes, I believe he did. But I haven't seen any of them in town since then. Maybe they were killed by the Croix," said Mason.

"Or by the Wendigo," said Samuel who was with Bones.

Mason smiled. "Maybe, but I'm not one of those who believes in such things."

"The Wendigo?" Samuel asked.

Dr. Cook turned to his young protégé. "See, I'm not the only one who's a skeptic."

"I think it's more likely they're still out there—probably looking for the creature," said Mason. He stopped and thought for a moment. "Then again, they could'a just vanished."

"Just vanished?" asked Samuel.

"That happens sometimes, you know. People just vanish around here. One day they're in town at the General Store buyin' corn meal; the next day, town folk are asking why they haven't been seen a church lately. Worried, they go out to their cabin and find 'em gone—disappeared without a trace."

"Have there been others recently?" Bones asked.

Mason smiled. "We had ... let's see ... about five during the last year alone. There was Luisa Maye Percy last year, Adam Clyborne about six months ago, Edwin McMillan about then too. Then, there was Alma Douglas and her sister Katie. Never did find them either. Of course, Edwin may have been a special case."

"Why's that?" Bones asked.

"It was well known that Edwin was never playing with a full deck, if you know what I mean. He was missing some cards. When I found out he hadn't been seen in quite a while, I asked the sheriff to go up to his cabin and check things out."

"And?"

"The sheriff said things looked normal there, except for the fact that his gun and a bunch of ammo were missing, but nothing else. His horse was still tied to the post outside his house. Thank goodness he had a trough of food and some buckets of water nearby or he wouldn't have made it."

"Do you know where this Croix village is?" Bones asked.

Mason pulled out a map and showed the doctor exactly where the village was supposed to be. "This is where it's registered to be, but that doesn't mean it's there. The chief moves the tribe around now and again just to keep it safe. It's on all these maps, so everyone would know where to go to harass them or worse."

"What would they do to them?" Samuel asked.

"In my youth, we used to go ridin' out into the woods for some fun. It's not a good thing when you mix a bunch of young, crazy men, liquor and guns together. They feel invincible—like they have somethin' to prove to the world and each other. You understand what I'm sayin'."

"I'm afraid I do," said Bones.

Samuel looked at the doctor with surprise. "Is there something you haven't shared with us, Dr. Cook?"

"Plenty," Bones answered, "but you're not going to get it out of me now … or ever."

Bones thanked Mason, and Samuel and he returned to the lodge.

While Bones and Samuel talked with people in town, Missy went to the schoolhouse. It was a whitewashed, single room building with worn, weathered doors front and back, simple wooden tables with short, mismatched chairs, and a fireplace with a stone hearth tucked away against the far wall—one still burning from the morning's stoking. All grades were taught in the same room—first through eighth. It was a lot to handle by one teacher and one assistant as there were as many as thirty children in the classroom at one time. Yet, Allison Metcalf was an experienced teacher having taught at several rural schoolhouses during her life and nearly twelve years alone in Wadena.

Missy arrived shortly after classes had been dismissed for the day, finding Ms. Metcalf sitting at her desk at the front of the classroom looking through classwork done on handheld blackboard tablets. She looked up, surprised at the new visitor, but glad at the same time.

"May I help you?" Allison asked, smiling as she put down one of the boards.

"Hello. I'm sorry to interrupt, but I was wondering if you had a few moments to talk."

The teacher was more than happy to share what she knew. In fact, she was so talkative, Missy spent most of the rest of the day with her. Yet, the conversation was mutually beneficial. Although Missy gathered good information about the town and its people, she also offered a sympathetic ear, having been on her own and taught in Texarkana for a few years.

"Recently, I saw a group of men come into town—strangers, in fact," said Allison. "They looked army, but they didn't wear any rank insignia—just the blue uniforms. There have been army men through here before, but they never stayed, only passing through. This lot was different. They didn't pass through. They camped just outside of town. I don't know how long they stayed, but I hear they left a few days ago."

"How many of them were there?"

"I think there were five. One was definitely the leader—a big guy with a bushy beard and silver glasses. The others were from Duluth, I think. They didn't look like the most upstanding citizens of that fine city; I can tell you that."

The teacher went on to talk about Jenkins and what he claimed he'd seen. She told Missy that the town had been in an uproar over it, but when no one else had seen the creature in the woods—either before or after—and no one had been attacked, things died down. She went on to say that the legends of the Wendigo came from the Indian tribes that lived in the area.

"But that's where most people learn about them," said Allison. "Again, I'd say most people don't believe them. There are a lot of Indian myths that you hear about—all likely intended to scare the children and make them behave. Luckily, I haven't had to use any of those on my students." She laughed.

"You heard about them from the Indians?" Missy asked.

"For me, it was from my grandfather, Charles Coleman. He was the mayor not long ago, and he had an interest in it. The He-Chunk and Croix were the predominant tribes here, and he was sympathetic to them. Not many townspeople agreed with that approach though, and he wasn't in office very long. However, he got to know the local chief of the Croix, and they traded stories. That's when he found out about the legend of the Wendigo."

"Is it true that it eats humans?" asked Missy.

"That's what my Grandpa Charles used to tell us when we were kids. Like I said, I always thought he was trying to scare us into behaving. And, it worked pretty well whether it was true or not. But there was one story he told us that even scared my father."

"What was that?"

"As I remember it, our grandpa was out hunting for white tail, and he came across a dead buck. But he hadn't shot it; it was already dead when he found it. Anyway, that wasn't the strange part. What was odd was that it had been gutted—all the insides were gone, but none of the meaty parts had been touched. Almost all carnivores will eat the meaty parts too."

"That does seem strange, but it's not crazy. Perhaps it was a black bear that had started eating its kill but got scared off by a hunter. There are probably a dozen reasons that might have happened, right?" said Missy.

"Maybe, but what happened next was something he never could get out of his head. It haunted him. There were tracks of some creature around the deer that he'd never seen before—huge tracks. And as he was looking over the deer, he sensed something in the woods nearby was watching him. He got nervous and picked up his gun to head back to the trail that would take him to Black River Falls. It was along this trail that the winds picked up and a cold breeze with frozen sleet began pelting his face."

"All right, but why is that weird?"

"It was September! We've never had snow or sleet in September!" said Allison, engrossed in her own story. "He said he remembered hearing a grotesque howling—like the cross between a bear and a wolf, but it wasn't either. Then, a deep mist blew through the forest, and it blinded him--he couldn't see a thing. But the last thing he remembered was that howling, shrieking sound that seemed like it was right behind him. He doesn't remember much after that. The next thing he knew, he was on the back of a wagon heading for Black River Falls. He had blood all over him, and there were deep bite marks in his arm. He said for weeks after that he had an irresistible urge to hurt people—to kill them."

Allison stopped, looking away.

"A Wendigo," said Missy.

"The Indian chief told my grandpa that the Wendigo was known to drink human blood and that a human bit by one would turn into one--a Wendigo."

"My god!" cried Missy, cringing at the thought. "Did your grandpa show any signs of ..."

"... of turning into a Wendigo? Thank goodness, no. But he did say it took him months to get over that feeling of wanting to kill other people. We were scared to be around him after father told us the story—who wouldn't be?"

"Yeah, I can understand that. No wonder you were terrified," said Missy. "So, do you think his story was true?"

"I don't know," Allison answered. "Grandpa didn't turn into one—so I have my doubts. Again, I think it was just a story to make us behave."

"How did he die?"

"Well, that was a bit strange too. The only thing our father told us was that he disappeared."

"Disappeared?"

"Yeah. One morning, he just wandered off into the woods. They never found him or his body."

Missy thought for a moment. "Did you know that Mr. Jenkins is missing? No has seen him in days."

"No."

There was a strange silence as both knew what the other was thinking.

"I'm sure he's just gone to see his relatives in Duluth or something," said Allison. "I think he has family there."

"Yes, you're probably right. He's just seeing family," Missy answered, trying not to fan the flames of hysteria.

Missy thanked the teacher for spending so much time with her. "You don't mind if I contact you later, if we need more information, do you?"

"Of course, not," Allison answered. "I'd be happy to."

When Missy returned to the cabin, she told Bones and Samuel all about her talk with the schoolteacher and the story about her grandfather.

"What do you think?" she asked.

"It's not far from what David Law told me today," said Samuel.

"Who's David Law?" Bones asked.

"Oh, it's Mayor Law, I guess."

"You met with the mayor? How did you do that?" asked Missy.

"I don't know. I went to the post office and saw a door marked *Mayor's Office*, so I went in. He was there working on something, and I just sat down and started talking to him."

Missy laughed. "That's my boy!" she exclaimed proudly. "You're learning pretty fast, Samuel."

"So, tell us what he said," Bones pressed.

"He told me there have been countless stories about the Wendigo in this part of the country. He said most were embellishments of simple bear sightings, but he added that he thought a few might be authentic. There was no good explanation for what happened. He said those came from upstanding citizens whom he had no reason to question."

"Did *he* have any stories?"

"He didn't have any personal knowledge, no. But he did say his uncle had an experience with a strange creature."

"Pray, tell us," said Missy, eager for another tale.

"Well, he said his uncle told a story about being out with a bunch of the 'boys' in his younger days. They had been carousing in Brainerd—not too far from here. They were drinking and carrying-on, and it was late. After coming out of one of the town saloons, they jumped on their horses to ride back to Wadena. However, when they were just outside of town, the horse of his Uncle Leroy's friend, Jake Talmont, got spooked. It reared back on its hind legs and pawed the air, nearly throwing him. But to his credit, he managed to get the horse under control.

"Thinking it was just a bear or something nearby, they continued, merely picking up the pace to put distance behind them and whatever had scared the horse. However, it was less than a mile up the road where the horse of his Uncle Leroy got spooked. This time, it threw its rider from the saddle, and he landed next to a big tree, his head missing the thick trunk by only inches.

"Well, at that point, they all knew something was in the woods spooking the horses. So, they got Leroy back into his saddle and tried to ride off; however, the horses refused to move. The mayor's uncle looked ahead. In the road, he saw something that chilled his bones."

"What?" asked Missy, now riveted.

"His uncle claimed it had red eyes, stood about nine feet tall on its back legs, and if that wasn't creepy enough, he said it looked half-human."

"Human?" questioned Bones.

"That's what he said. He told me his uncle swore the rest of his life that it looked like an emaciated, but hairy human with blood on its lips and evil in its eyes."

"What did they do then?" Missy asked.

"He said his uncle yelled for all of them to charge the creature. They were drunk, and when you're drunk a lot of stupid things seemed like the right thing to do, I guess. He said his uncle figured the beast would just jump out of the way if their horses were galloping toward it at a full tilt. The problem was —it didn't. The creature didn't move, and the horses balked fifty feet from it, refusing to charge and nearly throwing all the riders that time. Then they bolted into the deeper woods to flee."

"Wow," said Missy.

"It took them time to calm their horses, and when they got them back on the trail, they found it was empty. The creature was gone."

"That's some story," said Bones, grinning.

"What?" asked Missy. "Why are you smiling?"

"It's a story, a myth, a legend, like all the others," Bones said. "Yes, it's interesting—fascinating, in fact. But both are only stories."

"Then why are we here?" asked Missy, putting her hands on her hips. "We know you don't believe this stuff is true, so why are *you* here, Bones?"

"Just to be with my two favorite friends," said Bones, smiling.

"Bones!" cried Missy, now annoyed.

"Alright, fine. I find these stories interesting. I take that information, and I put it with all the other stories I keep on file."

"What are you going to do with it all?" asked Missy.

"I don't know. Someday I might get around to analyzing them—seeing common threads in stories from different tribes. I usually try to trace them back to some point of origin. Then again, maybe I'll write a book about them."

"*You*, write a book?" said Missy, skeptically.

"Yeah, why not?"

"What about calling it *Real Creatures That Aren't Real?*" asked Samuel. "That would make a good title."

"Yes, if we could only convince him that they are!" Missy answered, nodding toward their third partner. "I still don't know why we're staying."

"Then why don't we pack up and go home?" said Samuel. "Dr. Cook doesn't believe in them. I don't see a point now."

"Because I told Mr. Tillson I would do this for him. I agreed to try to find the creature—a creature—and prevent it from being captured by this private New

101

York group and their posse. I am a man of my word, and I will do that. It's up to you if you want to come along with me. I'm heading out tomorrow to find it."

"So, you're not worried about some man-eating Wendigo?" asked Samuel.

"I'm more worried about Mr. Jenkins and that Dalrymple group," said Bones. "I've found humans to be a lot more dangerous than any monster from folklore."

"So, if we confront the posse, we shoot, but if we confront the beast, we don't?" Samuel asked.

"You fire on whatever is the threat. I would wager it's more likely to be the trackers out here than it will be the creature."

"Will you place a bet on that?" asked Missy, holding out her hand.

"Yeah," said Bones. "A silver dollar says we have to shoot at a man before we ever shoot at a beast."

"You're on," said Missy. "I hope you brought a silver with you, 'cause my name is already written on it."

"Okay, so what's next?" said Samuel.

"Just as we did in Texarkana," Bones began, "I think we need to talk to the local Indian chief. They're the best ones who can tell us which way Dalrymple and his men went. With Jenkins gone, there's no one else who can tell us."

"There must be another reason, at this point, Bones. Tillson wouldn't want you to risk your life with that posse group out here if there isn't a creature to be found."

"I'm feeling a responsibility to find Mr. Jenkins now," said Bones. "We've come this far. The least we can do is try to find him, and if he's still alive, we can bring him home."

"That's good enough for me," said Samuel. "So, what are we waiting for? As the saying goes, 'let's not let the moss grow under our feet.'"

"Who ever said that?" asked Missy.

Samuel shrugged. "I dunno. I thought I heard it someplace."

"Well, you're right," said Bones. "Let's get packed. We'll head out first thing tomorrow."

*****

CH 23 - Backup Plan

Although Mr. Phineas wanted his business partner, McGinnis, to address the surging activism on Capitol Hill, he didn't want him to abandon his responsibility in managing the project in Minnesota. And, when he didn't get an update report for weeks on end, he became worried.

"What do you know, Jorg?" asked Phineas, as he was leaving to go uptown.

"I spoke with Mr. McGinnis yesterday, sir," said his aide d' camp, Lungun Jorgenson or "Jorg," a tall, Norwegian who had been in Phineas's service for many years. Nearly six feet five inches tall with broad shoulders and a trim, athletic physique, Jorgenson was a second generation Norwegian after his grandparents emigrated at the beginning of the century. He had always been loyal and dutiful to his employer, and Phineas had always reciprocated, being unusually generous and kind to him. "Mr. McGinnis said he was going to send another telegram to Minnesota inquiring of Mr. Dalrymple's progress."

"I thought we'd have that damned beast in New York by now. I'll not wait any longer!" It was obvious that Phineas was terribly unhappy with the progress being made. He nervously tapped the tips of his fingers on his top hat while he stood waiting for his private coach to pull around and take him into town. "Send someone out to that damned little town now. I want another set of eyes on what's going on out there. It's taking too damn long."

"Who shall I ask Mr. McGinnis to send, sir?"

"Who do we have who can go with such short notice? Do we have any young, unmarried man who can handle himself in the wilderness?"

"You mean in the Midwest?"

"Whether in the Midwest, the wilderness or the jungles of a big city, I don't see much difference anymore."

"Well, there's Potter."

"No, he's too timid for this kind of job."

"What about Stewart?"

"We need him to coordinate the tents and setup."

"The only other one I can think of is Timothy Campbell. He's only twenty or so, but he's always looking for another challenge."

"Great! Put him on it. Tell McGinnis I said so. If Campbell needs to find men out there to go along with him, that's fine. He's authorized. I just want this exhibit in my show as soon as possible! Do you understand?"

"Yes, sir. I'll let him know, sir."

"You do that and tell him he'd better not let me down."

"Who sir? Mr. McGinnis or Mr. Campbell?"

"Both!"

***

McGinnis took the train down from New York City; it wound along tracks laid decades earlier through Trenton, Philadelphia, Wilmington, and Baltimore before creeping into Washington's Union Station. He hated going there, as he considered it a backwater marsh with nothing but self-absorbed politicians and clueless bureaucrats who thought they were important to the world but in his view were only barriers to the greater success of his company and the country.

The reality was that political positions on Capitol Hill were still only part-time. Congressmen and senators were in the nation's capital only about four months during the year drafting legislation and bickering over giveaways that would sweeten the pot enough for someone to vote for it. The rest of the time, members of Congress worked their other jobs in their home states.

Most senators came from wealthy families, and increasingly so did their counterparts in the House. Their pay was $5000 per year for only part-time efforts. This contrasted greatly with the average compensation of $580 paid to unskilled and semi-skilled laborers for a full year of work. Even then, members of Congress rarely spent more than six hours per day on the job when they were in Washington. This was half of the time the average laborer put in each week—usually sixty hours or more.

McGinnis took a carriage from his hotel suite at the Willard to Capitol Hill where he had made appointments to see prominent senators and congressman. Phineas had pressed him hard on two fronts—the hunt in Minnesota and the pending legislation in Congress—and it was all he could do to keep up with everything. He was well aware of the other parties lobbying to push through legislation to ban the use of animals in entertainment venues as well as other, more far-reaching, restrictions on their deployment. Since entertainment was McGinnis's company's livelihood, he understood the severity of the threat and took every meeting with those who would determine his fate as a life and death struggle. As Phineas had told him, "If you give them an inch, they'll take a mile. We don't want them to pass *anything* of this sort on the Hill. It's a slippery slope, and once they sink their teeth into this issue, there's no telling where it might lead."

"Senator Groome, thank you for seeing me," said McGinnis shaking hands with the Maryland senator. James Groome was the junior senator from that state and was among a handful with the notorious distinction of missing almost as many vote sessions as he had attended.

"Always a pleasure to talk to one of my constituents," said Groome, sitting back in his office chair.

"Thank you, senator," answered McGinnis knowing full well that as a resident of New York he was not a constituent of the senator's. "Sir, I'm at the Capitol talking to various members of Congress about a bill being proposed that I feel would be very contrary to the heart and spirit of capitalism which, as you know, is the very basis and foundation of our nation."

"Which bill are you referring to?"

"It's currently in the House. It's bill number HR2339. It makes it illegal to use domesticated animals. Think of that! To outlaw the use of animals?" Of course, McGinnis was exaggerating the intent and scope of the bill to suit his argument. There was no proposed bill to outlaw the use of domesticated animals. The proposal would only have addressed cruelty to animals.

"Outlaw the use of animals? Well, I've heard some crazy ideas up here, but that one must take the cake," said Groome. "How could the farmers survive without domesticated animals?"

"Exactly," said McGinnis. "And there are many more who would be put out of business. Just think, such a law might even prohibit you from putting your dog on a leash when you walk him down the city sidewalk. Imagine that! Being arrested by a patrolman for taking your canine for a walk. It's absurd."

McGinnis went on to tell the senator other possible, if not implausible, scenarios involving the use of animals by their owners.

"So, it's important that if such a bill comes up that you vote it down," said McGinnis. "We can't have these half-cocked ideas gaining momentum in the halls of an institution whose purpose is to make our country a better place in which to live. Banning animals would make things hard on farmers, on people in cities who rely on horse-drawn carriages, and on other people who use animals for the betterment of their families and our country."

"You have my support," said Groome, getting up from his desk and extending his hand.

"Thank you, senator."

McGinnis left Groome's office and went down the hall. All the senators' offices were located in the Capitol building, as were those of House congressmen. It was becoming increasingly crowded, and although the senators enjoyed larger offices than those of their House member counterparts, they still complained of needing more space for themselves and their staffs.

McGinnis's next stop was Senator Charles Jones of Florida. He too had a murky history of missing votes. In fact, he had missed more sessions than he had attended.

Reviewing the proposed bill, McGinnis again made claims about the legislation that were far from true. This time he launched into the ill-treatment of horses used for coaches in the cities and in general transportation by just about everyone, whether in urban or rural settings.

"Can you imagine denying someone in Columbus, Ohio, the ability to use his horse to pull a wagon filled with feedstock from the town center out to his farm to feed his hogs, chickens, and sheep? What about using them to plow his fields and plant crops? How can we place such a burden on the American citizen? The American farmer? It would likely spur wide-spread discontent and, quite probably, a revolution—one not unlike the Tea Party in Boston. How could you vote for such legislation knowing it would destroy millions of American families and starve their children?"

As with Groome, Jones was utterly convinced by the arguments presented by McGinnis and without hesitation gave his support in opposing the legislation.

McGinnis spent the rest of the afternoon roaming the halls, walking into the legislators' offices and sitting down with as many as had time available to talk to him. These included influential members such as Howell Jackson of Tennessee, Thomas Baynard of Delaware, and Henry Dawes of Massachusetts.

When McGinnis reported back to Phineas, the old man was pleased.

"That's a good start my dear fellow. Now, we must keep up the pressure. We can't let the other side gain any momentum on this issue. It's too important."

"Yes, sir," McGinnis answered.

"And who is it again that is spearheading and promoting this bill?"

"It's a man named Tillson—William Tillson."

"Is he from Washington?"

"He worked at the Department of the Interior. He was an assistant director, if I recall. He left recently to pursue this ridiculous path."

"Yes, well, let's make sure he doesn't succeed. We can't jeopardize everything we're working so hard to build. This business is worth a fortune, you know, and won't let anyone take it away from me."

"Yes, sir. I am fully aware."

*****

CH 24 – Discovery in the Cupboard

"How is he?" Esther asked, taking off her shawl and gloves and handing them to Clarence, her butler, who had come with her and was standing next to her on the Orville's doorstep.

"Dr. Moorhead says he's not doing well, but I'm always optimistic," Claire answered. "I'm sure he'll pull through."

Orville's flat, which was once immaculate, was now a complete wreck. With trash piling up in the kitchen, a pungent smell permeating the room, and the scattering of dirty clothes on the floor and the furniture, it was an apocalyptic scene of which Esther was not accustomed. Worse were the soiled undergarments on the dining room table and the muddy shoes on the white chair cushions.

They went upstairs where Esther entered Orville's bedroom, drawing nearer the patient. Orville lay unconscious—his eyes shut and his mouth agape. His body shook uncontrollably even though he was not awake. Next to him was Dr. Moorhead, his hand on Orville's wrist taking his pulse.

"Claire tells me you still don't know anything," said Esther, turning to the doctor.

"I don't," Dr. Moorhead answered. "For the life of me, I can't figure out the cause. It's baffling and frustrating."

"You said it's a poison."

"Yes, I think so, but …"

"So, he's getting worse?" asked Claire.

"Yes, I'm afraid he is," said Moorhead.

"I'm worried about him," Claire said.

Leaning over Orville, Esther whispered to him. "Can you hear me, Orville?" she asked. Orville only groaned. "How do you feel?" she asked. This time there was no reaction. Esther studied his ruddy face, taking her hand and stroking his flushed cheek. Then, she lifted one of his eyelids and then the other.

"What is it?" asked Claire.

Esther glanced at the doctor but then shrugged. "I … I'm not sure." She got up and quickly started to leave the room.

"Where are you going?" Dr. Moorhead asked.

"I need to use your washroom," said Esther, looking at Claire. "Is it downstairs?"

"Yes ma'am."

Madam Grey went downstairs and shut the door to the lavatory but without going inside. Then, she headed straight for the kitchen. There, she quietly rummaged through the cupboards, opening several containers and sniffing each one. Finally, she found one with tea leaves and popped the cork stopper that kept them fresh. Putting it to her nose, she pulled back suddenly, put off by something inside. Then, pouring the contents out onto the dining room table, she began parsing through the fractured ingredients using a kitchen butter knife that she'd found in a drawer. When she finished, she went back upstairs.

"Ah, thank you very much," she said to Claire. "Well, I believe I should go. I will pray for poor Orville here. And Dr. Moorhead, I need to talk to you about my sciatica. I'm afraid it's back. Would you be able to take a look at it now?"

"Yes, of course. I have a few minutes," said the doctor.

"Good. Let's go downstairs so we don't disturb your other patient," Esther answered, motioning toward Orville.

Clarence was waiting for her downstairs, and after instructing him to bring the carriage around, she took Dr. Moorhead into the kitchen.

"Madam Grey," said Dr. Moorhead, scratching his head, "I didn't recall that you have sciatica. Do you? I'm puzzled."

"Dr. Moorhead, do you recognize this leaf?" Esther asked probingly as she held up a fragmented piece of something dried and cracked.

The doctor leaned in, examined the shard and shook his head. "No, I'm afraid not. I'm not familiar with it," he answered.

"It's nightshade, doctor. I know all about it as it is what my cousin died from twenty years ago. He was poisoned by his wife, poor man. He was never a saint, mind you, but he never deserved to be taken out from this life like that. It causes tremors and dilates your pupils. It also leaves you with dry, reddened skin—all symptoms shown by Orville upstairs."

"He's being poisoned by this?" Moorhead asked, taking the piece of the leaf between his fingers.

"Yes, I'm afraid he is," she answered.

"How could something like that get mixed in with those tea leaves?" The doctor pointed to the tea leaf mix strewn across the table in front of them.

"By someone living here … someone who wants her brother dead for some reason. I don't understand it, but I can't help but think about something Orville said shortly after Claire recovered from her bout with TB."

"I don't recall. What was that?"

"He said that she'd changed. She wasn't herself."

"She seems perfectly normal to me," said Moorhead.

"I don't know her well," answered Esther. "But as you know, appearances can be deceiving. It's all very bizarre."

"Quite," said the doctor. "Orville's life is in danger, then. We should alert the authorities."

Esther stopped him. "No, we need to get Orville out of here now! Away from his sister. *That* is the imperative." She paused, and then added, "Dr. Moorhead, I think there is more going on here. How does someone go from an honest, caring, church-going person to one that schemes and murders."

"What are you saying?"

"I'm saying that I don't think the person upstairs is Claire."

"I don't follow you."

"Let's get Orville away from her first. I'll suggest that Orville be moved to my manor, just as I did for Claire. You will agree and insist that he can be better cared for there. After that, we'll address the Claire matter."

"All right Madam Grey. Whatever you say."

Dr. Moorhead and Madam Grey told Claire they would be taking Orville to the Grey mansion for observation and on-going treatment. As expected, Claire protested, saying she was the best person to care for him. However, the doctor insisted, stating that those were his explicit orders, and they should not be countermanded. Having no choice, Claire relented.

Orville was moved that very day, and Clarence was given strict orders to be in his room upstairs at all times when Claire was visiting. She was also not allowed to give her brother anything while she was with him.

*****

CH 25 - Meeting with the Chief

Bones's meeting with Chief Kewaydin did not go well. It was unfortunate that the chief's previous meeting only two days earlier with Dalrymple had gone so poorly. It put the chief in no mood to talk with another white man about the same subject.

"I already gave your other white friend information he need," answered the chief. "He threaten me at muzzle of his gun. Now, you ask me to give you same? I don't think so. I not help you."

"Please, chief. I don't know this Dalrymple fellow. He is not a friend of mine, and from what I can tell, he's not a good fellow. But I can assure you that we mean no harm to you or anyone."

"So, you tell me you are different? You are good?"

"Yes."

The chief laughed. "Why should I believe you? After all the lies of white man, why should I believe a word coming from your mouth?"

"You shouldn't," Missy answered, speaking up. "But I think there is an Indian saying, 'it doesn't take many words to speak the truth.' Is that right?"

The chief's eyes lit up. "Ah, someone who is learned about my people."

"I had much time in New York City this past year and spent time in the library studying about Indians and your culture," Missy answered.

"Then, you also know the Cheyenne saying, 'Do not judge your neighbor until you walk two moons in his moccasins.'"

"Yes," she answered, "and we don't presume to understand how you must feel about the white man after what's been done."

"Good answer," said the chief. He paused and looked deeply into the eyes of the three sitting in front of him. Then, he said, "I must also put on my moccasins and walk with you in order to understand you as well."

Bones smiled and nodded. *This man is wise*, he thought, *very wise indeed*.

"I tell you what I told other white man and leave it to you. The creature can be in many places at the same time. Where we have seen it is in the hills surrounding Black River Falls north of here. It about sixty miles on horseback."

"Is that where the other white man was headed then?" asked Bones.

"I suppose, but I do not know. We did not track him after he left our village. Now, go. I do not wish to see another of your kind anytime soon."

Like Dalrymple, Bones, Missy and Samuel headed north, following the same overgrown trail used days earlier by the posse. But it wouldn't be long before they found something—just not what they were hoping for.

*****

CH 26 – An Unexpected Find

Once they revived Jeeter, he was able to verify what Leroy had already told them. It had taken time to calm him: he was a mess, twitching and convulsing with shock over what he'd seen in the deep woods.

"So, you found Clyde's body? Where was it?" asked Dalrymple, taking another shot of whiskey from his silver flask—now trying to finish it with some urgency.

"It was about a half mile from here," Jeeter replied, stammering. "We followed his tracks through the mud. Then, they stopped all of a sudden where there was broken bushes. But we kept goin' 'til we saw dark splotches on the leaves. Leroy here wiped one with his finger to see what it was."

"It was blood," said Leroy. "Blood!"

"Then what did you do?" asked their leader.

"Then," Jeeter began, but stopped. He began breathing fast and shallow, hyperventilating, and his eyes started to roll up into his head again.

"Take it easy, Jeeter. Just tell us what you saw," said Dalrymple.

"There was drag marks in the earth where someone was drug off from the trail and into the forest."

"I think it was the heels of his boots," said Leroy, piping in.

"Yeah, I think you're right, Leroy. But then when we got far enough into the bush, I saw it—Clyde's body. It was torn limb from limb. It was awful, it was."

"What did it look like?" asked Eddie Johnson, usually the most cowardly of the group.

"Parts was up in a nearby tree; other parts was on the ground around another big pine. There wasn't much blood right there in that area, but we didn't stick around to look. It was the most horriblest thing I's ever seen!"

"What could do something like that?" asked Leroy, shaking his head. His face was still gaunt and blanched. "Do you think this the creature you're looking for?"

Dalrymple knew if he said yes, his men would flee immediately back to Wadena or to Duluth. He couldn't let this incident interfere with his capturing the beast and collecting on his payday. That was something he couldn't—no, wouldn't—let happen.

"Heck no," their leader answered. "The Wendigo doesn't do things like that. It's pretty harmless. It's only dangerous if it's cornered. Only then might it lash out to defend itself and any young ones. No, this sounds like a big black bear of some kind."

"Bears don't do things like that," said Jeeter, shaking his head. "That weren't no bear."

"Well, I've heard of bears takin' a swipe at a guy's head and knockin' it clean off," said Dalrymple. "I'm sure the big ones can take a man apart fast. They can climb trees too, so it makes sense to me since you saw parts of Clyde stuck up in the tree limbs above ya'."

"What about there bein' no blood around once we got to where the body parts were?"

"You said you saw some on the trail."

"Yeah, but not by where his body was, and there weren't much on the trail either—not what you'd think from a dismembered body!" said Jeeter.

"It's probably there or just got soaked into the ground," said Jack Peters, jumping in to side with his boss. "It was dark. How you gunna' see blood spots in the dark? Come on men. Think!"

"And the rest of Clyde's body?" asked Leroy. "We didn't find no head."

"No head?" asked Eddie, beginning to rock back and forth uncomfortably. The magnitude of what they were facing was quickly sinking in.

"Well, bears don't like to eat those parts," said Dalrymple. "It probably tossed it someplace. It rolled under a bush somewhere. There are answers to all your questions—answers that don't involve this Wendigo thing." Dalrymple stopped and sat back, taking one last swig of his whiskey. "No, I think this is pretty clear, boys. It was just an unfortunate bear attack. We need to be more careful out here, that's all. We'll keep the fire goin' tonight, and if you want, one of you's can be on look-out. We can take turns. How's that? Does that make you feel better?"

The other men looked at each other warily. What their leader had said made sense, but they were still uneasy about all of it. Yet for now, they agreed on taking shifts just in case whatever it was that took Clyde apart was still lurking nearby. For all, morning could not come too soon, and when dawn broke, they began looking for any other signs of the rest of Clyde's body. However, this time they found nothing—not even the bits and pieces Jeeter and Leroy had

114

claimed were in the dark limbs of the trees above. All the evidence had vanished.

*****

CH 27 - Confrontation

Once Orville was safely resituated at the Grey mansion, it was time for Esther and Dr. Moorhead to address the potential danger posed by his sister, Claire. She was still staying at Orville's flat, hoping she could still persuade Esther and Dr. Moorhead to let her brother return home. "He's better off at home in familiar surroundings," she had pleaded to no effect.

Armed with the discovery in Orville's kitchen, Madam Grey and her doctor paid a visit to Reverend Benton at the church.

"Thank you for seeing us," said Esther.

"Please make yourselves as comfortable as you can in my most-uncomfortable, yet affordable, chairs," said Benton, laughing.

Esther gracefully placed herself on one of two cane chairs resting in front his desk and smiled. "These aren't so bad, reverend. I'm sure they're more comfortable than the seats in your confessionals."

Benton's chortle was loud and robust. "Very good," he answered. "I'll have to remind my parishioners of that the next time they complain about those seats or the church pews. Now, what can I help you with today?"

"We've come to talk to you about one of your staff, reverend," said Esther.

"Oh?"

"Yes. It's about Claire Cook."

"What about her?"

"This is a sensitive matter, so please don't say anything to anyone," Madam Grey asked. "This discussion should not leave your office."

"I understand," he answered. "So, what about Claire?"

Madam Grey told him about the severity of Orville's illness and what she had discovered in the container of tea leaves in his kitchen.

"So, you see why we moved Orville to my estate," said Esther. "We feel it's essential for his wellbeing."

"Of course," said Benton. Then he became quiet.

"Is there something wrong?" asked the doctor.

"Yes, actually. You say Claire was staying with him."

"Yes."

Benton rose from his chair.

"I take it from your comments that you believe Claire is involved in this."

"Yes. We think she is involved," answered Dr. Moorhead. "Why?"

"Then why not take it to the police?"

Esther leaned forward in her chair. "I understand from others that you had sudden illnesses and deaths at your church—and recently too. Is that right?"

Benton was quiet for a moment. Then, he replied, "Yes. That is true."

"And did you take those to the authorities?" asked Esther.

The reverend walked to the window and gazed outside, putting his hands on his hips. "For a period after Claire returned from her sickness," Benton began, "we did have many problems with illnesses here at the church. Those falling ill seemed to come down with it after our Sunday services. Thank goodness the problems stopped within a few weeks, and we haven't had any since." He was skirting the question, which was obvious to both Esther and her doctor.

"But you think Claire was involved," said Esther, pressing the matter.

Benton turned back from the window to address them more directly. "I did wonder if there was a connection somehow to Claire. Don't get me wrong. Claire has been a model deacon at our church. The people love her. But ever since she came back, she hasn't quite been, well, ..."

"... quite herself," said Esther, finishing his thought.

"Yes. Not at all. Many people in the congregation have commented to me about it too. She's been much colder and more distant. It's like there's an invisible force between her and me when we talk—like trying to push two same-charged magnets together. Orville told me the same thing."

"So even her brother noticed," said Dr. Moorhead.

"Yes. He didn't tell me in confession, so I feel I can share that with you." The reverend took a seat once more before continuing. "This attack on her brother is quite troubling. I can't imagine what could have changed in her to make her do something like this."

"That's why we're here. That's why we haven't gone to the police yet either," Madam Grey responded. "I think it's something more ... much more."

"Possession," said the reverend, almost matter-of-factly without a change in tone or pitch. "I didn't want to believe that such a thing is possible, but somethings cannot be explained any other way."

"You think she may be possessed too?" Esther asked, putting her hands on the desk and drawing closer.

Benton leaned back in his chair. "Yes, I think it may be an explanation, although maybe not the only one. The Devil can hide within a person and not show himself until the time is right," he answered. "However, we Methodists don't have a way to deal with something like this. It's the Catholics who have the resources and experience in this area."

"What do you mean?" Dr. Moorhead asked.

"Exorcism of demons requires special training and priests with experience. I've never witnessed one, but there are countless stories and incidents of people becoming possessed by evil like this. Sudden changes in a person which cause him or her to become evil may be manifestations of demons that have taken hold of their bodies and pushed out the person who once occupied it. Exorcism is a deadly-serious business—not just for the priest but also the person possessed. It can decide the ultimate fate of not only their body, but also their eternal soul."

"What do we do, then?" asked Esther.

"First, I think we should confront Claire with this," said Benton. "We will need a lot more proof before we can convince the local bishop to allow an exorcism and dispatch an experienced priest. For now, however, we should arrange a meeting with the three of us and Claire to talk about it and see how she reacts. It is possible that this could all be a misunderstanding—that it's nothing more than a series of coincidences."

"It could be, reverend, but I don't think so," said Esther.

"How soon do you think we can arrange a meeting?" asked Moorhead.

"As soon as we possibly can," Benton answered.

***

Reverend Benton stopped Claire one day while she was at the church working with some parishioners to prepare host wafers for those who were invalid or otherwise unable to come to the church for Sunday service.

"Claire, do you have a few moments?" asked the reverend. "I'd like to talk to you about a few things in my office."

Claire followed the reverend to his study, and when she entered, she saw two others already waiting for her. However, neither of them had happy, calming expressions on their faces. Instead, they were stiff and anxious, as if bracing themselves for something more to come.

"What's this?" Claire asked nervously.

"We thought it best if the three of us talk to you about things we've noticed lately—things that are not in keeping with the person whom we know, or thought we knew, as Claire Cook." The reverend spoke softly, but directly. "Please have a seat."

"I think I'll stand," Claire shot back, her demeanor changing instantly and her posture becoming rigid and cold.

"Claire, we're concerned about you," began Esther. "That's why we thought we should talk to you about it."

"I don't understand why you are concerned," Claire answered. "There's nothing to be concerned about. I'm fine. Perfectly fine."

"Are you?" asked Esther.

"Yes. I'm fine!"

Dr. Moorhead held up a glass bottle with some dried leaves crushed inside. "Do you know what this is?" he asked.

"No. I have no idea."

"It's nightshade," the doctor answered. "Madam Grey found it mixed in with Orville's tea leaves. It's deadly in large doses and can cause severe illness in smaller ones."

"What does this have to do with me?" she asked, ignoring the implication with her brother's illness.

"This is a serious matter, Claire," said Moorhead. "If Orville had continued taking this tea, it most certainly would have killed him."

"Were you aware of the nightshade being mixed in with his tea?" asked Esther, watching for Claire's reaction.

"Of course not! How could you accuse me of ..."

119

"I'm not accusing you," said Esther. "I was just wondering if you knew there was something else mixed up with his tea."

"No. I had no idea."

"But you are the only one living with Orville. You're the only one who has been with him during these past several weeks," said the doctor.

"How dare you accuse me of …."

"Now, Claire, we're just trying to find out …" began Benton, trying to de-escalate the situation.

But it was then that Claire's face transformed into something they hardly recognized, contorting and turning scarlet red. Even the irises of her eyes changed from a beautiful chestnut brown to a milky white and then a glowing red.

"You don't understand what you're up against," snarled Claire, her voice now deeper and harsher than before. She cackled like a horned witch before she spat on the finely finished wooden floor of the office.

"You're not Claire Cook, are you?" asked Esther.

"*Ha!*" said the body standing taller and bolder behind one of the two cane chairs. "What do *you* think?"

"Then who or what are you?" Madam Grey asked.

"I am *Jahi*," it said, now with a male voice, the mouth twisting to make the sounds. "You have no domain over me. You will be cursed … every one of you! And I will take you with me down to the depths of hell!"

Claire, or whatever she had become, let out a fiendish laugh, and ran from the office, down the central aisle of the parish and out the double front doors of the nave. She ran down the street but mysteriously vanished into nothingness as if she had found a portal into an ethereal world beyond.

Horrified, Esther trembled as she watched it all unfold. But as soon as her eyes came unfixed from the empty doorway, she heard a thud.

"Doctor!" she cried out.

Benton glanced over to where Moorhead had been standing. His body was lying on the floor, face down. He was dead, his heart having exploded at the very moment Claire had bolted from the office.

*****

CH 28 - Extravaganza

Now it was Tillson's turn to apply some pressure on the Hill. He had learned of McGinnis's trip to the Capitol to visit with senators and try to sway them to vote against the proposed legislation on animal abuse. However, Tillson was not disillusioned about the colossal fight he faced. McGinnis had money, and Tillson knew of his partners in New York and the vast extent of their wealth. It was clear he had his work cut out for him.

"Senator Riddleberger," said Tillson, "it's a pleasure to meet you."

Senator Harrison Riddleberger was from the Commonwealth of Virginia and had served as a captain in the Confederate Army during the Civil War. Having been captured by Union forces in 1864, he spent a year as a prisoner of war in various fort prisons until the war concluded in 1865.

Only in his forties, Riddleberger had a severely receding hairline which was more than accommodated by his long, fashionable, beard which extended down to the lapels of his suitcoat. Broad-faced with narrow, brown eyes, he had a stern disposition and came across as equally austere. However, those who knew him understood him to be very open to special causes and movements. A member of neither the Democratic nor Republican parties, Riddleberger was the junior senator to William Mahone, both of whom belonged to the Readjusters Party. The Readjusters were focused on more equity for blacks and increased funding for black education—particularly within Virginia.

"Mr. Tillson," said Riddleberger, "please have a seat. Now, what is it that I can do for you?"

Tillson explained the problems with the abuse of animals, giving much the same presentation as he had given those in attendance at the church fellowship hall a week earlier.

"So, we are trying to raise awareness in Congress about these most abusive conditions," Tillson began, "and we need our leaders to pass laws to criminalize such behavior."

"Those are shocking incidents you cited, Mr. Tillson. Shocking. I was not aware that such things were going on in this country. But isn't it the states' responsibilities to address these things? You said some states had already passed laws—New York, and others. Isn't that the place to focus your energies?"

"With all due respect, senator, traveling to all the states would be quite impossible as you know. It would take years to get the state legislatures to pass the laws necessary, and in the meantime, how many horses, dogs, cats, and other domestic animals will be beaten, starved, or otherwise left to die? How many more of these animals will be subjected to horrific treatment at the hands of their owners? I believe this is something that is necessary *now* and can only come from Capitol Hill."

"I understand," said Riddleberger. He stood and extended his hand. "I will see what I can do. It is a calamity of monumental proportions—something that needs to be addressed."

"Thank you for your time, senator. I will continue to write, sending you information that may be helpful to you in persuading others on the Hill to move quickly on this."

Just as McGinnis had done, Tillson moved on, up and down the halls to the offices of others in Congress. He and Amanda—much to her dismay—made the rounds in D.C., talking to anyone who would listen. They met with Senators John Logan of Illinois, John Mitchell of Pennsylvania, and Elbridge Lapham of New York, along with Congressmen Martin Haynes of New Hampshire, William McAdoo of New Jersey, and Oscar Turner and John Carlisle of Kentucky, the latter of which was the Speaker of the House at the time. Those men, in addition to the other politicians already involved—Senators Ferry, Sawyer, and McMillan, and Congressman Coswell—were rapidly growing into a formidable power. And by the fall of 1883, legislation was well on its way through committee in the House.

However, McGinnis and Phineas were not going down without a fight.

***

Dear Senator Cockrell,

It is with pleasure that I invite you to a gathering we are having at the Willard Hotel on 22 May. Many of your fellow members of Congress have been invited and are arranging to come. There will be plenty of exquisite food and beverage for all.

In addition, for those attending, we will be making contributions of $500 to your campaign fund as we support the causes in which you have *interest. At this occasion we will be interested in contributing to those causes and will also bring to your attention some interests of ours that we believe deserve consideration.*

Very sincerely,

Phineas Taylor

RSVP

This note, written on expensive stationery and personally delivered to the residences of each member of Congress in Washington, raised much attention. Given the amount of the campaign contribution offered, McGinnis received a large number of positive responses.

The night of the event was planned as an extravaganza. Phineas had left nothing to chance and had spent thousands on the room, food, beverages and the reserve fund to funnel money into the campaigns of those who attended.

Outside the Willard Hotel, the black carriages of members of Congress were lined up, dropping off their important guests and their wives who were dressed in long gowns for the night's festivities. None would be disappointed.

The grand ballroom of the hotel was decorated magnificently with patriotic bunting, candles, centerpieces, and other garnishments. Draped from the center of the ceiling was a huge American flag, reminiscent of the Star Spangled Banner that flew over Ft. McHenry in 1814, but was now in the care of Eben Appleton, the grandson of one Major Armistead who fought at the battle.

Beyond the festive trappings of the hall, there were hors d'oeuvres that were simply to die for. In addition to the Oysters Rockefeller, devil's eggs, crab salad tapas and crab and salmon canapes, there was boiled shrimp, raw oysters on the half shell, and countless other delicacies. Not to let the food outshine the beverages, Phineas had ordered the best brandy, whiskey, bourbon and scotch he could find. And for those oenophiles, he imported fine Bordeauxs, Burgundies, and Champaigns, as well as other wines from Portugal, Spain and Italy. Each was deemed exquisite, and a rare treat for those not accustomed to Beluga caviar and fine Madeira.

"Mr. Phineas, this is a grand event, I must say," commented Senator Fair. "We don't get a lot of seafood in Nevada, nor do we get fine wine like this," he added, lifting his crystal goblet.

Phineas gently patted the senator's shoulder and replied, "No, senator. I imagine you don't, and that's why we had it brought in especially for you and your lovely wife."

Fair burst out in laughter, having already imbibed several bourbons earlier during the evening and was now working on his second glass of Jerez sherry. Of course, McGinnis and Cooper were on hand as well, working the crowd and discussing their opposition to the animal abuse bill being circulated on Capitol Hill.

Finally, as the evening drew to an end, Phineas went to the front of the room and had his partners clink their glasses to draw everyone's gaze toward him.

"May I have your attention," began Phineas. "I hope all of you had a lovely time tonight. We certainly enjoyed arranging it for you. I trust we have your campaign information so we can make a generous contribution to support your continued efforts on the Hill." There was widespread chuckling in the audience. "Tonight, we have discussed many issues facing our great nation, and, hopefully, we have raised awareness of the hardships people will face if this animal control legislation is put through Congress. I think we can all agree that domesticated animals used by our farmers and others need to be treated well; however, we cannot prohibit their use in the course of planting and harvesting food for our dinner tables. This is the way Nature intended it to be. This is the way God intended it to be.

"Like other animals on this great and wonderous Earth, we nourish ourselves with the produce from them—whether directly or indirectly. Without the use of these animals, farmers would be unable to till the soil to grow corn, beans, wheat, barley and the rest. Ranchers would be unable to raise cattle, hogs, chickens, and sheep. We would have no meat, no grains, no milk. We could not sustain ourselves.

"There are many half-baked ideas circulating out here in Washington. We're seeing big movements—activism—that we've never seen before. Many threaten the very heart of our nation. They undermine the fabric which holds together all of us as one people, one country. If we allow these ideas to take root and grow, we risk losing all that our Founding Fathers established nearly a hundred years ago. Our young men bled for this country—not only to free us from the tyranny of King George III but also to eliminate slavery on our shores. No, we can't let these crazy people sell us on these so-called "societal betterments." We can't let ourselves be taken in by this progress for progress's sake. It's time we push back on the tidal wave of reformers promising us their vision of utopia. Rarely do they stop to think about the unintended consequences of their actions. If we allow this, then I fear we will drown in a fomenting, churning and violent sea of our own making.

"I'm sure you will support our fight against such lunacy, and when the bill comes up in committee or on the floor you will vote *No*. Thank you."

Phineas got a roaring round of applause. He was in his element, and he was very much pleased with himself.

"I think that went swimmingly well," he said to McGinnis after stepping down from the riser at the front of the room.

"Yes, sir. I believe it most certainly did."

*****

CH 29 – Another in the Woods

After meeting with the chief, Bones, Missy and Samuel set out in the direction where Kewaydin had said they would find the Wendigo and, perhaps, Dalrymple and his men. They were a few days behind the posse, but Bones hoped to catch them, traveling lighter without a wagon and other supplies the chief had seen with the group. And while Bones was good at tracking, he was not an expert, and several times, Samuel had pointed out where they had missed a turnoff, spotting a broken limb, bent grass or the faint depression of a horse's hoof in the hard ground, suggesting the posse had taken off in another direction.

"We should have brought a guide," said Missy, who, like Samuel, was keeping her eyes peeled for any signs of where the group had gone. "Couldn't we have asked the chief for someone to help us?"

Bones shook his head. "I'm afraid the chief was in no mood to help us with anything," he admitted. "It was good of him not to have his warriors haul us off and roast us for supper."

"Come now, Bones. That's a bit of an exaggeration," said Missy, riding behind him. "You know well that the Indians don't …"

"… yes, yes. I know," answered the doctor.

"They're not savages, you know," said Missy.

"No more than any other human," added Samuel. "We're all savages. Aren't we?"

"Perhaps," said Bones. "Perhaps."

By the second day on the trail, Samuel was beginning to complain.

"Dr. Cook? How sure are you the chief was telling us the truth? Couldn't he have lied just to get rid of us?"

"Yes, but I don't think he did. He knew too much about Dalrymple. He knew about his search for the Wendigo. He wouldn't have known all that without meeting with him."

"He doesn't like the white man though," said Samuel. "Maybe he sent both of us off on this wild goose chase just to get even. This is awful out here."

"Bones, I don't know about what the chief intended," Missy began, "but I think we've lost the trail of Dalrymple and his men. I think we're just out here wandering aimlessly."

Missy and Samuel had continued looking around for more clues that others had traversed the path they were on; yet, at that point, they were finding nothing. They had lost their tracks.

"I think we're on the right trail," Bones answered.

"Well, it sure doesn't look like it," Missy said. "We haven't seen anything for hours. I think we should turn back."

"I agree," said Samuel. "I think we should go back to the chief and …"

"… and what?" Bones snapped, also growing weary. "He won't be any happier to see us a second time than he was the first. Why would he suddenly change his mind and be willing to give us help?"

The mosquitoes and black flies were taking a toll on them at night as well as during the day. It was a relentless attack, and adding warm, muggy air to the mix only made a recipe ripe for the pot to boil over. Everyone was agitated and annoyed—with the environs and each other.

"All right, then," Samuel answered. "But will you promise to turn back if we don't find the posse's tracks by the end of today?"

"*Shhh!*" Missy said, stopping her horse.

"What is it?" Samuel asked.

"I heard something. Something ahead and off to the right."

Missy slid her rifle out of its scabbard, and Samuel and Bones did the same. They moved their horses slowly ahead, plodding forward and listening for another sound. But after about ten minutes, they heard nothing.

"I guess it was just a deer or something," said Samuel.

"Or maybe a big bear," said Bones laughing.

Bang!

A bullet hit the trunk of a tree next to Bones's horse, bouncing off after shearing splinters of bark from the side.

"Take cover!" Bones shouted, jumping off his ride and pulling it behind the next largest tree.

Missy and Samuel followed his lead, hiding behind a log that had fallen nearby providing them some protection. Two more shots rang out, missing their marks and soaring deeper into the woods.

"You don't belong here!" came a thunderous disembodied voice. "Go back to where you came from!"

The man's English was clean and articulate, and although raspy and halting, it was clearly the voice of a white man.

"We don't intend any harm," Bones shouted in reply. "We didn't know this was your property."

"It's not my property. It belongs to Mother Earth. Now get yourselves out of here!"

"We're not here to hurt you or anything else. We are not trappers or hunters."

"Then why are you here?"

"Perhaps we could meet with you and tell you in person?"

"You'll just ambush me. You stay where you are."

Bones began moving toward the voice. He pointed his rifle barrel down at the ground as he walked.

"Don't' come any closer! I'm warning you!" said the man.

"We're following some men—some bad men," said Bones. "They're trying to capture some rare animals out here, and we want to stop them. Like you, we're trying to protect Mother Earth and her creatures."

"Why should I believe you?"

"You shouldn't, but I'm telling you the truth. Would I bring my family with me if it weren't true?" Bones was lying, but he didn't want to get anyone shot either.

"Well ..."

"You can see I have my wife and my son with me. Can't you?" Bones hesitated. "Come out, and we'll talk," he added, still walking.

Not more than one hundred feet ahead of him, an old man with a grisly white beard and wild grey hair that look like it could catch fire at a moment's notice emerged from behind an immense elm tree. His rifle barrel was pointed directly at Bones, and he chambered another round just to make his point.

"What's your name?" Bones asked.

"Put your gun down," said the man.

Bones complied, putting his rifle down on a nearby, flat-topped stump.

"And what about your two friends? Tell them to come out and do the same."

Missy and Samuel stood from behind their log and placed their guns on the timber as well.

"Well, come on. Get over here where I can see you better," said the old man.

"I still didn't get your name," said Bones.

"John Larrabee Winston," he answered.

"And do you live out here by yourself, Mr. Winston?"

"That's none of your business," said the man. "Now, I suggest you get back on those horses and ride out from here."

"Do you know of a creature called the Wendigo?" Bones asked, hoping for a reaction, and, indeed, he got one.

"What do you want with a Wendigo?" the man shot back.

"Those men we're following ... they're tracking one. They want to capture it and put it in a cage. If you're a man of planet Earth, I'd assume that would bother you."

The man thought for a minute and then said, "It's none of my business what they do with a Wendigo."

"But you were upset with us for traveling peacefully through the woods here, and we weren't harming anything."

"That's different."

"How so?"

"Well ... it just is, that's all," said the man, still pointing his gun at them.

"Have you lived out here long ... all by yourself?"

This time the man answered. "Yes. It's been many years now, and every time I come across people like you, I chase them away. People who come out here are up to no good."

"What makes you different?" asked Bones.

129

"What do you mean?"

"Why is it all right for you to be out here, but not us?"

"Because I look after Nature out here. You are just looking to destroy it," said Winston.

"Like those men I told you about—the ones we're trying to stop from doing the same thing."

"I don't know that," said the man. "To me, you're all the same."

"We're doctors," said Samuel, piping up. "We help people. That's what doctors do, right?"

Missy felt a little uncomfortable being included in the "doctor" group, but she didn't think it wise at the time to contradict her nephew.

"This is Dr. Cook, and I'm Dr. Stinson."

Then the old man looked at Missy.

"Oh, yes, and this is … is Dr. Grey."

"I see," said the man. "You're all doctors but you're trying to stop bad men from trapping an animal. Doesn't make sense to me."

"I study Indian folklore. It's a hobby," said Bones.

"Yeah, so?" said Winston, getting agitated.

"Listen, that's the truth," said Missy becoming impatient. "Now, will you help us or not?"

"Help you? Help you do what?"

"Help us find those men who want to hurt your forest and the creatures in it."

Missy began moving toward the man, and upon seeing her close-up, he started to lower his rifle.

The man's black, bushy eyebrows nearly met in the middle of his forehead. They had speckles of gray that matched the rest of his mane. But what struck Missy was that his eyes were of different colors—one blue and one brown. The brown one twitched slightly as he chewed on some tobacco, spitting a little bit out every so often which landed onto a patch of dead, brown leaves he was standing beside.

"Help you, huh?" he said.

"Yes. Help us," Missy repeated.

"All right, but you have to do what I say. No funny business. Do you understand?"

"Can we get our guns?" asked Samuel.

"Fine, but just don't shoot anything ... especially me."

Bones, Missy and Samuel retrieved their guns and got back on their horses. Meanwhile, the old man took off briskly down the path in the general direction where Bones and company were already heading.

"How many men were in the group?" asked Winston, striding ahead of them.

"We don't know. Several," Bones answered, his horse plodding right behind.

"Several as in a hundred or several as in four or five?"

"Probably five to ten, but not more than that. We've been tracking them, and ..."

"You have? You're a scout?"

"No, no. I just notice things," said Bones.

"So, you noticed that I just passed where they turned off?" asked the old man.

"What?"

"Yeah, I was testing you to see if you knew what you were doing. You don't." The man then pointed behind them. "Your posse friends turned off about fifty feet back and went that way into the woods."

"Then why are we going this way?" asked Samuel.

"Because they came back out of the woods right here, where we're standing. See that depression in the leaves on the ground back there? That's where they trampled them. I'd say they were here probably a day or two ago. There was a heavy rain last night, so it's hard to tell unless you know what to look for."

"See Dr. Cook, I told you ..." Samuel began, but Bones ignored him.

"Well, good," said Missy. "I feel better knowing we have a true scout in our midst." She laughed heartily at Bones's expense.

"This way then," said Winston, motioning to them.

Bones noticed that the man was missing the tip of one of his fingers, so he asked him about it.

"Oh, this?" said the old man, raising his hand. "This is a souvenir from our great war. I was a Union lieutenant in General McClernand's army before he was dismissed by General Grant. It was during the siege of Vicksburg in '63 that I got this little memento. Attacking the north wall of the city along the Mississippi, I got my finger blown clean off. I was lucky, though. There were many during that battle and the war that came back without arms, legs, eyes, and much more. Many others didn't come back at all. I count my blessings it was just this."

"It was a brutal, unthinkable, and sad event in our nation's history," said Samuel.

"You're right about that young man. I hope to God your generation never has to go through something like that."

"That's quite a story, Mr. Winston," said Missy.

"You can call me Larrabee," said the man, looking at her and giving her a slight smile.

"And you live nearby, I presume?" she asked.

"Near enough. I won't be going too far with you—just far enough to get you lost." Again, the old man laughed at his own joke, but none of the rest thought it was particularly funny.

The trail seemed endless, and Bones was careful not to pepper the old man with questions about the Indians out there, what it was like to live in isolation, and about the Wendigo. But by the end of the day, the old man stopped and said, "It's time I leave you. You should stay on this trail until it splits ahead. If they know where to find the Wendigo, they will take the left fork. Watch for signs they've gone through there. I'll leave you with that."

"But it's late," said Missy, "why don't you stay in camp with us until morning. You can have supper with us."

"What are you fixing?" Winston asked.

"Will you allow us to shoot a rabbit or two for supper?" she asked him.

"It's all right if you eat what you kill."

"Good, then I'll go round up some stew for us," she answered.

Missy took her rifle and marched out into the woods by herself.

"You're going to let her go out there alone?" the old man asked Bones, surprised by her independence. "I thought she was your wife?"

"She wouldn't want it any other way," said Bones with a smile.

Winston checked the tin pot next to the fire to see if the water was boiling. Then, he added some coffee grounds and waited for it to steep before pouring it off into his tin cup.

"Pipin' hot," he exclaimed, taking a sip. "Just the way I like it."

Shortly, Missy returned with two hares and tossed them at the feet of her nephew. "Ever cleaned a rabbit?" she asked.

"No," Samuel replied, shocked at the question.

"Well, get out your scalpel. You're gunna' learn something today."

"I'm really startin' to like her," Winston said with a grin. "She reminds me of my daughter."

Missy was brought up in a well-to-do family, but she was always determined to be independent. When she went to Texarkana to teach school, she had learned a number of things—from hunting and fishing to gutting and cleaning. And while Missy showed Samuel how to prepare the meat, Bones continued his conversation with the old man.

"Larrabee, you never told us about your family," Bones asked. "You mentioned your daughter. Where is she?"

The old man lit his pipe and puffed a few times to get it going.

"My daughter lives with her husband and five children in Chicago. She left home when she was only sixteen—ran off with a boy to go to Chicago. She didn't end up marrying him, though. She found someone else there—a hardworking young man who had a good job working construction. He's a smart lad and worked his way up the company ladder to become a construction foreman and then management. As for my two sons, they live in Duluth. One owns a general store and the other works for the government. He's the postmaster there."

"And your wife?" asked Missy.

"Maude?" The old man grew quiet as tears welled up in his eyes. He brushed them aside quickly as if they were an embarrassment. "I loved that woman," he answered. "She died after we had Alan, my youngest. It was a terrible accident, and one I blame myself for."

"I'm sorry," said Missy. "May I ask what happened?"

"We were all on a riverboat, heading downstream to Chicago to visit family. The weather was awful and with all the rain the river was high and flowing fast. Well, it was late at night and the boat struck a bridge pier—the captain had dozed off and let his second mate take over. The mate had also fallen asleep and let the boat slam into the pier. We only had a little time to abandon the boat, and in the chaos, we lost my wife in the crowded mass of hysterical passengers. She fell overboard, and since I hadn't thought to teach her how to swim, she drowned. Things were never the same after that."

"I'm sorry," said Samuel.

"Yeah, it was hard on all of us back then. I had to raise the children, but Alexa, my daughter, was there to help. She was a godsend."

"So, how did you come to this place?" asked Samuel.

"Well, my daddy was a riverman on the Mississippi River, and he was lucky enough to befriend the son of one of the river's largest ferry operators. They became close, and soon after, Daddy was brought into the company. When the owner's son died tragically in a boating accident, my daddy became kind of a surrogate son to him and eventually ended up running the company when the owner got older. Without any heirs, the owner turned the company over to Daddy when he finally passed away, leaving that and most of the rest of his wealth to us. Needless to say, my daddy made sure we all got good educations."

"But you didn't stay on the river. You live pretty far away from it. Why?"

"Maude," said Winston sadly. "I couldn't bring myself to live on a river after what happened to her. Every time I looked at the calm and peaceful currents, they reminded me of the tragedy that night. So, we moved to Wadena. Then, after my daughter left and my sons were old enough to live on their own, I moved out of town. My daughter wanted me to move to Chicago to be near her, but I was never a city dweller either. No, this is where I belong. I like it out here—the solitude and tranquility, you just can't beat it."

Once the rabbits were gutted, skinned and readied, they were put on a make-shift rotisserie and roasted. As nighttime fell, they traded more stories while the campfire burned down to a thick layer of orange embers that crackled and popped in the cooling air.

"Have you seen one," asked Samuel, beginning to cover the fire with ash to keep it going all night. "I mean a Wendigo, that is?"

"I don't really know," Winston answered. "I might have."

"When was that?" asked Missy, snuggling up to Bones to keep off the evening chill.

"Oh, it was about six years ago, I reckon. I was in the woods hunting. It was broad daylight too, and I thought I saw a bear off in the distance, walking amongst the trees. But I knew something wasn't quite right about it."

"Why is that?" asked Samuel.

"It was walking upright, like a human."

"Was it big and hairy?"

"Yeah, but it was ape-like, not like what they say the Wendigo looks like. It's said to have a wolf-like head, fangs, and claws. This was, like I said, more like a big ape—like you'd see in a traveling circus."

"Did it try to attack you or anything?" asked Samuel, riveted to the tale.

"Nope. It just continued wandering through the woods paying no attention to me whatsoever."

"So, that was the only time you've seen something like that or heard about it from others?" Bones asked.

"Well, again, I don't know. There are a lot of stories that get passed along from travelers coming through, you know. Most of the people come from Michigan and Wisconsin and talk of strange man-wolf creatures they've seen in the woods."

"Ah, lycanthropy," said Bones.

Samuel looked at the doctor. "What?"

"Lycanthropy. It's the mythical ability of humans to transform themselves into wolves or other animals," Bones answered.

"Well, I don't know what it is, but I think I've seen man-wolf creatures out here too. One time was down by the river you'll be crossing tomorrow. I was fishing there and minding my own business when upstream I saw this creature. Again, I thought was a bear. It had its head down in the stream and was trying to swat its paw at a fish. However, after it looked up, it then stood and walked back into the woods on its hind legs."

"Bears do that," said Samuel.

"Yeah, they do, but only to sniff the air—not to talk around. This thing had the head of a wolf too with a long snout. Wolves don't walk like that."

135

"No, they sure don't," said Missy.

"Well, that's probably enough of the stories for tonight," said Bones, helping Samuel finish with covering the fire. "Many more of them, and none of us will be able to get to sleep."

"Shouldn't someone keep watch?" asked Samuel, by now nervous from the tales he'd heard.

"*Nah*," Winston answered, "nothin' out here we can't handle."

"Even a Wendigo?" asked Missy.

"Yeah, I think we could handle even one of those."

During the night, Samuel kept waking as he heard every flutter of a bat, every croak of a frog, every chirp from an insect, and every hoot from an owl. Eventually, Samuel's eyes burned like molten lead, and he finally fell victim to the Sand Man. It wasn't until the next morning that he got a gentle kick in the side by his aunt.

"Get up, Samuel. Don't be a lazy head. We need to get moving. The morning's late already."

After breakfast and a couple strong cups of hot java, Winston changed his mind.

"Ya' know. I haven't had this much fun in years," he said, slurping his joe.

"What are you saying?" asked Missy.

"If you'll have me, I think I'll stick around for a while."

Bones smiled. "Those were just the words I wanted to hear this morning."

Winston was quick to pick up the posse's trail after they had packed up camp and put out their fire. But it wasn't long before they happened upon a small, but swift, river which made them stop.

"Which way?" Bones asked.

The old man walked upstream and then downstream to find a sign of where Dalrymple and his men had navigated the watery obstacle, but when he returned, he was shaking his head.

"I must admit that I can't tell. There are broken branches and muddy footprints going both ways and then stopping a short distance as if they scouted each of them before fording it. But I can't tell where they went across.

136

Of the two, the upstream is shallower, so I'm thinking that's where they crossed. I think I'll have to go to the other side to know for sure."

The passage was far deeper than what he had expected, the water rising to the middle of the old man's chest. Winston struggled to keep his footing on the slippery rocks as he waded across. The current was swift taking with it tree branches, bark and even whole logs downstream. It was treacherous, and one slip or strike by a wayward wooden plank could have sent Winston on his way with no chance of returning.

"Be careful," exclaimed the old man as he finally reached the other side, trudging up the flat, but rocky, shoreline, dripping wet. "The water can take you pretty fast if you aren't ready for it."

Once Winston issued his admonishment, Missy followed, riding high in the saddle above the fast waters below. Bones went next, and although his horse slipped a few times on the slick, mossy stones, he made it to the other side. Behind him was Samuel who was by now in the middle of the stream and pulling up the rear.

"All right," said Winston, "so while Samuel is making his passage, I'll go see where the trail picks up again."

But just as Bones reached the shoreline, Missy heard a heavy splash back in the middle of the river. She turned to see Samuel's horse righting himself from a fall but without its rider. Samuel was nowhere in sight.

"Samuel!" she cried.

She watched as her nephew's head popped to the surface, but he struggled to keep it above the waterline, fighting against the fierce current. In less than a minute, he had drifted quickly downstream before vanishing out of sight.

*****

CH 30 — Demons

Without the nightshade in his tea, Orville gradually recovered. He was stunned by what Madam Grey told him about that day in Reverend Benton's office at the church and distraught over what had happened to his sister. The sheriff was notified, and the entire Boston police department put on alert for a young woman, small and fragile-looking with dark brown eyes, high cheek bones and long, chestnut hair, likely done up in a swirl on her head. However, a warning was also issued for all officers to take utmost caution as the suspect could "exhibit extreme and violent behavior on a moment's notice and without warning."

"But don't let them shoot her!" Orville had pleaded. "She's really a wonderful human being. I just don't know what's come over her."

"I've never seen someone change that quickly in all my years," said Esther bluntly. "She went from nice and normal to a monster within seconds. It was truly frightening."

"And then she ran from the church," said Reverend Benton, who had stopped by to see how the young man was doing. "No one has heard from her since then, and that was over a week ago."

"I am worried sick about her," said Orville. "She could be anywhere—in an alleyway, in a pauper's house, anywhere. I hate to ask, but have you checked the hospitals or the morgue?"

"Yes, we have," answered the reverend. "But no. No one with her description has been admitted to any hospital in and around Boston, and, thankfully, no one has been brought into the county morgue bearing her description either."

"At least that's comforting," said Orville.

But then Benton's face grew serious. "Funeral services for Dr. Moorhead are tomorrow," said the reverend. "Madam Grey and I will be attending."

Orville sighed. "I am so sorry for your loss," he said to Esther. "I know that he had been your family physician for a long time."

"Yes. Over forty years," said Esther, wistfully. "He brought all my children into this world. It's a tragic loss."

"Do you know what happened?" asked Orville, sitting up in his bed.

"The doctors say it was a heart attack," said Esther. "It took him quickly. He felt no pain."

"Madam Grey told me something before the incident arose, and I agree with her," said Benton.

"What" What is it?"

"This isn't easy to say, but we believe she may be possessed," said Esther.

"Possessed? You mean, demonically possessed?" asked Orville.

"Yes," answered the reverend, "and if that's the case, there may be only one solution: an exorcism." Orville looked shocked, and Esther put her hand on his arm to calm him. "Orville, it's not something that the Methodist Church gets involved with, but if Claire has become possessed by a demon, it may be necessary."

"Explain this demonic possession to me. How does that happen?" Orville asked.

"Demonic entities sometimes prey on those at a time of weakness. We believe Claire was in such a time when she was fighting consumption. This Jahi spirit entered her body during that fight and took over, forcing Claire's soul to go underground and hide. Demons often seek to find human hosts to give them substance in this material world. As ethereal energies, they are limited, bound by their own resources. Within a human body, they have access to much more and can influence others and spread their evil ways much more easily. This may also explain why her behavior became so erratic at church and why she caused others to become sick and maybe even die. Demons hate God and will do anything to cause death and destruction within His house."

"How did that happen?" Orville asked.

"I'm sorry to say, but I believe a poison was added to the Sunday communion," said Benton. "Of course, we don't use wine. As you know, our founder, John Wesley, was an early advocate for temperance, so our church adopted grape juice as a substitute for wine during communion. I think she poisoned it."

"What about the bread?" asked Madam Grey. "Who bakes that for you?"

"We get the bread from a local bakery. We've used him for generations—it's a family business. We've never had a problem, so I don't think that's the cause."

"But the grape juice?" Esther asked.

"That's made by our parishioners."

"And where is it kept?" she asked.

"It's prepared fresh each Sunday morning from grapes we acquire at the market."

"Who oversees that, then?"

"Well, that would be ... Claire." Benton stopped and looked at Esther.

"We just need to find her," said Orville. "If that demon is capable of killing parishioners and Dr. Moorhead, it can kill anyone."

"I fear you're right, Orville," said Reverend Benton. "It's only a matter of time before it strikes again."

*****

CH 31 - Towering Cliffs

As the posse left what remained of Clyde behind, Dalrymple told his men to keep a closer watch on the goings-on in the woods and those around them as they journeyed onward—pushing deeper into the thick brush and increasingly rugged and hilly terrain. The days were still warm, and the mosquitoes were still large and annoying. Even during the daylight hours, the little vampires, along with the heavy swarms of black flies, buzzed constantly, making life miserable for both the men and their horses.

That afternoon, after four uneventful hours on the trail, Leroy came running back to the group energized about something he had found. He had gone ahead of the main group—which was slowed and burdened by the wagon, crate, and other equipment—to scout for any signs of the creature. Out of breath, he was heaving and full of excitement as he stopped the entourage to announce his find.

"What is it, Leroy?" asked Dalrymple, pulling on the reins of his horse.

"I think I've found somethin' sir. Just up ahead. This way."

Leroy took Dalrymple and his men nearly a half-mile up the trail before kneeling and pointing to some deep animal prints that marked the soft, black mud. "Here," he said pointing, "and here." Then, he pulled back some tree branches and bushes to reveal other, similar prints leading away from the trail. "These leave the path here," said Leroy, "and go this way."

"What are those?" asked Dalrymple, getting off his horse to look more closely at them. "A big racoon, maybe?"

"I think those are the footprints of the Wendigo, sir."

If the prints in the mud were those of a racoon, they were one from a very large mutant. But there was an odd similarity to those of a human too, but with six toes rather than five.

"Wha-da-ya think of 'em?" Leroy asked, holding the tree branches aside. His hand was trembling with excitement.

"How big are those?" asked Peters.

"I'd say at least fifteen—maybe twenty inches."

"I don't know any racoon that's that big," said Eddie.

"No, clearly not," said Jeeter.

"And it's got, what, six toes?" Peters asked.

"Yeah, most animals out here have five," Leroy answered. "This ain't no bear either. Bears have a large pad that's part of their foot, along with five toes. These prints aren't those of a bear. The back part of the print is like a triangle with the pads spread out in front. Like I said, this ain't no bear."

The print was long and narrow. Its shape was human-like but with a very high arch and with six toes that ended in claws.

"Based on how big that sucker is, how tall would you say the creature is?" asked Dalrymple.

"Hard to say, sir," said Leroy. "That big a foot could either mean it's really tall—say over eight feet—or really heavy—over a thousand pounds."

"Or it could be both," said Jeeter, looking over Dalrymple's shoulder.

"I'd say that's a footprint from a hind leg," said Eddie, standing not far behind the rest.

"Well, let's follow it and find out," said their leader. "Clear this brush so we can get the wagon and supplies through here."

The team pulled away the gnarly brush and made enough room to squeeze the four-wheeled wagon through the newly created opening. Eventually, they lost the tracks but continued in the same direction on the trail in hopes of picking it up again.

"*Sh*t!*" said Dalrymple, finding a fresh set of tracks. "These seem even larger than the ones we saw earlier, and they were fresher. I don't understand."

"If it's human-like," quipped Peters, "it's probably over nine feet tall."

"Yeah, and it walks on its hind legs," said Jeeter.

"I'd say it's closer to ten feet," said Leroy. "This thing is a monster."

Eddie looked squarely at Dalrymple; angst written all across his face. "Sir, I don't think I'm cut out for trappin' somethin' like this. I think I'll head back to Wadena, if you don't mind."

Dalrymple pulled his gun but then quickly lowered it, realizing the mistake. "I tell you what," he said, re-holstering the pistol. "It does appear this creature is larger than we anticipated. So, what do you say if I double your wage for this little trip? Would that make it up to you?"

"Triple," said Leroy, folding his arms.

The other men nodded, except for Eddie who was still unsure.

"All right. Triple it is," answered Dalrymple, having no intention of paying them anything more.

"And double even if don't find the beast," said Jeeter.

"Fine, but we have to keep looking. I'm not givin' you a nickel more for stoppin' right here." Dalrymple turned to Leroy, and added, "All right, then. Leroy, you lead the way."

The posse moved along the path. But there was a change in the air. The horses, which had been docile and obliging, were suddenly on edge. Their ears were pitched up and their nostrils were flared. Every snap of a branch nearby or rustle of leaves set them—and the men—into a nervous frenzy.

"Calm down, girl," Leroy said to his horse, patting her on her shiny, black neck. "It's all right. It'll be just fine."

Soon, the air became thick with the barking of cardinals, the pecking of red-bellied and downy woodpeckers, and the rustling of limbs from the frolicking of brown squirrels jumping from fir to fir. Overhead, things grew more ominous as two goshawks circled, both expecting an easy meal to fall their way at any moment. Indeed, the woodlands were alive, yet oddly, inexplicably, as if sensing death.

After another hour of riding, they reached a rocky crest. The prints of the strange creature suddenly stopped at the point the hard dolomite and sandstone rock formation began to rise up from the forest floor. Although not mountainous *per se*, the landscape had changed to one more stony, craggy and steep than it had before.

"Well?" Dalrymple asked Leroy, impatiently. "I thought you were a tracker?" he said to Leroy. "What's the problem?"

They had lost the direction of the animal's prints and were wandering aimlessly on top of the first cut of the rocky outgrowth. The wooden wheels of the wagon were finding it increasingly hard to grip the surface and were sliding, putting it at risk of tipping over and possibly crushing the crate they had built.

Leroy got down on his hands and knees, examining the surface of the rock for traces of mud or any other clues that would show in which direction the animal had wandered. He eventually found tiny pieces of black earth that had been tracked onto the sandstone, and so they followed that. However, even that ended quickly after only a hundred or so feet. In frustration, Dalrymple surveyed the stony white cliff that stood as a formidable barrier in front of them and sighed.

"Well, what do you think?" he asked Leroy.

"I'd say the creature has found a place up there in the rocks, sir," said Leroy.

Dalrymple laughed. "Are you telling me that because you've lost the scent?"

"It's the only place I can see that it's gone, sir. Look, up there. Do you see those caves?"

Leroy pointed to three dark holes that suggested cave openings high up on the cliff face.

"They don't look deep enough to be caves," said Dalrymple. "Why would there be caves that high up anyway?"

"I dunno," said Leroy. "I've heard this area was once underwater—a big sea. So, anything could have made them if it's that old."

"You're makin' this sh*t up," said Dalrymple.

"Well, unless you have a better idea, I'd say that's our best bet."

The sun was falling toward the horizon and twilight was fast approaching. Dalrymple knew they had some decisions to make, and they needed to make them quickly.

"Sir, with that big of a critter, I don't think we should be out here after dark," said Eddie, his nerves beginning to unravel. "Can we find someplace to camp that's farther away?"

Dalrymple huffed, but he knew Eddie was right. It would be too dangerous to be out there at night near where they thought the creature lived, especially if it were a nine or ten-foot man-eater.

"Fine. Let's set the camp up back at the fringe line between the woods and these rocks. There are a lot more trees and brush over there. It will give us more cover than being exposed out here. We'll regroup and come back first thing in the morning."

So, they pitched their tents near a heavily wooded riverbank which gave them fresh water, protection, and quick means of escape, if necessary. They could hear the rush of water not far away downstream, and knew they were close to the Wendigo's hunting grounds. This was Black River Falls.

That night, Jeeter took the first shift as the campfire spat and sputtered but persevered to burn throughout the night to ward-off bears and any other creatures that might happen by—even those eight feet or bigger. But eventually, Jeeter succumbed to the call for sleep and nudged Eddie who reluctantly got up to take his position on duty. Soon, he too fell fast asleep, and it wasn't until he began snoring loudly that Leroy was awakened and decided to relieve him.

"Go on Eddie," said Leroy, "You're doin' us no good sittin' here snorin'. You might as well get some shuteye. I'll take the watch and then see if Dal will take the last one. Now git!"

As expected, Eddie didn't protest and went back to his bedding. Within a short time, he resumed sawing his logs which, at least, kept Leroy awake at his post.

It was the next morning when, as the first robins began to chirp, the men roused and began preparing coffee and breakfast. Peters sat checking and rechecking his guns and ammo for the day ahead. Yawning and stretching his arms, Dalrymple looked over the camp. In one area, there were wood shavings all around near the fire which had not been attended during the night and had burned out. Dalrymple was not happy.

"Say, where's Jeeter?" he asked gruffly, preparing to give a reprimand.

"I'm right here," came the answer, as Jeeter rolled over in his bed. "Why?"

"You let the fire go out."

"No, it was going when I ended my shift."

"Then, who took over for you after you turned in?"

"Eddie."

"Where is he?

"How should I know? I just woke up!"

Dalrymple glanced around the campsite for the others.

"Eddie?"

"I'm right here."

"Eddie?"

"Present."

"Then, what about Leroy?" Dalrymple asked, trying to account for everyone.

"I dunno, he relieved me just before dawn," said Eddie.

All looked across the camp at the empty straw where Leroy's bedding had been.

"Leroy?" yelled Dalrymple. "Leroy? Where are ya'?"

Dalrymple and the others began a new search—this time looking outside the camp perimeter for signs of Leroy.

"Nobody heard anything, then?" Dalrymple asked as they scoured the woods.

"Nothin' other than Eddie snorin'," said Jeeter, now anxious and out-of-sorts.

"Leroy! Leroy!" they called out.

Finally, Jeeter found a track. "Here," he called out. "I think it's his boot print, but then …" Pointing to the depression in the ground, he began shaking— nearly convulsing. "This … this … it's the beast. It was here."

Indeed, there was a boot print, but what was next to it was not. It was the same six-toed impression they had seen the previous day near the cliff.

"No," said Dalrymple, looking down at it. "It couldn't be. We would have heard an animal that big."

"That's the track all right," said Jeeter. "It musta' taken Leroy."

Dalrymple was quiet. "I still don't believe it."

"Well, the prints don't lie!" said Eddie, raising his voice.

"Let's get the camp packed up. If we can find the creature and capture it today, we can put it in the cage and be home in a couple of days. Remember, your wage will be tripled if we can get the thing back to Wadena and then to Duluth. There, we'll stick it on a train to New York and be done with this. Let's get going."

After packing up the camp, they returned to the cliff where Jeeter soon found the trail of the big animal once more. This time they parked their horses and the wagon at the edge of the tree line and began hiking up the rocky outgrowth following each other in single file. But midway across the expanse, the rocks became treacherous with loose shards and fine pebbles. There, the men began slipping, several times stumbling but catching themselves before anything became serious.

"Watch yourselves, men," said Dalrymple. "It's getting …"

Then, all of a sudden, Jeeter's boot slipped off the rock face, and he fell, tumbling down the escarpment and disappearing over the ridge. The men stopped and hurried down to the ledge where they'd last seen their friend. Dalrymple peered over and looked down at the crumpled body of Jeeter. He wasn't moving.

"What do we do now?" asked Eddie. "I should go down and see if he's all right."

"He ain't all right, idiot," said their leader, pained at the sight of another casualty. "He's dead."

Ignoring the calamity, Dalrymple turned back to resume their climb, insisting that his men follow. And as the incline became too severe to hike, they began grabbing onto the rocks and digging their shoes into any indentations in the cliff face to gain a foothold.

"Make sure you hold your footing before you grab for the next ledge," said Dalrymple. "I see a long ledge about thirty feet up. We just need to get to that. It's probably where the critter lives."

One by one they scaled the cliff, leaving the wooden crate below in the wagon and hoping to use it later once they captured the beast. It took over two hours for the men to climb the thirty feet to the ledge, and it was amazing that none lost their grip and fell as Jeeter had.

Finally, when all reached the ledge, Dalrymple turned and gazed into the colossal opening that disappeared back into the face of the hill. "All right," he said, "let's find that beast."

But there was another voice from below the cliff calling out.

"Wait!"

It was Leroy.

"Where have you been?" shouted Dalrymple, calling down to him. "We've been looking all over for ya'."

"Jeeter's down here, but we need to get him to a doctor," said Leroy.

"We'll put him on the wagon when we get back down there," Dalrymple answered. "Right now, you need to get your ass up here and help us."

"It'll take him too long," said Peters. "We gotta' go on without him."

Dalrymple sighed. "Crap. Fine. Stay down there. We'll be down soon."

Just then, Eddie's eyes grew wide, and his jaw dropped. "Did you hear that?" he asked.

"What?" asked Dalrymple.

There was the unmistakable sound of growling, and it was coming from inside the opening in the rock just behind them.

"It's not a bear," said Eddie, cautiously backing up. "I'm outta' here."

"You're right. That's no bear," exclaimed Peters. "I've never heard a bear make that kind of sound before."

"It don't matter. We won't get paid anything if we're all dead," said Eddie, turning to go back down the cliff.

But just as Dalrymple pulled his gun to stop Eddie, a ten-foot tall creature emerged from the cave. It didn't look happy.

*****

CH 32 — Retrieved

"Orville Cook?"

"Yes?"

"We have your sister. You need to come with me down to the station." It was the head of police, Chief Conway, who stopped by Orville's brownstone to deliver the news.

Orville had returned home from his quick recovery at the Grey mansion and had waited nervously, hoping to hear some news about his sister. Changing his clothes, he accompanied the chief downtown to police headquarters. There, they found Claire, sitting in a barred cell, her head down as if she were studying the labyrinth of cracks on the floor. As the cell gate creaked open, she didn't move—neither looking up nor flinching from the shrill, shrieking sound of metal scraping against cement.

"Claire?" Orville asked, hesitating before going inside.

Orville almost didn't recognize her. She was filthy—her hair in knots and tangled, covering her face which was black with soot. Her left eye was swollen and red from a burst blood vessel, and her clothes were torn and covered in mud and dirt. She looked worse than many of the sad homeless on the streets of Boston, and Orville's heart fell as he ventured inside the cell.

"Be careful," warned the sheriff. "The officer who found her said she was in an abandoned house littered with dead animals. He thought, perhaps, she had killed and eaten some of them."

Orville looked at his sister. "Claire?" Orville said, trying again.

Still, she didn't look up.

"Has she spoken since she's been here?" Orville asked.

"Nope. Not a peep. We only knew to contact you because you gave us her description. Otherwise, she'd be a Jane Doe sittin' in this cell until moved to one of the mental hospitals."

"Has she been charged with anything?"

"Not yet. Why? Is there somethin' she's done?"

"No, no, no. I just wondered," said Orville chuckling nervously. "So, can I take her home?

"I suppose so, but like I said, you'd better be careful. Something isn't quite right with her. I know she's your sister, but if I was you, I'd admit her to an asylum. I think that's the best place for her."

"Thanks for the advice, sheriff. I'll consider it."

Claire didn't fight him as he took her by the arm and led her out of the jail. Catching a carriage, they were delivered back at Orville's home where she promptly went upstairs. He didn't see her the rest of the night.

The next day, Orville sent a message to Madam Grey asking if either Missy or Marigold could stop by and help with her. It wasn't long before he received his reply.

> Orville,
>
> I'm afraid Missy left with your brother. If you recall, they both went to Minnesota with Samuel. As for Marigold, I will contact her and persuade her to stop in now and again and help as she can. I believe you will need someone full time to care for your sister until she is well.
>
> You heard what Reverend Benton and I had to say about her condition. We're not doctors, but we feel it is essential that you consider a priest to help with her cure. I hope you will let the reverend find the help you and your sister need . . . and soon.
>
> Warm regards,
> Madam Grey

Orville knew they were right, but he wasn't sure he could bring himself to put his sister through an exorcism. To him, that was a draconian measure that was a last option if everything else failed. *No,* he thought, *there must be another way.*

For the next week, things at Orville's flat were copacetic. There were no major outbursts or other noteworthy events, and Orville informed Madam Grey and Reverend Benton that he believed things had quieted. Claire had taken to herself, not wishing to go out or attend church services. She had locked herself in her room most of the time, asking Orville to bring her something to eat upstairs rather than joining him downstairs for meals.

"I don't believe there is any need for such a drastic measure as exorcism now," Orville said to Esther one Monday morning as he stopped at the mansion to return some linens he had borrowed.

"Well, just be vigilant," said Esther. "Let me know if anything changes. She can transform quickly into something unrecognizable as we've told you. I witnessed it firsthand."

But it was only a short time later that Orville had the experience of which Esther had warned, and it shook him.

"I had something strange happen the other night," he told Esther, "and I don't know what to make of it."

"What happened?" she asked.

"I was sleeping in my bedroom when I sensed a presence in the room with me, and when I opened my eyes, I saw a black, shadowy entity hovering over me. I couldn't see its face, and I'm not sure it even had one. It floated over the bed, and I saw that it had bright red eyes that were staring down at me. I could tell it was evil—I could sense it. I tried to call out, but I was paralyzed by terror. I could move my lips, but no words would come out of my mouth. I think I screamed, but there was no sound. At that point, I found myself wide awake but still unsure what had happened. It was really horrifying!"

"Has it come back?"

"No, but something else has," said Orville. "Last night as I was putting the dishes away in the kitchen, I noticed a shadow passing down the hallway to the back of the townhouse. I thought it was Claire going out the back, and I called to it, but it seemed to disappear. When I went to the back door, I found it was closed and locked. So, I went upstairs to check on Claire; she was in her bed fast asleep."

"Your mind is playing tricks on you, Orville. You've been under a lot of stress," said Esther.

"I would agree, but there's one more thing. When I returned to the kitchen to finish cleaning before turning in for the night, I discovered that all the cupboard doors were open. I certainly hadn't left them that way, and when I went to close them, they flew open again on their own accord. Unnerved, I hurriedly began slamming them closed, but that's when all hell broke loose."

"What happened?"

"Madam Grey, I don't know if I can go back to my home. It was demonic. I'm certain of it. Goblets and dishes began flying across the room and smashing into the walls. I had to duck not to be hit by them. I found myself hiding under the dining room table waiting until it stopped. I know you will think I'm mad, but I am not. It happened just as surely as I'm standing before you now."

"What are you going to do now? I think it's time we contact Reverend Benton."

"I spoke with Reverend Benton yesterday. He agrees that its time we found a priest. He said he would contact the bishop right away."

"Yes, yes. I feared this would happen. I believe it is the only way, Orville. I am so sorry. When did the reverend tell you he would have a priest?"

"He didn't know, but he did say that telling the bishop of my incident would present a strong case for an exorcism. He hoped it would be enough."

"The sooner we find a priest, the better," said Esther, wringing her hands with worry. "Where is Claire now?"

"We're still at my townhome, but I cannot sleep. Claire insists on staying in her own room upstairs. Every night, I hear strange noises coming from her room and, I swear, I see shadow people walking up and down the stairs. I can't take this, Madam Grey. I can't live this way!"

"Why don't you and Claire return to my estate," said Esther. "Perhaps you will find greater solace there."

"No, I think we will only bring the demon to your home. I could not live with myself if it caused even greater chaos there. No, I will wait with my sister until a priest is available. Only then can we battle this demon and drive him from my sister."

Orville took a carriage to pick up some of Claire's things from the church. But after talking to Reverend Benton, they decided that Orville should stay at the church rather than risk living with his sister again, particularly after the poisoning incident. Orville had protested, not wanting to leave his sister alone, but the reverend had made him understand that Claire could not get better if her brother were buried six feet below ground.

Arriving at his home to explain the change in plans to his sister, Orville got out of the carriage to pay the drive his fee when the front door to his brownstone flew open. His middle-aged housekeeper, who had been with him over six years, rushed out door screaming hysterically. With her hands flailing in the air, she scrambled down the brick steps and ran.

"Mrs. Livingston. What's wrong?" Orville had shouted after her.

The housekeeper didn't break stride, and with the hem of her dress pulled up to her knees, she turned the corner and vanished.

"Mrs. Livingston!"

But it was of no use. It was the last time Orville would ever see her.

Surprised and now more wary, Orville crept into his home and closed the door behind him. He shook, fearful of what he might find inside.

Standing at the bottom of the staircase, he glanced up and spotted Claire at the top looking down at him. The entirety of her eyes was black, demonically black, making them appear as empty sockets. But there was something else that was far worse. Claire wasn't just standing there. She was hovering above the floor, suspended by an invisible force, and in her hand was a long, kitchen knife. Her mouth was wide open, as though her jaw had become unhinged from her skull. It was surreal and petrifying. Orville's veins seemed to fill with ice, and he was frozen with fear.

"Orville, my brother," Claire began, her mouth moving in a ghastly, unnatural way, "it is good of you to come home. It is time you join me in the lowest levels of eternal Hell!"

Then, she expelled a most hideous laugh before floating down the stairs toward him. She raised the knife as her black, lifeless eyes stared intently at her victim.

The terror was overwhelming, and Orville's mind when dark.

*****

CH 33 – Campbell in Pursuit

Joshua Campbell arrived in Duluth several days after McGinnis had given him the order to execute the company's backup plan. Campbell was young—in his twenties—but his rap sheet with the police had begun many years earlier when he was only twelve.

Born and raised in a broken home without a father and with a mother who was a hopeless alcoholic, Campbell began his criminal career as a street pickpocket and moved up the world of outlaws to commit residential burglary and eventually bank robbery. It was in 1878 when he was arrested for attempting to rob the National Bank of Baltimore downtown that his run finally ended. The heist was thwarted when a patron's dog had attacked him as he was making his escape out the front doors. The money had spilled from the two sacks he was carrying and been blown across the wooden slats of the walkway. The police had arrived just as he was plucking the remaining notes from the mud.

"What do you think of Campbell?" McGinnis had asked another man under his employ—one known to be a killer for hire named Aldus Mercer. "Do you think he's up for such a task?"

Mercer had smiled and not hesitated in giving his opinion.

"Moe and I go way back. We're kinda' partners in crime, if you will. In fact, he and I pulled off a bank robbery in Philadelphia back in … when was it … '77. We were lucky with that one. We almost got caught. The problem was he took all the money—didn't give me a red cent. I suppose I should be bitter, but, hey, what do you expect."

"Why didn't you turn him in?" McGinnis had asked.

"What? I'm a man of honor, sir. I would betray a business partner of mine like that. Only criminals do things like that. Anyway, he finally paid me. We're good."

Taller than Mercer but thinner and more gangly, Campbell had a full head of wavy hair and a bushy beard that hadn't been trimmed in years. His thick eyebrows partly hid the darkness he held captive behind his mysterious, near-black eyes, and his rather bulbous nose and reddened ears suggested he enjoyed more than his fair share of drink.

Once a month, Campbell traveled the fifty miles north from DC to Frederick, Maryland, to see his ailing mother who still lived in the town where he grew up. He believed himself to be a good son and was careful to keep any news of his arrests and periodic incarcerations from her. Returning from prison the last time, he had only told her that he had "gone out of town on some important government business." She was old, but not stupid; yet, she allowed her son to believe he was successfully deceiving her.

Working for McGinnis, Campbell was making many times what he normally made doing odd capers with Mercer. And once he arrived in Wadena, he quickly went to work finding men who were willing to supplement their farm incomes and go on a two or three day trip into the woods to track down "criminals" wanted by the federal authorities. It was all a lie, but the story, as Campbell had concocted it, worked like a charm.

The three men Campbell found to go along with him were young and unmarried. Two worked as farm hands, and the third as an apprentice to the town's blacksmith. All were eager to make extra cash and signed on with little coercion. So, with more than sufficient funding from Phineas to pay for wages, a supply wagon, horses, food and equipment, Campbell was ready to go in short order.

Having received information from Dalrymple in an earlier telegraph, McGinnis informed Campbell of the trail his predecessor had taken to reach Black River Falls. And within two days of his arrival in Wadena, Campbell was already well on his way.

```
Mr. McGinnis STOP Arrived in Wadena yesterday and am
hitting the trail today STOP Should have creature in
crate ready to ship East in next two days STOP MOE
STOP
```

The weather was hot and muggy as the second expedition of Phineas & Company rolled out of Wadena. Campbell figured he would find Dalrymple's crew without much difficulty and, if still alive, would negotiate with him who would receive the bonus reward for the capture and return of the Wendigo. If things got ugly, Campbell was fully prepared to do what was necessary to secure the payoff money for himself, even if it meant killing Dalrymple and his posse. On the other hand, if they found the first expedition to be dead or didn't find them at all, the issue was moot.

What Campbell didn't know was there was another group between Dalrymple and himself—one with two doctors and a young woman.
*****

CH 34 – The River Takes Him

Samuel's horse scrambled up the riverbank, but it was without a rider as Missy looked on in shock. Coming to her senses, she shouted to Bones, "You go back and find Winston. Tell him what's happening. I need to find my nephew."

Missy galloped off along the shoreline downstream from the incident to try to spot her nephew in the roaring currents. However, soon the wild, reedy brush became too dense, forcing her to dismount and continue on foot. She ran along the embankment, her britches wet and snarled with the prickly briars, but, undaunted, she wasn't about to give up without a fight.

"Samuel!" she cried out desperately. "Samuel!"

Not seeing him, she began pulling back reeds along the riverbank checking for him or any sign of him. For several hundred yards she repeated the process until she startled a giant blue crane which leaped up from the cattails, took two swoops with its magnificent wings, and began to fly away.

"Aunt Missy ..."

The voice came through a parting in a sea of cattails. Its owner was a water-soaked young doctor who stumbled toward her. Rubbing his head, Samuel had a smear of crimson trickling down the side of his head, and he appeared dazed and confused.

"Samuel, are you all right?" she asked rushing to him.

Missy helped him to a spot higher along the shore and propped him up under a red pine tree that was leaning precariously over the riverbank.

"I'll be fine," he answered. "Just a bump on the head. Nothing requiring a doctor."

"But I am a doctor," Missy answered grinning, "at least that's what you said.".

Samuel laughed and then grimaced. "Oh, that hurt. Don't make me do that."

Soon Bones and Winston appeared with the horses.

"Is he alright?" Bones asked, getting off his horse and walking toward their newest patient.

"Yeah," said Missy smiling. "Unfortunately, he'll be back to his usual self."

Samuel laughed again. "Ouch!" he repeated, holding his head.

"Let's clean that and put some bandages on it," said Bones.

After taking care of the patient, they rested for an hour before Bones insisted that they keep moving. Winston had picked up the trail farther upstream, and soon they were back on course to hunt down the posse.

It was later in the day when they spotted tracks, but they weren't from the posse.

"Winston," said Samuel.

"What is it?" asked the old man.

"Over here."

Winston found Samuel and knelt to examine the tracks.

"What do you think?" Samuel asked.

The old man shook his head. "I've only seen tracks that big one other place, but it had four toes, not six."

"What was it?" asked Missy coming over to join them.

"Allegedly, it was a Wendigo. That's what the local trapper told me at the time, anyway."

"Did you ever see it?" Samuel asked.

"Nope. Never did. But the print was huge—just like these."

"What do you think we should do now?" Missy asked him.

"I think we should follow the trail," said Winston, "not the prints. If that Dalrymple fellow missed these tracks, then he would have continued along the trail."

"Are we following the posse or the creature?" Missy asked.

Bones hadn't expected to find any creature, so the mere finding of such strange tracks unnerved him. It was the first time in a long time that the doctor looked indecisive and confused.

"Are you alright?" Missy asked, taking Bones's arm.

"It must be a coyote or something," Bones mumbled. "I agree with Winston. We should follow the posse."

"I've never seen nor heard of a coyote that big," said Winston. "And coyotes have four toes with prints that are padded—not long prints like this with claw-like toes."

"What about a bear, then?"

"Bears have five toes," Winston answered, "not six."

"Maybe it's a mutant bear. We find mutant animals in nature all the time. Maybe that's what we're looking at here."

"Could be," said Winston. "There's always a chance of that, but it's rare, as you know."

"Or it could be a Wendigo," said Missy.

Bones stooped to examine the tracks further. "These tracks are perfectly even—each one is exactly the same. That's not normal. They look man-made, in fact."

Winston took another look at them. "You know, you're right. They do look too similar to be made by a casual animal. But who would be out here making fake animal tracks?"

"There's only one group out here that we know of," said Bones, "and that's Dalrymple."

"But why would he make faux prints? It makes no sense," said Samuel.

"If he knew we were tracking him, it might," said Winston.

"But he doesn't know we're tracking him. At least not that I know," said Bones.

"Well, whether it's the real McCoy—a Wendigo—or it's a fake made by Dalrymple, the answer is the same," said Missy.

"And what's that?" asked Samuel.

"We follow the posse," Bones answered for her. "They're the ones we have to stop."

*****

CH 35 – Addressing the Threat

Phineas had been quite pleased with himself after the blockbuster event he had thrown at the Willard Hotel. Many, if not all, of the nation's top legislators had attended, and feedback had been extraordinarily positive.

"Have you heard much after the little soiree of mine?" Phineas asked his third business partner, James Cooper.

"It was a great success, by all accounts," said Cooper. "We had to payout a lot of money for campaign contributions, but the votes we secured should more than cover anything the opposition can throw at us. I think we're in the clear."

"I'm not so sure," said McGinnis. "Tillson is still trying to persuade the senators' wives of their position. Pressure from the women and sympathy votes from the heart-string stories they're spreading are going to make this a battle, I'm afraid."

"What does he think he's doing?" said Phineas, exploding as his wife, Nancy, entered his studio carrying a telegram.

"I'm not very happy with you," she said to him, watching as he read the note. "What is wrong with you men?" Nancy was Phineas's second spouse, having married him after the death of his first, Charity, some ten years earlier. Nancy was young enough to be his daughter, but she was also highly spirited and outspoken. After giving her husband the note, she summarily left, slamming the door behind her.

"This Tillson fellow," Phineas began, "he's still stirring up a hornet's nest in Washington. Worse yet, he's pushing for the destruction of my business *and* my family. I just won't stand for it, McGinnis! What are you going to do about this!"

"I'll look into it, sir," said McGinnis, feeling the pressure.

"Look into it? You should be all over this! I've spent a small fortune wining and dining the senators down there on the Potomac. The least you can do is push our message harder, so we don't get lost in the noise. This is your responsibility as a business partner. You need to be in the loop with what's going on down there in D.C. You need to get down there again to shore up our position."

"Yes, sir," McGinnis replied, however not intending to travel any time soon. "I'll take care of it."

"While we're on the subject, what's going on in Minnesota?" asked Phineas, lighting a Partagas-Cifuentas cigar and blowing the blue smoke across the room. "You haven't updated me on our hunt for that creature in a while."

"The last telegram I got from Campbell was that he was venturing out from Wadena."

"And what about that Dalrymple fellow?"

"The last telegram from Dalrymple said he was heading out to a place called Black River Falls, wherever that is. But that was over two weeks ago. I haven't heard anything since. That's why we sent Moe Campbell to go there after him."

"How long ago was Campbell's telegram?"

"Got it yesterday."

"Don't you think we should have heard something from him by now?" asked Phineas.

"Phineas," McGinnis finally said, "you must be more patient. Things don't happen in the wild west like they happen here. They don't have Western Union offices stationed all along old Indian trails, you know."

"It's all taking too long!" said Phineas, thumping his fingers on his desk. "We've got two big projects and neither are coming to fruition as we planned. This is extremely frustrating."

"I know, Phineas. However, you must be patient. I'm taking care of them— both of them."

***

McGinnis did, finally, travel to D.C., checking into the Willard Hotel just off Pennsylvania Avenue and close to the White House. He knew he would never hear the end of it from Phineas if he didn't make the journey even though he felt other men he had hired in town were capable of putting pressure on those who worked on Capitol Hill. Yet, with the help of Phineas, McGinnis would be able to do something the others couldn't.

Although the president, Chester Arthur, was someone Phineas knew, McGinnis had never met the man. It had only taken one telegram to make the arrangements to have McGinnis visit 1600 Pennsylvania Avenue and meet with Arthur. With money, more often than not, came influence, and Phineas had become very influential.

Chester Arthur had taken over the presidency after the assassination of James Garfield two years earlier. Arthur had been a prominent figure during the Civil War—a highly efficient and capable quartermaster who had been promoted to brigadier general. After the war, Arthur returned to his law practice in New York before a mentor of his, ex-governor Edwin Morgan, was elected to the U.S. Senate. Through Morgan, Arthur became good friends with Roscoe Conkling, a Congressman who was a favorite of Ulysses S. Grant. As a result of Conkling's urging, Grant had appointed Arthur to the post of US Collector where he had served until Rutherford B. Hayes was elected president. Hayes had disliked Arthur and removed him. But Arthur had stayed involved in the nation's capital, and when the 1880 Republican National Convention was held to nominate a candidate for president, neither US Grant nor James Blaine could garner enough votes to become the nominee. So, the convention turned to a middle-grounder, James Garfield, who had served nine terms as a Congressman from Ohio. Then, when others had turned down the nomination for vice president believing Garfield would lose in November, Arthur had happily accepted. As fate would have it, Garfield was elected but within two hundred days of his inauguration was felled by the bullet of an assassin. Arthur was sworn-in and rapidly took the reins of power as President of the United States.

"The president will be with you shortly," said Fredrick Philips, who held the formal title of Private Secretary to the White House and the President.

McGinnis waited for over an hour but was finally led to the east side of the mansion and up to the second floor where Arthur and his administration ran the country. Arthur was working at his desk when McGinnis walked in, but the president did not look up.

"I will be with you in a moment," the president muttered. Finally, putting down his pen, he glanced up without smiling. "I understand that you know a mutual acquaintance: Phineas Taylor. He's quite a salesman and businessman, isn't he?"

"Yes, Mr. President. He and I are business partners."

"Well, Mr. McGinnis, I don't have a great deal of time, so what can I do for you today?"

"Mr. President, we have come to understand that there is an effort—a movement, if you will—in town that wishes to impose laws on businesses which would severely hurt that in which Phineas and I have spent much time nurturing and developing. We believe that such laws—while well intentioned—would be misguided."

"To what exactly are you referring, sir?"

"I'm referring to efforts to pass legislation on the use of animals in agriculture and commercial businesses. These laws would force a great many people out of business and thereby take work away from the people who can least afford to be without a job. It would also make private farming almost impossible. Thousands of farmers would lose their family farms. I don't think this is something that will make you very popular with the voters."

Of course, Phineas had coached McGinnis on the approach he would take with the president. Telling the full story would not have elicited the response they wanted, so they decided to tell only part of it.

"I am aware that New York City has been at the vanguard of this and children's protection efforts. Is that what you mean?" asked Arthur.

"Yes, Mr. President. We are all for the protection of children and, of course, animals, but the way they are going about this is wrong. We shouldn't punish honest farmers and businessmen and take away their livelihoods. We believe there must be a better way to address the issues they've raised, and that the current bills should be tabled until there is further discussion from all sides."

"I see," said the president. "Well, I'm not as familiar with the efforts to protect animals as I am with women's suffrage and other matters. I'm also not aware of any issues or problems with the treatment of animals."

"There are very few issues, I can assure you—none which require the federal government's intervention."

"And what would you like from me?"

"We ask that you support our position when the bill comes up on Capitol Hill—to redirect those efforts to something more ... useful?"

"I suggest you contact Eldridge Gerry in New York City. He established a Children's Protection Society there in the 70s. If you recall, his grandfather died in office as vice president under James Madison. Perhaps that is a better cause to which you and I can direct our efforts."

"Yes, absolutely," McGinnis answered. "That's a fine idea. Thank you, sir. I shall."

It wasn't exactly what McGinnis had hoped for, but it was a start. Next on his dance card were to return to members of Congress. Many he had already met and talked to about the matter. However, after meeting with the president, he could argue much more effectively against the bill and the movement.

Days passed, and McGinnis was making slow headway to sustain their opposition against the animal right's bill. There was a growing wave of anti-business sentiment which had developed from the rise of the industrialist tycoons like Rockefeller, Carnegie, Mellon, and others. This attitude was spilling over into other issues with the business community and the matter of child and animal protection was gaining traction. Even with Phineas's soiree, the wives of Congressman had become a potent strategy by Tillson and one that was paying dividends.

"What is happening down there?" Phineas barked, growing increasingly impatient at the lack for progress. "I'm reading the newspapers, and it seems support is *growing* for this legislation, not diminishing."

"Things move slowly in Washington," said McGinnis defensively. "You should know that, Phineas."

"I don't care! You need to stop this movement. You need to kill it."

"Yes, sir."

"And I don't care how you do it. Just do it!"

"Yes, sir."

Just outside of Washington was a place called the Red Fox Inn and Tavern located in Middleburg, Virginia. There, McGinnis had arranged a meeting with Aldus Mercer, his man for doing odd jobs and those so unsavory that few others were willing to do them. Aside from his robbery gigs with Campbell, Mercer had been in prison for the swindling of an eighty-two-year-old grandmother, Patricia Langsdon, leaving her and her family penniless. He was looking for work when McGinnis contacted him.

"When do you want this done?" Mercer asked, wiping his mouth on his sleeve after slurping some cool ale.

"As soon as possible," said McGinnis.

"I'll make it happen," said Mercer, "but I want half up front."

"Here," said McGinnis, sliding two gold pieces across the table. "You'll get the other three when the job is done."

Two days later, Tillson came out of the south wing of the Capitol where the House of Representatives resided. He was in a hurry to find a carriage for a ride home. It had been a long day, and, having been through a marathon of meetings with reps and senators, he was ready for a hot meal and share a glass of Madeira with his wife, Amanda.

"Are you Mr. Tillson?"

It was a short man with a heavy beard and a wildness to his eyes and manner. He was wearing a dark overcoat but not a top coat, vest or cravat as was the style and tradition on the Hill.

"I am," Tillson replied.

Suddenly, the man pulled out a revolver and fired it twice, hitting Tillson in the center of his chest. The former deputy secretary fell to his knees, looking shocked and bewildered. Then, he collapsed.

"Maybe that will make it harder for you to ruin someone's business," said Mercer, turning to run.

Tillson lay faceup on the ground, his eyes open and unmoving. Hearing the shots, others passing by ran to him to help. In the meantime, Mercer sprinted off, hoping to escape without being caught. However, he hadn't needed to worry about the police. Later the following day, he was found in an alley with two slugs to the head. Dead, he would tell no tales, and no one would ever be identified as his killer.

Phineas and company had taken care of business in Washington and tied up all loose ends. The dirty business of business was completed, allowing their empire to move forward, continuing to grow and prosper.

******

CH 36 – Summoning a Priest

Orville fled the house, just like his housekeeper. Immediately, he found his way back to Trinity Church where Reverend Benton was conducting a baptism for a prominent church family. After the ceremony, Orville hurried to the baptismal fount where he pulled the pastor aside.

"Reverend Benton, I need to speak to you. It is most urgent."

Orville was still shaking as he told the pastor about the frightening incident at his home and how he had fled for his life. Benton listened intently before raising his hands and pressing them together in prayer.

"So, as I feared," said the reverend. "It is time, Orville. We must act quickly before it's too late and she becomes lost forever."

"Did you find a priest?"

"Yes. The bishop listened to my plea, and he had no hesitations. There are two Catholic priests who perform exorcisms in Boston. I will contact them today and let you know how we should move forward." The pastor put his hand on Orville's shoulder. "Stay strong. The demon working within your sister is no match for the power of Christ. It will be driven from her. I promise."

"I hope you're right, pastor."

"You must believe, Orville."

***

Within three days, all had been arranged, and Orville arrived back at his brownstone with Reverend Benton defending his flank as he walked toward the red-bricked porch. Meeting them there were two priests from the dioceses which covered all the parishes within several local counties. These were Fathers O'Shaughnessy and Wentworth, although they went by their first names, Father Patrick and Father John, respectively.

"Very nice to meet you both," said Orville, shaking their hands. "I presume Reverend Benton has apprised you about my sister and what she's capable of?"

"Yes, Orville. Father John and I have conducted many exorcists here in Boston, and we've seen more than you can ever imagine. The power of the Devil is strong, but it is nothing compared to that of our Lord. There is nothing he can throw at us that we can't handle with the Lord behind us."

"Shall we?" said Reverend Benton, gesturing for them to go inside.

Both priests carried large, black bags as if they were medical doctors. However, once inside all they could smell was the pungent odor of sulfur. Orville leaned over and began to gag, but Father John quickly handed him a handkerchief.

"Here, use this if it gets too overpowering," the priest said, "I warn you that it will only grow worse as the ritual unfolds. Now, where is your sister?"

Father John was the shorter of the two men. Both were dressed in long black frocks with the traditional white collars. The frock buttoned from the neck to below the knees and came with billowy long sleeves. The older of the two priests, Father John, was quieter and more introspective than his counterpart. A gentle man, his demeanor was kind and unassuming. Deferential to all, Father John still commanded respect, if not by his age and his experience alone, then by his piety. For his age, he had a more hair than most, and what hair he did have was dark, albeit with a bald spot in back which cleared a pathway forward toward his forehead. His face was replete with wrinkles fissured by a history that few would understand, and then there was that fading, two-inch scar across the side of his face—its origin from an exorcism the father no longer wished to discuss. He played endlessly with the silver rosary that hung gracefully around his neck—either a nervous habit or a faith act that helped him when battling demons.

On the other hand, Father Patrick was youthful and energetic. He was taller than Father John by three or four inches, and much thinner by comparison. Although only in his early thirties, he too was losing some of his wavy brown hair although he retained a plume or two in front which he combed to the side across his scalp. With bright blue eyes, he had a glow about him that exuded confidence, security and trust. His broad smile brought out the tiniest of crow's feet around his eyes, making him appear friendly and approachable.

"My sister should be upstairs in her room," said Orville. "Follow me."

Orville took the men upstairs, but as they climbed, the air grew noticeably colder, damper, heavier than it had been below. By the time they reached the spare bedroom door, they could see their breath and shivered as they opened the door. A cold blast of air roared from the room, knocking Reverend Benton to his feet and nearly blowing the other men down the staircase. Orville held fast to the door handle, while the two priests—trained to anticipate everything—braced themselves for what lay ahead.

"Oh my God!" said Orville, and as he opened the door, he began gagging from the putrid smell of urine and feces that permeated the room.

Yet, that was not the only shock.

Levitating two feet above the bed was Claire. As they entered, she turned her head and stared at them. Her eyes were coal black as they had been when she had drifted down the stairway threatening Orville with his life. Her face had aged into that of an old hag, tinged with a sickly gray-green palette that itself was haunting. However, more disturbing were the stubs of horns beginning to grow from her forehead. It was a hideous sight, and one that made Orville run from the room to vomit.

"Ah, so you finally came to see me," Claire growled in a guttural, almost animalistic, tone. "Good. Soon you will all find yourselves begging for your pathetic God's mercy only to find you are all condemned to join me and Claire in eternal hell."

She cackled and, as if possessed by a dragon, let a stream of fire shoot from her mouth, spewing flames across the room and igniting the heavy woolen curtains by the windows. Father Patrick rushed to put out the blaze before it could spread while Reverend Benton looked on in horror. When Orville returned, he witnessed only the priest attempting to squelch the flames.

"Orville, I must leave!" said the trembling reverend, already overcome by the enormity of the evil. He immediately ran from the room, shuffling quickly down the stairs and out the front door.

Even Fathers John and Patrick stared at each other. Neither had seen anything this powerful and disturbing before.

"Don't go!" Orville cried to the reverend. "Don't leave us!" But his plea was in vain. Reverend Benton sprinted down the street as far as he could before finding a carriage to return him to his church. There he would pray in the chapel for the next two days without eating or sleeping.

The three remaining men left Claire's room and went back downstairs.

"Orville," began Father John, "we will need to rethink this."

"What do you mean?"

"Neither Father Patrick nor I have witnessed this level of demonic behavior before. The manifestation of fire like that is beyond anything we've experienced or read about, and I'm not sure ..."

167

"Oh, no. You're not going to tell me that you can't do this. You're not."

Father John looked again at Father Patrick before answering. "All right. We will try, but we will require more supplies." They went on to tell Orville what they would need, and when they had finished, Patrick asked, "Do you have those items, or can you get them for us? We must have them before we start."

"I have those and perhaps other things that might help you," Orville answered. "I'm an inventor, and I've come up with many useful things over the years. I'm sure we can find something that will come in handy."

*****

CH 37 – Last Moments

The attack had been swift and merciless. The creature had leaped from the cave and within seconds had devastated Dalrymple and his ranks.

Dalrymple recalled seeing a giant, hairy mass before hearing a scream from Eddie before his mind went blank. The next thing he knew, he was lying at the bottom of the cliff as if he had fallen, but not hard enough to kill him. He rubbed his head and felt a gash on it as well as pain in his ribs and leg. He was afraid he'd broken both but forced himself to sit up anyway to assess what had happened.

"Hey?" he called out, his vision blurry and mind foggy. "Anyone else down here?"

It was Leroy whose face came into view as he leaned over his boss.

"So, what happened up there?" Leroy asked.

"I don't know," Dalrymple answered. "The last thing I remember is a huge creature that came out of the cave."

"The Wendigo?"

"I think so. It all happened so fast, I'm not sure what I saw. So, who are we missing?" asked their leader.

"You're the only one who fell off the ledge, boss," said Jeeter, limping over to where Leroy stood.

"You're alive?" said Dalrymple, surprised to see Jeeter all in one piece. "I thought you died in that fall of yours."

"I feel like I did. My leg's broke and my rib's probably cracked," he answered.

"And Eddie and Peters?"

"They must still be up there," said Leroy, pointing up the ledge.

There was no movement or sign of life up on the cliff, and they could only assume the worst.

"That thing, that creature, must have eaten them," said Jeeter, sitting next to Dalrymple and curling up in a fetal ball.

"Maybe," answered their leader, "but I guess it don't matter now. At least we know that damned creature is real."

"Well, I'm outta' here," said Jeeter. "My leg's busted, but I'll have to make it back to Wadena to have a doctor look at it."

"I'm not sure how far we'll get in the condition we're in," said Dalrymple. "At least we have the wagon in case somebody can't walk or ride their horse."

"We do?" asked Jeeter. "The wagon's over there, but I don't see our horses."

Sure enough. All were gone.

"Well, I think it's every man for hisself," Leroy said answered starting to walk away from the group.

"You can try, Leroy, but you aren't going to make it out of these woods alive by yourself. You need us to help you. How are you going to stay awake all night to make sure that Wendigo doesn't grab you and drag you up and into its lair?"

Leroy stopped and slowly turned around.

"Yeah, I thought so," said Dalrymple. "Now, help me to my feet. We need to get back to our campsite and figure out how we can get home."

Leroy helped Dalrymple get up, and together with Jeeter they hobbled back into the deep woods, moving ever so slowly to their former campsite.

The afternoon passed quickly, and the dread of nighttime fell upon them before they were prepared for it. For all three, it was a moment they never wanted to come as darkness wiped away the last remnants of light and hope.

Leroy found a couple squirrels, and they had those for supper. Yet, even as the fire crackled and kept the camp warm and illuminated, they felt little safety or consolation. They still had whiskey left to drink, and it went quickly, leaving little extra time for conversation.

Dalrymple got up to move things around to make room for his bedding. He picked up his saddle bag which he had left behind earlier in the day and then reached for Leroy's.

"What's this?" asked their leader, seeing a long handle sticking out of Leroy's pack.

Dalrymple set the pack down and extracted something that had an odd appendage on the end. In his hand was a wooden model of a six-toed animal's foot.

"We've been hoodwinked!" exclaimed Jeeter.

"Where'd you get this?" asked Dalrymple.

"I have no idea," said Leroy. "I've never seen it before."

"Liar!" shouted Jeeter. "You're the one who made those animal tracks we followed!"

"You planted it in my pack!" said Leroy. "You're trying to set me up!"

"*This* is what we've been following," said Jeeter. "You duped us! You son of a bitch!"

Jeeter tried to lunge at Leroy, but in his condition, he was only able to take two steps before he fell, nearly toppling into the fire.

Their posse leader recoiled. "Stop it!"

Jeeter got up and pulled his gun. "You did this! You did this to all of us!"

"What did I do?" said Leroy. "I didn't force anyone up on that cliff. I didn't leave two of our own up there to die." He looked at Dalrymple. "You did that. Not me!"

"Why? Why?" asked Dalrymple.

Leroy smirked. "Me and Peters figured you didn't know what the hell you were doing out here. It was only a matter of time that you would have an accident or get yourself killed. If that didn't happen, we were going to help you along."

"Kill me?"

"Peters and me wanted the prize money. We're the most experienced trackers of the group. Why did we need you lousy pieces of baggage? Why should we split the money with all of you?"

"You were going to get rid of me too?" said Jeeter.

"Yeah, but you almost took care of that for us, didn't you?" said Leroy.

Leroy pulled his revolver and pointed it at Dalrymple. "Let's make this quick and easy, shall we?"

The shot came, but it wasn't Dalrymple who took the slug.

Jeeter's gun smoked after he'd fired the fatal shot, and Leroy fell over stone dead.

"Well, I guess that solves that," said Jeeter, pleased with himself.

"It does and it doesn't," answered Dalrymple. "Now we're left with the two of us, neither of which can walk more than about a hundred yards without having to stop and rest. How long do you figure it will take us now to get back to Wadena?"

"Crap!" Jeeter said, "But he would'a shot us both before we got there anyway."

"Probably so. I guess, if we're lucky, we'll come across someone else on the trail who can help us. You better start prayin' for that Jeeter."

Jeeter put his palms together. "I already am, boss."

It was Jeeter who took the first watch. Unlike previous times, it wasn't hard for him to keep his eyes open. Dalrymple too couldn't sleep after what they'd gone through that day, and for much of the evening both were awake and twitched with anxiety.

"I'll take over now," said Dalrymple, grimacing as he sat up and took his gun back from Jeeter who relinquished his watch and returned to his spot by the fire.

It was well into the night, after Jeeter had relieved Dalrymple for another shift, when Jeeter heard a twig snap nearby.

"Boss!" he exclaimed, the pistol shaking in his hand. "I heard somethin'. Somethin's out there."

The posse leader sat up and began listening.

"Give me my gun," said Dalrymple, not trusting Jeeter to be steady with a shot if the beast came their way.

"I've got this," said Jeeter, not wanting to give up the gun either.

"No! I said, give me my gun!" said Dalrymple.

Dalrymple grabbed for his gun, and the two men wrestled. Quickly, there was a shot.

Bang!

Dalrymple's face showed one of stunned pain. He clutched his chest and fell forward next to the fire. He didn't move.

But what happened next came so fast that the last remaining posse member didn't know what hit him. There was a savage roar in the woods, and the Wendigo leaped into the camp, striking Jeeter across the face with its huge, mangy paw. Its six-inch claws nearly decapitated him, leaving only a few vertebrae and a mangled mass of tendons to hold his head to his body. It was over within seconds, and in the aftermath, there was little left to be found in the camp aside from the burning fire embers which seemed not to notice. The flames continued their macabre dance, bouncing merrily on the hot burning logs. They wouldn't die out until the early morning hours, when they would join the rest of their campmates

*****

CH 38 – Final Meeting

McGinnis hadn't met with Phineas for several weeks, and when they finally got together, the meeting was less than cordial.

"You haven't delivered the Wendigo as you promised," thundered Phineas. "I've made commitments to people here in the city, and they want to know when to expect it so they can plan the exhibition."

"I haven't heard back from Dalrymple or Campbell," said the junior business partner. "I'll wire the sheriff in Wadena to see if he knows anything. But Phineas, I took care of our Washington problem, so give me some credit! We've succeeded at delivering a crushing blow to the animal rights activists and their movement to derail our business plans. Congress is not going to act on the Animal Protection Act. They're too focused on other matters now. We can continue moving ahead with our expansion."

"Well, that is good news," Phineas answered. "Perhaps you are worth keeping." The older man smiled, and his face softened. "Not only do I want to exhibit the most bizarre and rare animals in the U.S., but I want to display other oddities in this world—both human and animal alike. I want to go beyond New York and other big cities, showing them in England and other parts of Europe."

Just then, a knock came at the door to Phineas's office.

"Yes?"

"There's a Mrs. Tilson here to see you," said Jorg, his assistant.

"Not now. Send her away," said Phineas.

"She says its important, sir."

"I said, send her away," barked the old man.

Yet, it wasn't a minute after Jorg had closed the door that he was back.

"I'm sorry, sir, but …"

Barging Into the room behind Jorg was a middle-aged woman dressed in black. Amanda Tilson entered, and the calm instantly turned into hostility.

"Good day," she began, her voice trembling with rage.

"Good day madam. What is it that you want?" asked Phineas.

"Justice," she announced, pulling a small, ivory-handled derringer from her purse and pointing it at them. "You killed my husband," she added.

Phineas took a step back and raised his hands. "I don't know what you're talking about," he muttered. "Just don't do anything stupid like fire that gun at us."

"Stupid? Really? I have every right to shoot you as you stand before me," she answered. "You shot my husband!"

In the meantime, Phineas's assistant backed out of the room as the drama heightened.

"PT," Amanda continued, "you must believe you are invincible and that you can get rid of anyone who gets in your way. Well, you're wrong! You may have succeeded in derailing our efforts on animal rights, but you won't live to see the fruits of that action. No, you and Mr. Bailey here must be stopped, and I guess it is up to me to do it."

"But the Ringling Brothers are doing the same thing," said McGinnis Bailey. "You'll have to fight them too."

"If I must, I must," she answered.

"Just put the gun down," said Phineas Taylor, who was better known by the public as PT Barnum. "It will do you and your children no good to kill us. They will arrest you, sentence you to death, and your children will be without a mother *and* a father. Is that what you want?" Phineas was a master at manipulation, and now he pulled out all the stops. "Even as we speak, we are rounding up a creature in the Midwest for our shows. It will be so popular no one will support your call to stop it. People like to be entertained. They *need* to be entertained. Circuses are here to stay. They will always be here, whether I am or not."

"I don't agree," said Amanda. "Most people don't like to see animals hurt. They don't like to see children hurt, and they will fight against it. You won't win this battle, PT, even if you survive my bullets. If it must be me who stops this, then so be it. Someone must."

Just then, the front doors to the mansion burst open, and two men in police uniforms stormed Phineas's study. Before Amanda knew what was happening, they had grabbed the gun from her hand and pulled her arms behind her back.

Jorg came in behind them, along with their third partner, Cooper. "It's a good thing I went to get them," said Cooper. "Your assistant ran into me as I was coming to see you. I hurried to the station which was right around the block. The chief is a friend and sent these two gentlemen right away."

"Take her down to the station," said one of the policemen. "We'll book her there."

"Good," said Phineas. "Book her for attempting to murder us all!" he shouted. "Put her away forever!"

But it was Cooper who intervened, aware of the ugly machinations of his two other partners. "Let's discuss this, shall we?"

"What's there to discuss? She tried to kill us—McGinnis and me!"

"She didn't fire at you, did she?" he asked.

"No, but she was going to!"

After getting everyone calmed down, Cooper got Phineas to agreed not to press charges against Amanda. Appealing to Phineas's only loyalty—which was to his business empire—he convinced him that the publicity of bringing charges against a recent widow with two young children would be bad for the family-oriented circus.

"If you ever show up here again," warned Phineas, "we will not hesitate to have you put away for the rest of your miserable life!" As Amanda was being escorted from the property, PT added, "And furthermore, you are to stop all efforts on your animal protection activism. I don't want to hear another thing about that. Do you understand?"

"Or what? What will you do?" Amanda shot back.

"He could have your children taken away from you," said one of the officers. "He's a powerful man. I wouldn't mess with him."

"And I'll make sure they're put in some abusive foster home and their lives will be horrible," said Phineas angrily before slamming the door.

The police took her to the station to spend the night behind bars and think about what she had done or tried to do. But, in accordance with Cooper's wishes, they didn't charge her. The next morning, she agreed to sign a statement that she would not return to New York City and would not agitate and inflame the citizenry with her "fabricated" stories of animal and child abuse. The case was closed. *****

CH 39 — In the Name of the Father

Coming up from downstairs holding an armful of treasurers was Orville. He had a trove of things—from conventional weapons and shields to electronic devices, energy projectiles and water guns. Orville laid them all out on the kitchen table and waited for any signs of interest.

"So, what's this?" asked Father John, picking at a couple of grey, ribbed robes he found within the pile.

"Well, the short answer is there was a man named Joseph Louis Gay-Lussac. Over fifty years ago, he soaked some garments in ammonium phosphate and borax. Amazingly, he found they were resistant to fire. I've improved on that a bit. Mine are made with that and stannic oxide. Mine don't wash out as much."

"As much?" asked Father Patrick. "Have they been washed at all?"

Orville laughed. "No, Father. But if you wear those, you still may wish to say a few prayers before you venture back into the room."

"Don't worry," the priest answered grimly. "We'll need to do more than that to battle this beast."

Wearing the cloaks and carrying other implements upstairs with them, Father John pushed open the door to Claire's room. The doorhandle was ice cold, and the air escaping from the room was like an Arctic blast ripping across the frozen tundra. Orville shivered as he followed the others inside.

Claire, or rather Jahi, was waiting for them.

"I didn't think you would return," she cackled, sitting up in bed. "I thought I'd scared you off!"

The scene was surreal. She sat on her mattress, but her legs were bent backwards over her head and dangling around her shoulders. Her head, too, was turned completely around, facing the opposite way as well. However, now, her face was inhuman. It was lizard-like with green scales on it, and the horns on top of her head were fully formed with masses of hair wrapped around them.

"You know, Father Patrick, you shouldn't have f*cked me the last time you were here. Now, I have a demon child—your child—growing inside me."

At that moment, Claire's lower abdomen began expanding like a balloon—making it appear as if she were pregnant and the fetus was growing at an astonishing rate.

"Enough!" shouted Father John. "In the name of Jesus Christ, our Lord, I command you to leave the body of Claire Cook." He immediately crossed himself and opened his Bible.

Claire growled at him and opened her mouth, blowing a flame of fury that struck him in the chest. Luckily, the grey robe did not catch fire, remaining unscathed as the blaze bounced off the surface. This only angered Claire, and she shot another blast his direction. This time, the priest covered his face with his sleeves and waited for the outburst to finish.

"Demon Jahi, you have no right, no claim, to the body of Claire Cook. Only our Lord, Jesus Christ and the Heavenly Father have such a claim. You will relinquish your control of her now!"

Claire snarled. "You have no claim over me, and I will never leave this earth-bound body. Never!"

Effortlessly, Claire then began talking in a strange language, spewing a chapter-long verse which no one in the room understood.

"*Harimbo katani morasu shahim. Orumo itsam para miktum losicrusix ...*"

Suddenly, the dresser on the far side of the room skidded across the wood floor, slamming into Father Patrick and pinning him to the wall.

"*Ah!*" he screamed in pain. With all his might, he tried to push the dresser away, but it wouldn't move.

Orville rushed to help him while Father John continued his exorcism undeterred.

"Christ, our Lord, came to Earth to banish the evil from our souls for those who believe in Him. He is the Light. He is the Goodness. He is our salvation. It is He who will vanquish the demon who dwells within this body. It is He who will drive it from Claire and from all corners of the Earth."

Unable to get close to the demon without risking another dragonian fireball, Father John took his long-handled aspergillum, which he used during mass to cast holy water on the parishioners and cast holy water across the room and onto Claire's head as she sat most perversely in the bed. She cried out in pain as each drop found its mark on her forehead, face and chest. As if burned, her body writhed in agony.

"You are nothing to the power of Satan. Nothing!" she screamed.

"In the name of Jesus Christ, I command you to leave the body of Claire Cook," Father John repeated. "I command you, unclean spirit, along with all your minions now attacking this servant of God, by the mysteries of the incarnation, passion, resurrection, and ascension of our Lord Jesus Christ, by the descent of the Holy Spirit, by the coming of our Lord for judgment, that you tell me the day and hour of your departure. I command you, moreover, to obey me to the letter, I who am a minister of God despite my unworthiness; nor shall you be emboldened to harm in any way this creature of God, or the bystanders, or any of their possessions. Amen."

"I shall never obey you or your god!"

"I say again, be gone you, hostile power—you demon from darkness. Release your control over this soul."

"Never!"

Then, Claire unwound her position and rose again from the bed, levitating with her legs crossed and her head down and determined. It was then that she, too, began her own incantation.

"Omini krustuos bali zophricon um tymoxis cromtus deca floran xuppototum erst non."

Orville cowered, gasping in terror.

Coming out of the walls were scores of hideous, black, dwarf-like men carrying battleaxes and holding long knives. Their faces looked like aged prunes, full of creases and pocked with boils filled with pus. Yellow and crimson mucous flowed from their black eyes, and when they opened their snake-like mouths, fangs of the same sort sprouted. Their cacophony of sibilating noises made Orville cover his ears as he watched in horror at what was unfolding.

"I adjure you, ancient serpent," continued Father John, "by the judge of the living and the dead, by your Creator, by the Creator of the whole universe, by Him who has the power to consign you to hell, to depart forthwith in fear, along with your savage minions, from this servant of God, for Claire seeks refuge in the fold of the Church. I adjure you again," he said, this time making the sign of the cross, "not by my weakness but by the might of the Holy Spirit, to depart from this servant of God, Claire, whom almighty God has made in His image."

The ogre-like creatures began moving closer to Father John as he spoke, their battleaxes raised. Yet, the priest did not flinch.

"Yield, therefore, yield not to my own person but to the minister of Christ. For it is the power of Christ that compels you, who brought you low by His cross. Tremble before that mighty arm that broke asunder the dark prison walls and led souls forth to light. May the trembling that afflicts this human frame, the fear that afflicts this image of God, descend on you. Make no resistance nor delay in departing from this woman, for it has pleased Christ to dwell within her."

Together, Orville and Father Patrick were finally able to push the dresser aside and free the younger priest, who hurried to protect his fellow clergyman. Yet, as they approached Father John, winds of hurricane force arose from nowhere, forcing open the window and blowing everything onto the floor of the room that wasn't nailed down. Orville and Father Patrick fought against the furious winds to reach the aging priest.

"Do not think of despising my command because you know me to be a great sinner. It is God Himself who commands you; the majestic Christ who commands you. God the Father commands you; God the Son commands you; God the Holy Spirit commands you. The mystery of the cross commands you. The faith of the holy apostles Peter and Paul and of all the saints commands you. The blood of the martyrs commands you. The continence of the confessors commands you. The devout prayers of all holy men and women command you, and the saving mysteries of our Christian faith command you."

But no sooner than Father John uttered these last words, the axes of the demonic entities fell upon him. Orville turned away, unable to watch and wanting to flee as Reverend Benton had earlier. Yet, as he closed his eyes, he did not hear a single scream or cry for help from the priest. There was only quiet. When he opened them, he saw only a grey robe, the crucifix Father John had worn around his neck, and his worn, black Bible lying on the floor where he had once stood. He was not there.

Shaken, Father Patrick rushed to pick up the Bible and the crucifix. Without missing a beat, he re-opened the Holy book and continued reading.

"Thou shalt have no claim to the body or soul of this servant of our Lord," said Father Patrick. He put down the Bible and began casting holy water on the demon once more. This time, when a droplet of the water struck the demon it cried out in even greater anguish.

"Ah! No! Stop hurting me!" This time it was Claire's voice, not the low, groveling one that had spewed from the same mouth only moments earlier. Additionally, the head and body had returned to that of Orville's sister. "Orville, do not let them hurt me! I am but a young woman—fragile and pious. They are trying to kill me. Stop them, Orville! Please, stop them!"

"You cannot deceive us, Jahi," said the priest, not backing off. "Our eyes are open to your deception. You still dwell within the body of Claire Cook, and you must depart at once!"

Claire's face instantly returned to the monstrous, serpent-like head that had taunted them before.

"You will pay for this, priest!" she shouted.

"You and your minions will not succeed in stopping the Lord, our God, and Christ, our Savior from saving this woman."

Then, Father Patrick began throwing the holy water on the ugly, dwarfs that had were regrouping and now encircling the younger priest with their weapons. This time, when the droplets hit them, each burst into a mighty ball of flame, crying out in agony as its apparition burned. The priest continued showering the demons with holy water, and one by one, they ignited, burning like a Roman candle and pooling on the floor like spent, gooey wax.

"Depart, then, transgressor. Depart, seducer, full of lies and cunning, foe of virtue, persecutor of the innocent. Give place, abominable creature, give way, you monster, give way to Christ, in whom you found none of your works. For He has already stripped you of your powers and laid waste to your kingdom, bound you prisoner and plundered your weapons. He has cast you forth into the outer darkness, where everlasting ruin awaits you and your abettors."

Seeing what was happening to her army of demons, Claire roared her anger. The room shook, and plaster began falling from the ceiling and the walls. Cracks formed as the walls separated, and a large piece of plaster fell from the ceiling, cutting the priest's face and causing him to bleed. A red flow streamed from the two-inch gash, yet he remained steadfast and determined.

Pressing against his wound, Father Patrick continued, "To what purpose do you insolently resist? To what purpose do you brazenly refuse? For you are guilty before almighty God, whose laws you have transgressed. You are guilty before His Son, our Lord Jesus Christ, whom you presumed to tempt, whom you dared to nail to the cross. You are guilty before the whole of the human race, to whom you proffered by your enticements the poisoned cup of death."

"You will not succeed!" shouted Claire, rising off the bed, but now moving menacingly toward the priest. When she reached Father Patrick, she raised her nightshirt and began urinating on him as a dog would relieve himself on a tree stump. "You are feces to me. You are trash. You deserve nothing and will get nothing from me."

Orville was repulsed by what he saw, yet he dared not intervene. Father Patrick merely wiped the discharge away with his sleeve and kept reading.

"Therefore, I adjure you, profligate dragon, in the name of the spotless Lamb, who has trodden down the asp and the basilisk, and overcome the lion and the dragon, to depart from this woman and to depart from the Church of God. Tremble and flee, as we call on the name of the Lord, before whom the denizens of hell cower, to whom the heavenly Virtues and Powers and Dominations are subject, whom the Cherubim and Seraphim praise with unending cries as they sing: Holy, holy, holy, Lord God of Sabaoth. The Word made flesh commands you; the Virgin's Son commands you; Jesus of Nazareth commands you, who once, when you despised His disciples, forced you to flee in shameful defeat from a man; and when He had cast you out you did not even dare, except by His leave, to enter into a herd of swine."

Suddenly, two more black, hairy ogres sprang from the wall next to Orville and ran at him, raising their sharp knives to cut him to pieces. Orville grabbed the aspergillum which Father Patrick had placed at the foot of the bed and snapped it with his wrist, flinging more holy water at them. However, there was no holy water left in it.

As the first demon steadied his knife to plunge it into Orville's chest, a ball of light descended through the ceiling and enveloped the beast. Turning milky white, the ball consumed it, and cries of pain could be heard from within it. The opaque ball then turned translucent once again, revealing nothing inside. The demon ogre was gone. Seeing this, the other demon dropped its knife and ran back through the wall from which it had come.

"And now as I adjure you in His name," continued Father Patrick, "be gone from this woman who is His creature. It is futile to resist His will. It is impossible for you to kick against the goad. The longer you delay, the heavier your punishment shall be; for it is not men you are condemning, but rather you are blaspheming Him who rules the living and the dead, who is coming to judge by trial of fire both the living and the dead."

The ball of light continued to hover in the room as if listening to every word spoken by the priest. And when the Father had finished that paragraph of the ritual, the bright orb moved toward him. It enveloped him as well and began burning like a thousand candles—a brilliance Orville had never seen before.

Afraid for this priest, Orville called out, "No! Don't hurt him!" But the sphere only grew brighter and hotter.

From within the ball, Orville could still hear the priest's unfaltering voice.

"Our Father, who art in Heaven, hallowed be Thy Name; Thy Kingdom come; Thy will be done on Earth as it is in Heaven. Give us this day our daily bread; and forgive us our trespasses as we forgive those who trespass against us, and lead us not into temptation, but deliver us from evil. For thine is the kingdom and power and glory, now and forever. Amen."

And as the priest said the final words of the Lord's Prayer, the bubble became milky white again and the image of Father Patrick inside vanished.

"Father!" shouted Orville.

"Now, it's just you and me Orville, my brother …"

The demon within Claire now turned its sights on her brother and drifted toward him. It laughed. Yet the sound seemed weaker and less haughty than before, and quickly the possessed body struggled to keep aloft, finally faltering and then crashing onto the bed's down-filled mattress. Claire lay there stunned.

"No! You can't have my sister!" Orville yelled. "In the name of Jesus Christ, leave her alone!"

The ball of light which had consumed Father Patrick began to change again. This time, the milky whiteness turned crystal clear and then dissolved, vanishing instantly. To Orville's shock, Father Patrick stood calmly beside the bed, still holding the crucifix and his Bible where the orb had just been. As if in a trance, his body was relaxed, his face was serene, and his eyes were closed. He was reciting the words from the Bible—this time from memory.

"In the name of our Lord, Jesus Christ, you will release Claire Cook. It is hereto commanded!" cried the priest, opening his eyes which were now on fire.

Father Patrick's body was glowing—scintillating all over—and he stretched out his hand, palms down, but with his long fingers pointed directly at the demon's reptilian face.

"No!" shouted the demon, trying to cling to Claire's body. Its protest was now feeble and panicked. "No! I … I …"

"You *will* ... you *must* ... you *shall* ... by the power of the Most Holy Father, the Son and the Holy Spirit, you will relinquish your hold on this child of God Almighty! You shall do it *now!*"

Claire's body went into convulsions, levitating once more but writhing in midair in ways not humanly possible. It began to transform again—this time from the green scaly monster back into the womanly form it had once held. Finally, the body lowered onto the bed, gently coming to rest. Claire lay quiet and peaceful, as if she had just reposed for a long winter's nap. The greyish green hue of her skin began to pinken, and life began to return to her cheeks.

"In the name of the Father, the Son and the Holy Spirit," said Father Patrick, "may the demons that have possessed our sister Claire never return." He then crossed himself once more and leaned over to make the same sign over Claire.

Orville glanced at the priest. "Is she ... you know ... is she all right now?" he asked.

"I pray to our Heavenly Father that our answer to that is yes."

"Claire, Claire, are you alright?" Orville asked urgently, coming to her side.

For what seemed like an eternity, she didn't answer. But finally, her eyelids fluttered, and she took a deep breath.

"Orville?" she asked, opening her eyes. "Is that you?"

"Claire, how do you feel?"

"I feel ... well ... like I've been in a boxing ring," she answered, sitting up and holding her head. "What happened? Have I been asleep? It seems like I have for a long time and with such horrible dreams. I can't tell you how horrible they were."

Orville turned back toward the priest. He was on the floor on his knees, hunched over and holding his abdomen. He seemed to be in immense pain.

"Father Patrick, are you alright?" Orville asked.

The priest looked up at him. His face had now turned a greenish grey and was contorting into something inhuman. There was evil in his eyes.

*****

CH 40 – Bloody Mess

"How long since they were here?" Bones asked Winston who was kneeling next to a charred, but cold, campfire. They had followed the tracks for a long time, until they had ended at the foot of a series of high, rocky cliffs.

"I'd say a day at the most," said the old man. "The fire is stone cold, but it rained yesterday, so their tracks have deteriorated some from the water softening their footprints."

"So, they aren't far," said Samuel.

"Yeah, if we put in a long day today, perhaps we can catch them," said Bones. "Hopefully, they've been stalled or delayed somewhere along the way here."

The foursome headed out again, but it wasn't long before they reached another campfire. This one was still warm.

"Why would they camp again so soon after the last one?" asked Bones.

"I don't know. It's odd," Winston answered. "All I can guess is that either they went quite a bit farther up the road and then came back here, or they found something around here that caught their attention."

"A Wendigo?" Missy asked.

"Could be," said Winston. "As you can tell, this one is fresh. They probably left here earlier today."

Winston wandered off to look for traces of the men, and after a few minutes returned.

"Find anything?" asked Missy.

"Plenty," the old man replied. "I found more of those strange tracks that lead off toward a cliff not far from here. It's likely that they spotted them too and headed off after them."

"What do you make of this?" asked Bones, holding something in his hand. It was a mangled pair of silver glasses.

"I don't rightly know," Winston answered. "Maybe he didn't need them except to read and dropped them."

"But they're thick and concave," said Bones. "This suggests myopia or nearsightedness. This person can't see things in the distance."

"Did you find anything else?" asked Winston.

"It just looks like there was a struggle of some kind," said Bones. "There are drag marks that lead away from the campfire and into the woods, but we can't figure out what made them. I'd say boot marks. But we found no bodies nearby, and they disappear just outside the camp perimeter. The underbrush is just too heavy to tell."

"There's still plenty of daylight," said Winston, looking to the sky. "We should follow them and see where they went. Make sure your guns are locked and loaded. We don't want to get surprised by something that's big."

"... and hairy?" asked Samuel.

"Yeah, that too."

Determined, they set out to follow the tracks, but now it was Winston who saw a problem. "Dr. Cook, I see another problem with our prints. The gait isn't right for such a big animal. The tracks are too close together. I think that backs our theory about them being manufactured."

"Maybe the creature is injured and has a limp," said Samuel.

"Maybe, but there are too many other anomalies," said Bones. "I stand by my statement that these are manmade tracks."

"I think you're right," Missy said. "So, do you want to continue or stop? If there isn't a creature out here, then maybe we should call it a day."

"We still can find Mr. Jenkins," said Bones, "and if he's still alive, that would be a good reason."

"You heard the man," said Winston. "Onward!"

They continued on until they emerged from the tree line to find a wide-open expanse of hard rock that ran up to towering cliffs ahead.

"It would seem the prints lead that way," said Winston, pointing toward the steep climb. "And here are some others. They ain't from a monster."

Indeed, there were muddy boot prints that accompanied the other-worldly ones.

"The posse," said Missy.

"Looks like it," said Winston. "There are several different boot marks here. I'd say four or five men."

Samuel started walking toward the sandy, beige cliffs directly ahead of them.

"Where are you going?" asked Missy.

"I think I see something," her nephew answered.

He kept going until he reached the base where he stooped to pick up something. Turning he held up a torn, bloodied boot. "This could be one of the boots that made those tracks," he said, pointing back toward the others. Samuel looked straight up toward the ledge high above them. "Do you think something lives up there?"

"Could be," said Winston.

"It's likely just a big black bear," said Bones, dismissively. "It's not worth the climb."

"But what if it's Mr. Jenkins, and he's hurt?" asked Missy.

Bones looked at Winston but got no answer—only an unhelpful shrug.

Samuel moved closer to the rocky wall. "Look up there," he said gesturing. "Do you see that?"

About halfway up were the tattered remains of a gray, plaid shirt flapping in the wind. It was caught on the broken, leafless branch of a scrubby bush that had taken root in the side of the cliff face.

"Well, if we must go up ..." Bones began. Then, he turned and went back down to where the horses were tied. Moments later, he returned carrying a bulky, black bag which he threw on the ground and pried open. "I always get some things from my brother Orville before I leave. He sent some gadgets I think will help with this."

Bones pulled out some iron boot cleats and tossed them on the ground along with a strange-looking gun. It looked like a long pistol, but the black muzzle opening was three times the circumference of even the largest caliber long-gun. On the back was a tightly-coiled black spring which resembled some new fishing tackle being marketed in the big cities.

"What's that for?" asked Samuel.

"I'll show you, but you'll have to help me with it."

Bones withdrew an odd-looking bar from the bag. It had a round shaft that exploded into six separate arms with barbed tips, all curving into a mushroom-like shape. On either side of the rod was a series of three, two-inch wheels through which Bones threaded a very long, heavy hemp rope that held a sling on one end and a thick, Gordian-styled knot on the other. To the end of the new-fangled device he tied another heavy rope which he anchored to the gun. Then, he had Samuel help him rotate the lever on the spring to tighten it. When it was complete, Bones loaded the hook into the mouth of the short muzzle.

"Orville calls this his grappling hook gun. Let's see if it works. Hold this," he said, handing both ends of the pully rope to Samuel.

Bones pointed the gun toward the long, deep ledge high above them and pulled the trigger. There was a swooshing sound, and the hooked rod shot out the end carrying the rope up and over a cluster of boulders on one side of the ledge. Bones pulled on the rope until the grappling hook was wedged into the rocks above, then he gave it another two yanks to just be sure it was secure.

"Well, I'll be damned," said the old man. "That's a neat little gadget you got there."

"That's not all," Bones answered. He motioned for Samuel to unfold the burlap sling attached to the pulley rope and wrap it under the young man's arm pits and around his chest. The other end was then handed to Winston. "Here, pull on this."

Bones and Winston pulled on the rope, lifting Samuel quickly up the side of the cliff until he reached the ledge. It was as if he had walked up the cliff face on his own power, defying both gravity and the dangers of the climb.

But Samuel screamed all the way up the cliff side and only stopped once he got planted firmly on top of the ledge. He shouted back down to the group, "That wasn't nice! You didn't tell me you were going to do that!"

"If I had, would you have gone willingly?" Bones called out.

"Hell no!"

Bones laughed, and then said, "Lower the sling down, then tie the other end of the rope around a basket-sized rock that you can ease over the side from up there."

Samuel did as he was told, and as he was affixing the rope to the rock, Bones was busy fastening the sling to the next victim: Missy.

"Ready?" he asked her.

"As ready as I'll ever be," she answered warily.

Bones gave the signal to Samuel who eased the heavy stone over the edge. It tumbled faster than he expected, and he held his breath as he watched his aunt rocket up to the top to join him.

"Are you alright?" he asked, helping her get steady on her feet.

Although pale and sweaty, she knelt to collect herself. "Yes," she answered, shaking, "I think so."

Bones turned next to Winston. "You're up," he said.

Winston backed up. "I don't think …" he answered, raising his hands.

"I don't think we should leave anyone alone at this point. We all need to be together. If there is a bear or a Wendigo up there in a cave, we …"

"… we all need to die together? Is that what you want?"

"Dr. Cook!" shouted Samuel.

"What? What is it?"

"Those red rocks … they're bloody. They're smeared with it."

Winston stared at Bones, and the doctor stared back. Bones took back the sling and slipping it over his head and around his chest.

"Let the rock go," said Bones. "Haul me up, now!"

Samuel did as he was told, and Bones hurtled skyward until he stood alongside his companions.

"What happened here?" Bones asked, looking around the ledge.

In front of the cave were pools of deep crimson and a trail of smeared blood leading from the ledge's rim into the mouth of the cavern.

"By the looks of it, several animals were killed here," said Missy.

"Animals?" Bones asked.

"Animals and, possibly, humans," Samuel answered stiffly.

"A very big bear," Bones said.

"A Wendigo," said Missy, trying to correct him.

"What's going on up there?" It was Winston calling from below.

"There's a lot of blood up here," Bones answered.

"Any carcasses or bodies?"

"No. No signs of those—only a trail of blood into a cave," shouted Samuel.

"*Sh*t*," said Winston.

"What?"

"It has all the hallmarks."

"Of what?" Missy asked.

"Usually," Winston began, "the Wendigo kills its prey and then carries it off into the deep woods where it drinks all the blood but stores the body to eat later. Sometimes, it keeps the body intact if it wants to turn it into a Wendigo like itself."

"Dr. Cook, I don't like this. I think it's time to go back to Wadena," said Samuel nervously.

Even Missy was getting scared as she glanced into the dark recesses of the cave. "Maybe Samuel is right. Maybe it's time we …" she began.

Bones drew his six-round revolver from its holster.

"Be careful," Missy warned.

"Now, I think we're dealing with a mountain lion, instead of a bear. That's it. It's a mountain lion," Bones repeated.

"Yeah? Well, I think it's a Wendigo," said Missy.

"We don't have any mountain lions in Minnesota, doctor," said Winston, overhearing the conversation.

"Well, there's always a first," Bones answered.

Missy and Samuel pulled their guns too, and they watched as Bones crept closer to the cave. But just as he reached the entrance, he heard something that made his blood run cold.

*****

CH 41 - Recovery

Orville grabbed the Bible which had fallen to the floor when Father Patrick had collapsed, and as he rose, he felt the aspergillum in his hand. To his surprise, it felt heavier. There was more holy water in it—miraculously, it had refilled itself.

"In the name of the Father, the Son and the Holy Spirit, I command you leave the body of Father Patrick and never return to this house," shouted Orville. "Leave him and this family forever! Be gone!"

There was another rush of cold air as the priest exhaled—a breath that almost collapsed both lungs. He fell over and lay still. Orville and Claire watched as a sinister, black shadow peeled away from his body. It hovered briefly and then descended, seeping through the floorboards and disappearing from the room.

"Father!" said Orville, going to help him. He checked for a pulse just as his brother, Bones, had always taught him.

"How is he?" Claire asked.

"He's alive," said Orville, "but barely."

Orville helped Father Patrick up and got him into the bed once claimed by Jahi.

"Father, what happened? Are you alright?" Orville asked.

Father Patrick nodded weakly. "Yes. Thank you, Orville. You saved me."

"No, Christ saved you, Father. You can thank Him."

***

It took a few days for Claire and Father Patrick to return to normal. The incident had traumatized them, and Orville had grown deeper in his spiritual convictions, sharing the experience with his pastor, Reverend Benton. As for Father Patrick, the only lasting impact on him was the two-inch scar on his face—much like the one his colleague, Father John, had gotten after a similar, harrowing experience years earlier.

"You are lucky you weren't killed, Orville," said Benton. "It is far too dangerous for a layman to be involved in an exorcism. The priests should have had you leave before they started."

"If they had done that, then Claire would not have returned to us, and Father Patrick would not be alive."

"I suppose, but next time there is an exorcist, remember what I told you."

"The next time? There won't be a next time, pastor."

"Why is that?"

"I'm keeping a bucket of holy water at my bedside all the time. If anyone begins to show any sign of demonic possession, I'm going to douse them with it."

The reverend laughed. "Well, I hope you keep plenty of towels around the house, then." Orville laughed. "But what about Father John? I am very saddened by what happened to him. Can you explain that?"

Orville shook his head. "As you are well aware, there are things in this world we cannot explain, and this is one of them. The demonic creatures attacked him, and when I looked up, he was gone. All that was left were his clothes lying on the floor next to the bed."

"He couldn't just disappear."

"Well, he did. One moment he was there, and the next moment he was gone."

"But you said the demons began striking him up with their battleaxes. Is that true? Did you really see that?"

"I can't really say. I only assume that because I closed my eyes to the horror, and when I reopened them, he wasn't there."

"Well, the Lord moves in mysterious ways only known to Him."

"I think you're right, reverend. Only He knows what really happened, and it's probably best that way."

*****

CH 42 - Bitten

It pounced on him before he realized what had happened, sinking its sharp, poisonous fangs deeply into his calf. Bones reacted by instinct, swinging the barrel of his gun at it and firing one shot to get it off him. But it was too late. The six-foot rattler hissed before slithering quickly away, not waiting to see the aftermath of its deadly attack.

Bones dropped to his knees grabbing his leg in pain and calling out, "Missy! Bring me the emergency kit!"

"We didn't bring it up! It's still down there in my saddlebag!" she exclaimed, motioning down and over the side of the ledge.

Samuel rushed to the doctor and pulled out his knife. He cut two lines where the snake had punctured his leg and began sucking out the poison, turning his head and spitting out one mouthful at a time.

"Bones! Bones! Stay with us!" shouted Missy.

But Bones eyes went to the back of his head, and he slumped over, unconscious.

"Will he make it?" asked Missy.

But before Samuel could answer, there was sound that bellowed deep inside the cave. It was horrible, and it shook the entire cliff, causing a stream of small pebbles and fine gravel to avalanche down the side.

"What was that?" asked Samuel, sitting up and stopping his rescue.

"I ... I have no idea," Missy muttered, her rosy cheeks quickly blanching.

She pulled her hefty four-barrel Enfield and aimed it into the heart of the cave. Again, they heard the growling of something sinister and frightening coming from deep within.

"You're not going in there, are you?" asked Samuel.

"The hell I'm not," said Missy, her gun readied.

"I'll go," said another voice, coming up and over the ledge behind them. It was Winston. "Young ladies aren't supposed to be doin' stuff like this."

"I can handle myself," said Missy defensively.

Winston handed her the medical kit and took her pistol. "You can come with me if you want, but I suggest you stay here with your nephew and take care of the doctor." Then, Winston disappeared into the cave.

At first neither Missy nor Samuel followed, staring at each other. But quickly Samuel said, "You watch Dr. Cook. I'll go help the old man."

Winston hadn't made it far before the light had begun to fade and he found himself groping inch by inch toward the growling noise. Finally, he noticed a small stream of light coming down through a series of cavities in the cavern ceiling. By then, Samuel had caught up with him.

"Good thing you found some light," said Samuel. "I was wishing I'd brought a lantern with me back there."

Suddenly, another bellowing roar erupted from deeper in the cave, and both Winston and Samuel checked their guns to make sure they were loaded. Within a few yards, they came upon a grisly sight—one Samuel had seen before in the sewer system of New York City.

"My god," said Winston, looking at the scattering of bones and body parts along the way. "What kind of creature does this?" asked the old man. "It can't be human."

"It could be," Samuel answered him, "but I hope to God it isn't--not this time."

They crept quietly, farther down the throat of the cave and deeper into its deadly gullet. It revealed a nightmare—a massacre of men and animals at the hands of a creature too evil, too deadly, and too powerful to overcome. Winston stopped. He began having flashbacks from the war where he had witnessed men being torn to pieces by artillery and butchered by bayonets at the hands of the enemy.

"Are you alright?" asked Samuel.

"No, and neither should you," Winston answered.

It was then that Samuel tripped over a ridge in the cave floor and fell forward, sprawling face forward on his hands and knees.

"Shhhh!" muttered Winston. "What are you doing? Are you trying to be its next meal?"

"Stop!" said Samuel, getting up. He felt an immense sensation of dread, and it was overwhelming him. "We need to leave now, while we can."

"Not when there's a Wendigo in there!" cried Winston. "We have to kill it before it kills us. Your doctor friend is hurt. Do you want to leave him here for the beast?" He pointed behind him toward the cave's entrance.

"Let's just leave it alone. Let it be," said Samuel. "If we provoke it, it will surely come after us. Don't you remember all the blood on those rocks out there! That's us! We'll be next!"

But Winston just shrugged. "I don't see it that way, young man. I say we fight!"

Samuel shook his head. "I'm not following you. You're on your own."

Yet, no sooner had he stopped talking than a huge creature sprung from the darkness.

"Ahhh!" cried Winston, stumbling backwards and then staring straight up at it.

The monster dwarfed him. Standing on its hind legs, it was over ten feet tall. Although gaunt and emaciated, it was a force like neither man had ever seen. It had greyish skin, sunken eyes, and tattered lips. Its head was wolf-like with a long snout and sharp fangs that protruded on either side of its jaws. It was clear the creature had been eating, but at the same time, it looked like it hadn't eaten in months. Coated with long, grey hair that hung like an ill-fitting fur coat, the monster had milky white eyes and moose-like horns that protruded from the front of its skull. Worse than that, it had the foulest of odors: it smelled of death.

"No!" shouted the old man, shocked at the horrible image standing over him. He pulled the trigger on the Enfield, but the gun jammed. He struggled to free the round but dropped the pistol when the creature lunged at him. Winston put up his hand to stop it, but the beast bit into it, ripping it clean off.

Samuel raised his gun and pulled the trigger, firing a round. The slug hit the creature but had little effect. Firing again, he hit the beast once more before it swatted his gun away causing it to skid along the rocky cave floor behind him. By the time Samuel retrieved it, the beast had grabbed the old man and begun dragging him farther back into the cave.

"Help me!" the old man cried out. "Help me!"

Shaking, Samuel fire four more rounds, but none hit their mark. The Wendigo slowly trudged back into its lair with a fresh supply of meat.

With no more ammunition, Samuel ran from the depths of the cave toward the entrance where he found Missy still tending to the doctor.

"What happened in there?" she asked. "I heard this horrible yelp and shots. Are you alright? Where is Winston?"

"It's a Wendigo, and it killed Winston. I hit it a couple times, but it didn't even seem to slow it down, let alone stop it. I have no idea how soon it may come back out. We must get ourselves and Dr. Cook down off this ledge now!"

"Help me put Bones in the sling," said Missy. "We'll all have to go down together."

Together, they worked to get Bones into the sling and then wrapped the line around both of them to drop to the bottom of the cliff.

"Whoa!" shouted Samuel on the brisk ride down.

Their combined weight was too heavy for the counterweight rock, and they plunged down the hillside, bouncing off the rocks until they landed harshly on the ground.

Bruised and battered, Samuel got up to check on the others.

"You alright?" he asked his aunt.

Dazed, but not badly hurt, Missy untied herself from the device and turned toward Bones. Still unconscious, he seemed to have weathered the fall, but his breathing was increasingly shallow and labored.

"We must get him to a doctor," she said.

"It looks like there's a wagon just over there," said Samuel, pointing toward the wooded ridgeline. "Let me hitch it to one of the horses and bring it over here."

Samuel returned with the posse's wagon, and they lifted Bones into the back. Then, they set out for Wadena which now seemed very far away.

The first few miles were tough with Bones lying motionless in the bed of the wagon which creaked and groaned with every turn of its wheels. Even though it was warm outside, the doctor's body shivered as the poison traveled through his system making him weaker and sicker. Missy covered him with blankets and stayed with him as Samuel drove the wagon with the horses tied up and following behind them.

"How is he?" asked Samuel after a few hours.

"Not good," Missy answered. "We may need to get him to Duluth as I'm not sure there is a doctor in Wadena, is there?"

"There was none that I found when we were there," said Samuel. "I have my training, but we don't have the supplies we need to treat him. We need something to counteract the venom, and I doubt they have anything in Wadena."

"Then I guess we'll be riding night and day," Missy answered.

"Whatever it takes," said Samuel. "Whatever it takes."

*****

CH 43 - Poor Moe

It was dark, and Moe and his two hired mercenaries had just found the strange, six-toed imprints heading toward the cliff. Not much farther down the trail, they also stumbled upon the last site where both Bones and Dalrymple had camped during their journeys.

"They was here," said Clem Thompson, one of the locals Moe had hired for the job. He stood up after putting his hand on the cold campfire to check for heat.

"How long?" asked Moe.

"I'd say at least three days. There are a lot of prints around here though. How many did you say were in his group?"

"I was told five."

Thompson shook his head. "Well, I don't know about that. I see more boot marks than that."

"Well, I think we should bed here for the night and start fresh in the morning," Moe answered.

The night air was warm and sultry as the summer season was still in full swing. Occasional wisps of clouds passed across the full moon, allowing the stars to pop in their brilliance during the intervening moments. All around, the crickets were busy with their mating calls, nearly drowning out the other sounds of pond frogs croaking, bats fluttering, and owls hooting. Now and again, the call of a wolf pack would send shivers through the men, but they kept close to the fire knowing the canines wouldn't come near it.

"There's a cliff nearby," said Thompson, taking a spoonful of camp beans. "Them tracks lead directly to it."

"Alright, then after supper, let's start lashin' together a cage," said Moe. "Mr. McGinnis said the Wendigo can get pretty wild, so we need to make it real strong."

"Wild ain't the word for it," said Miles Rogers, another of the locals. "Indians say it's the most blood-thirsty thing out here."

"Yeah, yeah, yeah," said Moe. "I've been up against eight-foot Grizzlies before. This thing don't scare me."

"It don't have to scare ya'," answered Rogers, "All it's got to do is rip your throat out, and we wouldn't hear a peep to know you went missin'."

"Well, let's just stick to the plan. We got guns. It don't."

"But you said we're not supposed to kill it," said Thompson.

"We don't have ta' kill it. All we's gots to do is injure it, so it can't hurt us none. Then, we'll stuff it in the cage and haul it back to Duluth. Mr. McGinnis has people there who'll take it off our hands and get it back to the big city."

"Good. The sooner we get rid of it the better," said Rogers.

The men cleaned up and worked on their cage, lashing wooden poles together that they'd freshly cut from saplings nearby. Then they rolled out their bedding to get some sleep.

It was a few hours later when an owl landed in a big red pine just at the perimeter of the camp. The hoots woke Moe, who grumbled before rolling off the mat and loading his gun. "Damn thing," he muttered. He sat up and took a few shots at it to scare it off. The sound shattered the peaceful order of the night, breaking the rhythms of nature and the harmony in the universe.

Rogers and Thompson leaped out of bed, rubbing their eyes. "What the hell is goin' on?" Rogers shouted.

"Nothin'," said Moe, "just tryin' to get some shuteye and that damned owl keeps botherin' me."

However, the hooting didn't stop, and when Thompson and Rogers woke up again, they found Moe's bedding empty and his gun missing gun.

"Where did he go?" asked Thompson.

"He probably wandered off lookin' for that stupid owl," said Rogers. "Either that or he's takin' a dump."

"Should we go after him?"

"Nah. He'll come back as soon as he's taken care of his business."

The two men rolled over and went back to sleep.

But within moments, they heard another, other-worldly, growling sound at the edge of their camp.

Grrrrrr ... grrrrr ... grrrrr

"What was that?" shouted Thompson.

"I dunno. What do *you* think it was?" asked Rogers, now scared.

The growl was guttural and vibrated so low as to make the earth seem to shake.

"I've never heard anything like that in my life!" yelled Thompson. "Grab your gun!"

"I'm gettin' the hell outta' here," said Rogers, scrambling to roll up his bedding and pack his things on his horse.

The last thing either man saw were the milky white eyes and long fangs that leaped from the darkness. It struck suddenly, violently, and without mercy.

*****

CH 44 - Duluth

The distance to Duluth was too far for one full-day's ride, especially with Bones's injury and the wagon, so Missy and Samuel stopped to catch some rest. Samuel had remembered his medical schooling at Harvard about restricting the blood flow and circulation of snake bite venom by applying a tourniquet above the bite which they had done before getting off the ledge. But they needed to relieve the pressure periodically to allow some blood to flow; otherwise, Bones would likely end up losing his leg.

After quickly building a fire, Samuel helped Missy tend to Bones, who was perspiring heavily and shivering from the effects of the poison. Even though Samuel had managed to extract much of the venom, enough remained to pose a grave danger to the Harvard professor.

"Go down to the creek and fetch some cold water," Missy asked her nephew.

When Samuel returned, Missy took a grey rag and dipped it into the cool liquid before applying the compress to Bones's forehead.

"I'm just trying to keep his fever down. He's burning up," she said. "What else do you think we should do?"

"I think this is all we can do," Samuel answered. "In medical school, I read an article about the French who are working on an antivenin serum, but I don't think they've succeeded yet."

"Well, we need to find a hospital in Duluth, or I'm afraid we might lose him," said Missy, stroking Bones's hair. She looked lovingly at him, fearing the worst but praying for the best. She realized how much this man meant to her, and she couldn't think of life without him.

That night, none could sleep, and they rose early with the dawn and headed out. By the next evening, they arrived in Duluth. There, they found the newly built St. Francis Hospital, which had been founded by the Franciscan Sisters of the Perpetual Adoration. Although a more well-known hospital, the Mayo Clinic, was only seventy miles west in Rochester, Minnesota, the distance was too far. They knew Bones would never make it there. As it was, the doctor was deteriorating rapidly, and there was little more they could do.

Taking Bones off the wagon, the two brought him inside the hospital hoping he would be looked at promptly and that there might be a cure to save him. Missy and Samuel took turns at their friend's bedside, watching for some change, some improvement. The attending physician, Dr. Johanne Brut, had come to Duluth from Germany. He had trained in Frankfort, but had spent a year in Paris at the prestigious Sorbonne.

"What do you think?" Samuel asked.

"He is in grave condition," said Brut with a heavy German accent. "However, I did work briefly with researchers there at the Sorbonne. Some were researching the antivenom you speak of. Perhaps we can still save him. In the meantime, we will keep him in a coma and see."

The day passed, and Missy and her nephew found a boarding house near the hospital and took rooms. Missy sent a telegram to her mother explaining what had happened and that they would be staying in Duluth until Bones recovered. On the third day, there was a knock on Samuel's boarding room door. He opened it to find a young nun.

"Good morning, sir," she said. "I was sent to tell you to come to the hospital right away."

"What's wrong?" Samuel asked.

"I don't know, sir. I was only asked to give you that message."

Samuel went to Missy's room which was just down the hall and urgently pounded on it to awaken her.

"What is it?" she asked. "We aren't supposed to leave for another half hour or so."

"It's Bones," answered Samuel. "Someone from the hospital told me we should go as soon as possible."

Together, they rushed the few blocks down the street to the hospital where Missy went directly to the front desk. There sat another, older nun, who was crocheting with two thick wooden knitting needles and a spool of pink yarn in her lap.

"Good morning," said the nun. "Can I help you?"

"We were told to come at once. The patient is Dr. Reginald Cook," Missy said. "They said he was in a dire condition and that we should see him."

"I don't know but come with me. I'll take you to him," the nun answered, putting down her needlework and rising from her chair.

Even though they knew the way, Missy and Samuel let the nun escort them down the long corridor that led to the gymnasium-sized room where all the patients were held. Bones's bed was the eighth one down on the right side, but a curtain barrier was in place around it.

Missy felt sick to her stomach.

"The doctor will be with you shortly," said the nun, leaving them.

Samuel started toward the barrier.

"Don't!" Missy cried out. "I can't bear it!"

"Bear what?" came a voice from behind the curtain.

Samuel rolled back the barrier. There was Bones, awake and sitting up in his bed. He looked haggard but was conscious and seemed to be in a good mood.

"Bones!" screeched Missy, overjoyed with his recovery. She rushed to him and kissed him on the cheek.

"I guess I've had a few rough nights. That's what they tell me," Bones joked, smiling.

"We've *all* had a few rough nights … and days," Missy answered, catching her breath. "How do you feel?"

"As well as can be expected. Dr. Brut said I will need to rest for the next few days to regain my strength, but that I should fully recover. I guess your medical training came in handy, Samuel. The doctor said that without the torniquet I wouldn't have made it. Thanks."

"You're a good professor," Samuel answered.

"I don't think I taught you anything about snake bites in my class, did I?"

"No, but I thought I'd tell you that just so you'd feel better sooner," said Samuel, grinning.

Missy took Bones's hand and squeezed it lovingly. "I thought we'd lost you," she admitted.

"Sorry to put you through that," Bones said. "Did I miss anything?"

"No, not much," said Samuel. "Just the man-eating Wendigo, the massacre of the posse members we were following, and the one-hundred-mile journey carrying your sorry ass in the wagon back to Duluth. Other than that, no."

"I think you planned this just so you would miss the grand unveiling of the monster—just like you've managed to do every other time," said Missy.

"What do you mean?" Bones asked.

"The Wendigo. You missed seeing the Wendigo," said Samuel.

"Yeah, right."

"No, really. I saw it Bones. It was …" started Samuel.

"Don't tell me. It was ten feet tall, fangs as long as a sabretooth's, evil red eyes, hairy and mangy, and … well, does that about sum it up?"

"Yeah, pretty much," said Samuel.

"And you. I suppose you saw it too," said Bones looking at Missy.

"Well, actually …" she began.

"I saw it Dr. Cook. It killed Winston. You remember him, don't you?"

"Of course. Winston died?"

"Yes, I'm afraid it killed him."

"Did you see it kill him?'

"Yes," said Samuel. "It was terrible."

"Then I guess I'm three for three. You got me there," said Bones, crossing his arms.

"You don't believe me, do you?" asked Samuel.

Bones laughed. "Oh, dear lad, you'll have to come up with a story better than that to make me believe you."

Samuel shook his head and chuckled before looking at Missy. "You're right Dr. Cook. You saw right through me. Maybe next time, we'll *really* find a monster in the woods for you to see."

"Either that or you'll come up with a better story to tell me," Bones answered.

*****

CH 45 – News from Wadena

"Dead?" exclaimed McGinnis.

"Yes, and the whereabouts of the other team is unknown," said Phineas.

"And how did you come by this information?" asked Cooper who was in the room.

"I cabled the sheriff in Wadena," said Phineas. "That's what he said in his reply."

"What did he say, exactly?" McGinnis asked.

"He said that he hadn't seen or heard from the group in weeks. He said the chief of the Iroquois tribe out there told him they were all dead. When he asked the chief where they'd been found, he was told someplace near Black River Falls."

"How were they killed?" Cooper asked.

"He didn't say but suggested that the Indians may have had something to do with it," said Phineas. "At least that's what I think."

"Of course ... them, red-skinned bastards!"

"Well, there's nothing we can do about it now. Have you heard from Campbell?" Cooper asked.

"The last cable I got said he knew exactly where Dalrymple and his men had gone, and he was riding out to find them," said McGinnis. "Black River Falls was where Dalrymple had said they were going, and I assume that's where he and Campbell went."

"The sheriff said there was another group out there?" asked Phineas.

"What other group?" McGinnis asked.

"The sheriff said there was another group—a woman and two men—snoopin' around and asking questions about Dalrymple. He told me to recall my people. He didn't want them in his town—nobody did."

"Who is this other group?" McGinnis asked again.

"He said it was a doctor, a young woman and a younger man. They told him they were there to find Dalrymple and his men. They seemed to know about the mission to capture the Wendigo too."

"Why?"

"I don't know," said Phineas, "and either the sheriff didn't know or wouldn't tell me."

"We need to notify Campbell," said McGinnis. "We need to warn him."

"How? You said he was out in the wilderness. There's no way to get a message to him," said Cooper.

"From what you've said, James," said Phineas, "Campbell is a resourceful young man. I'm sure he can take care of himself—especially up against a doctor, a woman and a young lad."

"What if we paid the sheriff to ride off after them and see what's going on?" asked Cooper.

"I tried that," Phineas answered, "but he was in no mood to do that."

"Not even for a hundred dollars?" McGinnis asked.

"Not even for a thousand," Phineas replied. "And one other thing," he added, "the Indians reported finding bodies scattered around the woods near a tall cliff. How they were killed in such a remote area is baffling."

"How many?" Cooper asked.

"Several."

"Several? How many is several?"

"I don't know, Cooper. Several!"

"Shouldn't he go out to investigate?" McGinnis asked.

"Like I said, he won't," said Phineas. "Anyway, what good does it do me? It doesn't really matter does it?"

"I don't think you can believe the Indians," said McGinnis. "They're a bunch of ..."

"Now, now, McGinnis," said Cooper. "They are just like the rest of us. Some you can trust and others you can't, right?"

"They're savages," said McGinnis. "They'll always be savages."

"So, where does that leave us, Phineas?" It was McGinnis who was worried— not only about Campbell, but also about their quest to capture the Wendigo.

"Unless your buddy Campbell comes through for us, it leaves us, my dear McGinnis, with a circus of elephants, lions, giraffes, baboons, ostriches, and a bunch of other animals that won't sell in the big city."

"So, we stick to a vagabond circus, entertaining the *hoi polloi*? That's it?" asked McGinnis.

"No strange creatures in cages?" asked Cooper.

"Not unless you're stepping forward to volunteer," said Phineas, smiling.

***

Nine months later, the U.S. Army's 3rd Cavalry Regiment came through the area at Black River Falls, finally deployed by the Secretary of War at the request of Phineas. While they found a broken crate and other artifacts left behind by both companies of men, none of them or their remains were ever found … nor were any Wendigo.

*****

CH 46 – Bones & Missy

Madam Grey was still not happy with Bones for taking Samuel with him to Minnesota, but there had been so many other things that had happened during the interim that it had been hard for her to stay really angry at him. With Missy's pleadings, Esther agreed to forgive and forget, and her desire to see Missy finally married—to him or any eligible bachelor at that point— outweighed any animosity she continued to bear.

"Dr. Cook," said Esther, greeting him at the door after Clarence had taken his wraps, "it is so good to see you again—and in one piece."

"Madam Grey," Bones answered, kissing her hand. "Thank you for allowing me back into your home."

"Oh, *tisk, tisk*. That's water under the bridge—a mere triviality in the scheme of things. So, I assume your brother filled you in on your sister?"

"Yes, he told me that she's been lovely and hasn't raised a peep since I've been gone. I'm quite surprised, as he can be hard to live with, you know. "

Esther studied Bones's face and found no trace of irony. So, she merely laughed, letting it pass. "Well, I guess that's one way to look at it. I'm just glad that she's feeling better?"

"Yes, Orville told me she's returned to the church and seems to be back to her old self."

"And Reverend Benton?"

"He is too, I understand. Orville mentioned that he's thinking of becoming a deacon at the church."

"Is that so," said Esther. "Well, I think that suits him. He and Claire will be great helpers at the church. I'm sure of it."

It was then, when Missy came into the room—all smiles.

"Dr. Cook," she said formally, curtseying in mock respect, "it is so good of you to grace us with your presence."

"Ha!" said Bones. "Well, then, I am humbled by your invitation to join you and your family for dinner."

Samuel also emerged from the hallway and greeted Bones warmly.

"Dr. Cook, so good of you to come," he said. "I see you've recovered fully. As your doctor, I did insist that you rest and recover your strength, but I see you chose to ignore my guidance."

Bones laughed. "Yes, doctor. I never did make a good patient."

The group had supper and talked about their adventure in Minnesota. While Missy and Samuel continued to contend the Wendigo was real and that it attacked Winston, Bones would have none of it.

"I'll believe it when I see it," he said, scooping the rest of his desert into his mouth.

Later, Bones took Missy for a stroll along the Charles River which flowed along the back of the Grey estate.

"Bones?" she asked, holding his hand.

"Yes?"

"Don't you think you will tire of searching for all these monsters you don't believe in?"

Bones released her hand and stood back. "What are you saying?" he asked.

"You … we … have been doing this for a few years now, and you're no closer to believing in their existence than you were before all this started. So, what's the point? Why continue?"

"Because you're there with me," he said, smiling. "It wouldn't be the same if you weren't there. I learned that the hard way in New York City."

"I don't understand," she said.

"I go on these trips because I know you will be with me."

"But …"

"I spoke with your mother before I came tonight. I talked to her about things."

"Things? I don't know what you're saying."

Bones dropped to one knee. He reached into his pocket and withdrew a small, black velvet box.

"I know it's not much. But Missy? Will you marry me?"

Missy put her hands to her mouth in astonishment. She was speechless.

"Is that a yes?" he asked.

Breaking down in tears, Missy grabbed Bones and began kissing him. He pulled her close, and they continued the love.

But then, Missy pulled away from him, holding him at a distance.

"What's wrong?" he asked.

"What's wrong is you haven't uttered the three magic words required for me to say yes."

"I asked you to marry me, didn't I?"

Bones looked confused, but Missy offered no help.

Finally, Bones said, "Ah," as if a light had gone off in his head. "Missy?"

"Yes, Dr. Cook?" she said, now smiling.

"Can I borrow your pistol?" he laughed.

Missy frowned. "That's five words, and they're not funny, Bones!"

Bones grabbed her and kissed her. "Missy, I love you. I love you with all my heart. I'm sorry I didn't tell you that earlier, but I do. I love you, and I want to marry you. Will you accept me?"

Missy's face softened, and she kissed him passionately. "Yes, yes, a million times yes!" she said. "I love you too, Bones. I can't imagine loving anyone else as much."

*****

Appendix A:

1892: Ringling Brothers parade in Wisconsin

Charles Van Schaick/Wisconsin Historical Society // Getty Images

In the late 1880s, families anxiously awaited the arrival of acrobats, exotic animals, and other performers on Circus Day. Each time that a circus came through town, their arrival would be marked by a parade along the main street. In this photo, residents of Black River Falls, Wisconsin, line up on either side of Main Street to watch the procession of the Ringling Brothers' Circus, including several elephants.

1888: Executive committee members of the International Council of Women

In 1888 the International Council of Women became the first organization of women to promote the advancement of women's rights and equality on an international level. The organization's birth and activity were a natural result of the growing discourse around gender-based injustice that was taking place in the latter half of the nineteenth century. In this photograph, members of the organization's first executive committee, including famous women's rights activist Elizabeth Cady Stanton, are shown during their first meeting in Washington D.C.

Next Book

Book IV

The author continues the series with another story about Dr. Cook and Missy Grey. Together, with Samuel, they will take more toys from Bones' brother, Orville, and pursue the tale of a different monster stalking innocents in another part of the country.

*****

About the Author

Alex Ross Carol is a pen name used by the author. He lives with his family near Chicago, Illinois. Mr. Carol began writing for enjoyment at the age of fifty and has written many other novels and fantasy series, including *The Strange Treasures of Gramma Zulov, Blue Monkey Quest,* and others.

He hopes you enjoyed this story and will read many more yet to come.

****